Imagination of the Heart

Brandon Originals

Imagination of the Heart

Vincent McDonnell

BRANDON

First published in 1995 by
Brandon Book Publishers Ltd
Dingle, Co. Kerry, Ireland

© Vincent McDonnell 1995

The moral rights of the author have been asserted.

British Library Cataloguing in Publication Data
is available for this book.

ISBN 0 86322 215 3

This book is published with the financial assistance of
the Arts Council/An Chomhairle Ealaíon, Ireland.

Cover designed by
Public Communications Centre Ltd, Dublin
Typeset by Koinonia, Bury
Printed by ColourBooks Ltd, Dublin

For my brother, John, who first showed me the lights

And the LORD smelled a sweet savour;
and the LORD said in his heart, I will not again
curse the ground any more for man's sake;
for the imagination of man's heart is evil
from his youth; neither will I again
smite any more every thing living,
as I have done.

Genesis 8:21

1

I returned to Castleford on a cold November evening. On the journey from Dublin I dwelt on the past, recalling to mind people I'd once known, and in my own way had loved. As I drew near my destination I began to think of ghosts, of the tormented shades of the dead who remain forever trapped in the place where they met their deaths, imprisoned by the fields of energy generated by the violence of their dying. I gave no thought to what was now drawing me back. So pre-occupied was I with the past, with the ghosts which mercifully now rarely troubled my dreams, that the proposed piece I planned to write on the recent killing took second place.

I had the car window wound down so that I could smell the countryside spread out in the darkness around me. The air smelt crisp and clean, like freshly laundered sheets, and I was surprised; I'd half expected it to be tainted, to have the stench of corruption and death.

In the darkness I tried to pick out the familiar, but it wasn't until I crested the hill outside Castleford and saw the lights below me that I knew with certainty where I was. It was then, too, I smelt the sea − predominant smell of my childhood − and, mingled with it, the smell of something putrefying out there in the darkness.

As I pulled onto the hard shoulder and stared at the sodium lights below me, I thought that the stench was what I'd expected to find, as if the corpse of the child which had brought me here should have contaminated the air. It was not the reasoning of a normal mind, but just then I was far from normal. Castleford was my home town. It was here, out beyond that sprawl of lights, I'd spent my childhood and teens. Here I'd found a boyhood dream and encountered the horror that destroyed it and which still haunted me.

For a moment I thought of the man who had been instrumental in bringing me here, who stalked the dark countryside, stalked the children with his lust for sex and blood. He was satiated for now, but how long would it last? How long would it be before the ghost of another child haunted the darkness as the ghost of Majella Hawley surely haunted it tonight?

I wound the window back up – to shut out the smell I told myself. But deep down in that part of us which belongs to the dark ages of the past when our ancestors were hunted, down there where terror lurks, I felt afraid. I imagined a wraith materialising out of the darkness, a hand reaching for me through the open window. Not the hand of Majella Hawley, nor that of the missing schoolgirl, Jacinta Devlin, but the hand of another child long since dead. Or maybe the hand of an old man, a charred hand with that smell of burning I would never forget...

I shook myself and wondered what Jones would make of me and laughed in that way we use to convince ourselves that we're not afraid. He would think me a fool like D'Arcy. 'It's the story of the year,' Jones had said this morning. 'A child's murdered in a west of Ireland backwater. Another child's been missing for months and it doesn't take a genius to work out that she's been murdered too. And look at what D'Arcy's given me. "Gardaí Are Baffled." Good Christ, they're shitting themselves, and that asshole gives me "baffled".'

'He's one of your senior journalists,' I pointed out. 'He

went to Trinity – defied the ban and all that. A man who uses an apostrophe...'

'Christ protect me from educated morons!' Jones's blush-red complexion changed to a livid shade of crimson and then to the colour of calico. 'I want something better,' he went on. 'I want fear... terror... *Sunday Chronicle* readers being sick into their muesli.' He threw the front page of the paper onto the desk. 'Did you read it? Such shit!'

I didn't tell him that I hadn't read it. I didn't want to be sick into my muesli, which is the sort of effect his paper had on me. I didn't tell him because I needed a job. He wasn't giving me the assignment out of love. He knew I was from Castleford, that I knew the area and the people and would have a distinct advantage over other journalists. He knew that I would get him what he wanted. I also knew there was a government crisis brewing, and he wanted D'Arcy back in Dublin to cover that.

'A monkey'd have done better,' he went on. 'And I would-n't have to put up with his bloody whinging about the weather. I told him to buy an umbrella and get me some fuck-ing headline material. With two little girls abducted and brutally raped and murdered, he should've been able to come up with something better than "Gardaí Are Baffled".'

I remained silent, not bothering to point out that we could only be certain that one child had been brutally murdered. And as the Gardaí were reluctant to divulge details, we didn't know if she'd been raped.

'Now,' Jones said when I didn't respond, 'I want the kind of detail that sells newspapers. I want to whet appetites. I want colour, atmosphere, details of what was done. How many times. How many different ways. I want the exact number of tears shed, how much hair's been torn out. And don't give me that "sexually assaulted" crap. Now I'm relying on you, Willie. You know the area and the people. They're your bloody lot after all.'

I didn't bother to point out that they weren't mine, those people he had so disparagingly referred to, down there where the glow of the sodium lamps hovered over the town like orange fog. We'd been interlopers here, outsiders who'd taken their land. That it had been for sale for years and no one here had bought it didn't count. Well, they had it now, the scrawny fields and the cut-away Mayo bog my father had greened with love and care and more important still, with his life. And the Paddy Kavanagh hills that the poor poet I'd once dreamed of being hadn't wanted to darken with his shadow.

I put the car in gear and edged back onto the road. On the journey I'd dwelt on the inevitable memories of a past I'd been running from for so long, but now I pushed them away and looked forward to finding myself a room at the hotel, something to eat and a Guinness. There was little chance of another child going missing tonight. There had been two months between the first and the second and, according to some expert, the third wasn't due for at least another five weeks.

I turned off the new bypass about three hundred yards outside the town and came into Castleford through a long avenue of beech, the road here unchanged since childhood. The stone wall of the estate edged the left-hand margin, crumbling and patched with ivy. On my right, the secondary school was chequered with light. Here the streetlights were of the older type, and in their dim glare the leafless trees stood like skeletons, the branches joined together over my head to form a canopy, creating in the summers of my childhood a cool green tunnel through which splintered rays of sunshine fell like knife blades. Here one autumn a man was killed during a storm – some foreigner here for the fishing. He was crushed to death by a falling tree, his fishing basket smashed open so that he was found with his catch dead beside him. The tree was cut up for firewood and one of the legends that grew up around the event had blood seeping from the timber instead of sap.

What legends, I wondered, would grow out of the recent events; what children would be touched by them? Soon children would walk behind the coffin of Majella Hawley as I'd walked behind the coffin of another child. They'd walk behind Jacinta Devlin's, too, when her body was found. That she was dead, I didn't doubt. What others might they yet walk behind before the present terror abated?

The wind bent the tops of the cypress trees which sheltered the parish priest's residence as I came into the town proper, past the Catholic church and on into Main Street, the turn-off to my left leading down to the Garda station, the one on my right to the railway station, where sycamores and nettles had flourished between the rails and in the dilapidated buildings long before I ever left here.

The familiar never fails to touch one, and as I looked at memories of another time, I too was touched. The shopfronts were modernised now but most still had the names I remembered: Moran's hardware shop, Flanagan's drapery, Kelly's and Vaughan's groceries and bars. Ida Doyle's sweetshop was gone, as was Brown's toyshop in whose window a model train had run in the weeks before Christmas. Further along was Brogan's newsagents where I used to buy my pens and paper and stare at the books on the shelves and dream of one day seeing my own name there.

As I drove down Main Street I caught a glimpse of a poster stuck on the telephone box. "Have you seen this child?" The black-and-white image of a young girl's face stared back at me. Beneath the picture the print was too small to decipher. Along the street her face stared out from numerous other posters. There wasn't a living soul to be seen, only this image which might be for me alone. The corners where the men had gathered in my youth were devoid of human presence. Fear was out there. I sensed it in the dark recessed doorways, sensed it like the stench which was assailing my nostrils through the closed car windows.

I drove through the square, not a square at all but a large triangular area edged with kerbing stones and on which the town water-pump still stood, along with the weighing scales which dated back to a time when there was a market here. I continued down Bridge Street, over the hump-backed bridge and left into Strand Street to go down by the river, past the pair of black cannons which were said to be from the Spanish Armada, wrecked off the coast four hundred years before, many of the survivors, the Spanish sailors and soldiers who'd come from warmer climes to this God-forsaken place, butchered by the people as they came ashore, if one could believe the stories.

There were heavy black chains slung between concrete posts along the river. In my day it had been open yet I never remembered hearing of an accident. Except for that one drowning, the death of that child, the river had been a benign presence.

The Bridge Inn Hotel was on my right, opposite the monument erected to the memory of two local men who'd been killed in an ambush. A Black and Tan had also been killed that day, but there was no monument to him here. I'd often thought of him, coming from Liverpool or Manchester to die on a lonely stretch of road. What mark had that incident left, apart from the monument with its inscription – the names of the dead and some phrases in Irish about death and freedom that I no longer remembered.

An alleyway gave access to the hotel car-park, the large number of vehicles there a sure sign that the hotel was doing brisk business. The tourist season was long since over but there were attractions now other than the sea, the solitude and the scenery. I was drawn here like those others, and it wasn't inspiring to think that I'd been reduced to this – the boy who'd dreamed of being a poet like Yeats or Kavanagh, now trying to earn a living from the misery of others.

I got out of the warm cocoon of the car and the wind and the stench struck at me. I locked the door and retrieved the laptop and my shoulder-slung luggage from the boot. I hurried across the car-park and made my way to the hotel entrance, elaborate and ornate woodwork painted in dark blue. There was a poster stuck on the window, identical to the one I'd seen earlier, the face of the child staring out at me, the features blurred in the blow-up. Underneath, in the small lettering which I had been unable to decipher from the car, was a description of Jacinta Devlin. As I stopped to read it I realised that it could have been the description of any ten-year-old little girl.

I entered the foyer, which ran through for about fifty feet, carpeted in a rich red floral pattern. On my right there was a large room with a log fire burning in a huge fireplace, a scattering of tables and a self-service counter. On my left was the dining room, frosted glass in the door so that I had but an impression of vague human shapes beyond. Further along on my right was the reception desk.

The receptionist confirmed that she had a vacant room. Later I learned that most of the other journalists were staying at the Castleford Hotel and the Gardaí were billeted with bed and breakfast establishments – a ploy on the part of Superintendent Halligan who was in charge of the investigation. He had felt that a couple of officers in a private house, mixing with the family, would learn a lot more than they would gathered together in the hotel discussing overtime payments and the problems of being separated from their families.

I signed the register and told the receptionist I'd be staying until the weekend at least. She'd already noted the laptop and could decipher from that why I was here. She would have seen enough of us by now – the perpetual transients who spend our lives in strange hotel rooms, digging into the private lives of people.

I asked her to order a cheese and mushroom omelette with brown bread and butter and a pot of tea. I'd take it in the dining room in ten minutes. 'I must apologise for the awful smell, Mr Leitch,' she added. 'Something went wrong with a sewer today.'

I nodded and, taking my luggage and key, made my way through the foyer to where swing doors gave access to the lifts and stairs. My room was on the second floor overlooking the street. The furniture, the usual to be found in any rural hotel without the urge to be pretentious, was in a mahogany finish and could be considered adequate. The portable television worked and the bathroom was clean and functional.

I put away my laptop and the few bits of clothing I carried with me, had a quick wash and went back downstairs to the dining room. The food was bland, only the bread meriting comment, and for a moment I was reminded of home. Instead of the tables all around me, I saw the kitchen of my childhood with its old Stanley, the top glowing almost red hot and my mother stooping down to take out the soda bread, juggling the cake in her hands until she placed it on the wire stand to cool. And my father cutting a slice from it while it was still warm and the melting butter running down his chin and she wiping it off with the corner of her apron and scolding him and laughing while he winked at me over her shoulder. Guilt, regret, shame – they touched me for a moment, but I'd long been practised in the skills of pushing them away.

After I'd eaten I peeped into the bar and saw a gaggle of journalists who must have known each other by now better than they knew their families. I saw the rake-thin figure of D'Arcy among them, and drew back. I didn't want to start drinking with them. One drink would lead to another and didn't I know only too well the dangers that that entailed?

I slipped out of the hotel, crossed the street and walked along by the river, the black water reflecting pools of orange light which shimmered in the eddies of the stream. I heard the water sloshing and sucking at the bank and the urgent rush of it as it raced through the narrow arches of the bridge. As I crossed the bridge I heard faintly beneath me the echo of my footsteps, which seemed to follow me as I came into the square and turned right down Market Street.

I pushed open the door of Dempsey's bar and entered, heads turning to see who it was, a head of patently false blonde hair swivelling in my direction from a seat by the fire. She was the last person I would have dreamed of meeting here, and recognition, even after all the time which separated our last meeting and this, dawned in our eyes simultaneously.

How long ago was it?

Twenty-three years last August my memory told me, long years in which I'd grown harder and colder, more cynical and uncaring. 'Willie?' she called across the space, across the cigarette smoke, blue in the lights, across the years and the memories and the other events and people who'd touched our lives since then, the first to speak as she had been that first time we met outside the Astoria Cinema.

'Deborah!' Somehow I managed to instil a lightness in my voice – there was no need to attempt to instil surprise – and then she was rising from her seat and edging between the tables towards me, the few patrons raising their eyes from her to me, while the eyes of the man who sat beside her never wavered for a single moment from my face.

I had a feeling of horror that she would grab me in her arms and kiss me. I stuck out my hand as she came within range and she reached for it. It was only then that I thought that I might feel the scars and tried to pull my hand away. But she held on and I was aware that she was trembling – a vibration was running through her body and my hand was an instrument for measuring it.

'Willie,' she repeated, not a question now but a statement of wonder. She held my eyes for a moment, and then she swung away and spoke to the man who still watched me. 'It's Willie, Bren,' she said, and even then I detected in her voice not only triumph and what I took to be hope, but a malignancy, another manifestation of what I thought I'd seen in her eyes, as if a small sick creature were hiding in her body.

2

If there was one person I never wished to see again, it was the woman before me. And as if to avoid looking at her, I stared around me.

The pub had an old-fashioned aura with blackened beams and a stone fireplace, imitation oil-lamps and turn-of-the-century prints of Castleford on the walls, but the effect was pathetic and false. Thirty years ago it had possessed a high counter and old beer handles, forms about the walls and heavy wooden tables. Now the oak half-casks which served as tables were pretentious rather than fashionable.

I took it all in – a few men by the bar, some couples at the tables, boredom beginning to settle about them again after their initial interest in me. Yet despite the sense of normality, inexplicably I felt afraid. The hairs at the back of my neck tingled. With an effort I turned to look at her.

'Come and sit by the fire,' Deborah McQuillan said to me, 'and I'll get you a drink.' She behaved as if the events of that August night were all part of some bad dream she'd long since forgotten. Earlier I'd thought about meeting ghosts; I'd tried to prepare for such an eventuality, but I'd never considered meeting the living.

'I'll buy my own,' I said but she persisted, and as interest focused on me again I told her I'd have a pint of Guinness.

'Go on,' she said. 'Sit down there with Bren. We can have

a chat about old times.' She laughed and I knew it was the moment to make my excuse and leave, but something held me. I looked at her, astonished that she could laugh at what she so easily referred to as old times, but to my surprise and relief I found that I no longer hated her. Whatever loathing I had was for myself.

While she went to the bar I made my way across to the fire to sit beside another spectre from the past I hadn't recognised when I first entered. 'You here for the murder?' Brendan Callen asked when I was seated, staring at me in what I took to be puzzlement.

I nodded and turned away from his bloodshot eyes which bulged beneath his dark hair. It was already thinning, combed back in a style long out of date. From the flush spreading across his grey face I knew he'd consumed a great deal of alcohol, but as yet he wasn't drunk.

'He's here for the murder,' Callen said to McQuillan when she came back.

'Isn't he a reporter?' she said. 'And him coming from here and knowing us and that...'

She turned to me, her breasts thrusting against the buttons of her blouse. Once, so long ago now that the memory was overlaid with so many others, I'd unbuttoned her blouse, and when she'd pulled up her bra, her breasts had dropped under their own weight into my cupped and trembling hands. Did she remember? I wondered, the memory like emery paper scraping an open wound.

Callen still stared at me and I wondered too if she'd ever told him about us – not everything of course, but the fact that we'd been lovers in the days of the flower people, 'Are you going to San Francisco' on the juke-box in Lennon's shop where the old threepenny bit would get you three plays, the same as for a shilling.

Just then the barman brought my pint and I turned away from Callen and rummaged in my pocket for money. 'It's my call, Willie,' she said, rooting in her handbag. 'You're the stranger here now.'

Earlier I'd avoided looking at her hands, but as she reached across me to give the barman his money, I couldn't help being drawn to them. I saw that time must have healed the scars, or perhaps she used some cosmetic to camouflage them. She wore no wedding ring, but a number of other rings adorned her stubby, nail-bitten fingers.

I settled myself on the stool, acutely aware of my unease. I felt she was aware of it, too, and when she laughed I thought I sensed satisfaction in the sound. 'Cheers,' she said. 'Good luck to Willie and me – and Bren.' She added his name as an afterthought and laughed again. Only now there was no satisfaction there, but a little trill of bitterness couched beneath the laugh like a discordant note.

I picked up my glass and drank the Guinness, as the repeated use of the diminutive of Callen's christian name brought him more to life for me than his actual presence did. I found myself picturing, beneath the drink-bloated features, a younger version of the same face, the face of the boy whose stutter in moments of excitement matched the staccato rattle of the bren gun I then thought he was named after. It was he who'd enticed me under the disused railway bridge on the Duagh road, and at first with magazines, and then more graphically still, introduced me to the pleasures of sex. He'd given substance to the adolescent fantasies which were just then beginning to consume me and which were to be satisfied later by McQuillan.

My unease persisted. It was to do with meeting them, I told myself – the shock at realising that we'd been drawn together by death. After all, it was death that had separated us years before.

'Must be twenty years ago,' McQuillan said now as if she'd read my thoughts.

I nodded, wondering how it was that she couldn't remember to the exact minute. Perhaps amnesia was her way of coping with the past, of living as we all had to, from one day to the next. In the gloom her face seemed stern and I could see the beginnings of crows' feet around her eyes. They were cold, the pupils surrounded by greenish coloured irises, brown-speckled like the shell of a blackbird's egg. She was younger than me, but she seemed older, more worn by life. I hadn't loved her – for me it had never been a question of love – and I'd assumed that she hadn't loved me either; that she'd been using me as I'd used her, maybe seeing me as a means of escaping to a better life. In the end she had escaped, because after the tragedy she'd been taken off to Birmingham by her mother. What had drawn her back?

'Are you here on your holidays?' I asked, thinking this was the probable answer.

'No,' she said. 'We're living here now, at Bren's old place off the Duagh Road. We've been back a year.'

'Oh,' I said, unable to hide my surprise. They'd been lovers once, or so I'd then assumed, before McQuillan and I had become lovers. I also knew that Callen had gone to England shortly after McQuillan left, but I'd never considered the possibility of their meeting each other there. 'I didn't know you were home,' I said, trying to cover up my surprise. 'Mind you, I haven't been back here myself in twenty years.'

'Was that when your mother died?' she asked, and I realised that she must have made enquiries about me. How else could she have known when my mother had died? Or that I was a journalist? Yet wasn't it only natural, I told myself, that she should enquire about people she'd known?

'Just afterwards,' I said. 'I'd come back to sort out a few

things, some bits and pieces I'd wanted to take away. Books and that.' It had been my last gesture of feeling towards my mother – that I'd left my books until she died. She'd always thought that I'd come home. I didn't want to take that last hope from her, so I'd left the books and the other bits of my life until she was dead. I returned one weekend and took them away in cardboard boxes along with the wag of the wall clock which had never again worked and which now hung in the hall of my Dublin flat. What remained was auctioned along with the house and land. I didn't return for the auction, just signed the papers which were sent to me and banked the cheque when it came. I tried to forget Castleford, promising myself that I'd never return.

'You'd have known her father?' Callen said suddenly, as if not wishing to be left out of the conversation.

'What?' He'd caught me off guard and I turned to stare at him. Did he think of the past? I wondered. Did he remember that place where as boys we'd once hidden, where Sissy Bradley had come and Judith Kelly and what others? Maybe McQuillan, too, for all I knew.

'Joe Hawley,' he said. 'You must have known him?'

I nodded as I drank, the Guinness smooth on my tongue and throat. 'I went to school with him. He was a few years ahead of me.'

'You must have got a shock,' McQuillan said, 'when you heard.'

Although I nodded, in reality it hadn't been a shock. I remembered the news item and the first gut-stirring excitement we all experience when we learn of such an event, my excitement heightened by the familiar ring of the names. I'd actually wondered at first if it were Joe Hawley's daughter who'd been murdered, aware that there were many Hawleys in the area, and the doubts were dispelled the following day by the reports in the papers.

I'd stared at the blurred snapshot of a smiling child and tried to see if there was any resemblance to Joe Hawley, whose existence I'd once feared, but there seemed to be none. There had been a clearer picture of a taped-off area with the Gardaí on their knees among the trees in Castlewood, where as a child I'd played hide and seek. On seeing it, I'd realised that it had been tainted forever, not by what had been but a temporary grave for Majella Hawley, where perhaps she too had played, but by the monster who'd brought her body there.

'It must have been terrible for her,' McQuillan said, turning to stare into the fire where the flames leapt towards the darkness of the chimney. I looked at her, the blonde hair blackening at the roots. She kept staring at the fire.

'It must be worse for the Devlins,' Callen said. 'Not knowing...' I could have sworn that there was a trace of pleasure in his voice but assumed I was mistaken. 'They still hope she's alive,' he added, 'that some day she'll come walking in the door, safe and sound.'

'I suppose it's only natural,' I said, 'to go on hoping. But whoever killed Majella must have taken Jacinta, too. Surely it's the same sick mind at work?'

'There'd hardly be two, now would there?' McQuillan's voice was harsh. She raised her head to look at me, and I couldn't avoid the scorn in her eyes and something else that might have been loathing.

I drank some more of the Guinness and suddenly I wanted to get away. I mumbled an excuse and rose to my feet and made my way through the empty, rear lounge to a door marked Toilets. The Gents was off a hallway whose walls seemed to exhale the sour stink of urine and beer. The stainless steel urinal had brown stains the shape of tulip petals on its surface, and its outflow was blocked by cigarette ends. I heard the door open and Callan came up beside me. I was acutely aware of his size as I'd been aware of it when we were boys, when he'd seemed gross and pathetic and disgusting and, most frightening of all, damned.

'You going to be staying long?' he asked.

I shrugged. 'It depends,' I said. 'A few days I suppose, unless there's another killing.' He nodded and shook off the dregs of urine. He fiddled with his zip under the overhang of the belly. It was only then I noticed that the suit was threadbare, the shirt collar frayed.

There but for fortune... The words came to me, echoing in my father's voice. He was dead before I learned that they were only words from a song and not the wisdom of an old man I'd loved more than any other person I'd ever known.

'Did she send for you?' Callen asked now, bringing me back to the present. 'Was it her?'

I stared at him in surprise and with malicious satisfaction, seeing him in his old suit and frayed shirt, and with drops of his piss clinging to the toes of his scuffed shoes. Now he had McQuillan – had to make do with what I'd left him. 'No one sent for me,' I said. 'I'm here on assignment. I may even write a book about it,' I added boastfully.

'It's just that we're together now,' he said, 'McQuillan and me...' He adjusted the jacket and thought about closing the buttons. Maybe it had fit him when he first bought it, but it certainly didn't fit him now and he let it hang open. 'It's just that I don't want you bothering her. The past is over and done with. You'll be going away when this is all over.'

'It was all a long time ago,' I said. 'I won't be bothering her. I can assure you of that.'

'Ah.' His relief was acutely discernible. What he had wasn't going to be taken away. It was a long time now since we'd been under the bridge and he'd been the one with power.

'Where are you staying?' he asked and I told him. 'It's just

that we might have a pint sometime. No hard feelings then.'
He held out his hand, but I pretended not to notice and
walked back inside. I didn't cross to the fire but made my way
out. At the door I glanced back and saw Callen watching me
from the entrance to the rear lounge, while McQuillan
seemed caught in suspended animation, half out of her seat,
her eyes on him, her face in the gloom having what I might
have only imagined was a look of fear. Or perhaps it was only
frustration. I pulled the door closed behind me and was out
on the pavement before I realised that that was how I'd left her
before.

3

Even the stench from the sewer was welcome when I emerged and I gulped the stinking air deep into my lungs. After the warmth inside it was bitterly cold and common sense told me to return to the hotel, but I still didn't want to meet D'Arcy or the other journalists.

I was disturbed at meeting McQuillan and Callen – felt contaminated by them. When I'd left here for what I'd then thought was the last time, it had been partly to escape from the memories of the events I'd shared with them. Now it was a shock to discover that they were back, that they were lovers again. But it had nothing to do with me, I told myself.

I turned left when I emerged from Dempsey's and walked down Market Street. The town was hushed and my footsteps echoed in the still street. From the couple of pubs I passed, the buzz of talk fell on my ears like the murmur of bees among the flowers my mother had once grown in those summers when innocence was the only blessed thing I possessed. A yoke I'd thought then, wishing only to cast it off, aching for the knowledge I was to acquire from Callen, shedding both my childhood and innocence in the space of a year for the knowledge not of life, as I was to learn when Judith Kelly's body was washed up on the rocks, but of death.

I stopped at the end of Market Street where the sodium lamps gave way to the harsh glare of the older streetlights.

Beyond the light the darkness crouched like a great humped animal. I listened but there was only silence – I couldn't even hear the river. Was it the last earthly sound Majella Hawley had heard – the murmur of the water and the wind rustling in the trees? I didn't want to imagine the sounds her killer might have made – his heavy breathing and grunts of exertion and the rustle of his clothing...

I listened as if I might hear an echo from that evening when she'd disappeared, one week ago, or sense what she must have endured as her killer gratified whatever desires had driven him to abduct her in the first place. Unless of course the desire was not just for sexual gratification but for bloodlust and he'd only been satiated when her sightless eyes stared up at him. He was out there now, and I imagined him lurking in the shadows like the bogey man from childhood. But in reality I knew that he would seem as normal as myself.

I thought of the Devlins, enduring the nightmare of parents who have had a child go missing, the nightmare of not knowing whether he or she is dead or still alive and suffering. There isn't a single person with sexual experience who isn't aware of what hidden dark desires exist within themselves, and of what those desires might give birth to if they were unleashed.

I stared out towards Castlewood, sensed its presence beyond the edge of the town. In the summers of my childhood it had been a place of adventure, and I'd beg to be allowed to play there – cowboys and indians, hide and seek, dare, or true kiss and promise with the girls. Now no child would ever play there again.

I was about to turn back when I heard footsteps in the laneway which ran at right angles from this end of Market Street up to Barrack Street. I swung about to see three men wearing white armbands approaching and I recognised Hugh

Moran, a local councillor, from a picture I'd seen in the paper. 'Who are you?' Moran demanded. As befitted someone of his standing, he had appointed himself spokesman.

I stared at him, his body held rigid with his own importance. 'What's it to you who I might be, councillor?' I said.

He was taken aback that a stranger should not only recognise him, but should address him in such a manner, and it was left to the older of the three to explain. 'We're vigilantes,' he said. 'We're patrolling the town to ensure that there are no further ah... incidents. Mr... Councillor Moran here has organised the patrols.'

'Councillor Moran should know better,' I said. 'This kind of thing is illegal. Now if you'll excuse me.' I crossed the street and when I looked back they were whispering among themselves. Eventually they moved off up Market Street.

I felt shaken by the incident, by the reaction of the third man who'd stared at me with what I took to be naked hatred. I'd no wish to encounter them again and so I walked on, out by the new bungalows that had sprung up on either side of the road. They were stark boxes for the most part, but one was built in Spanish style, its windows and garden awash with light.

I passed the dark, cavernous national school and turned down the narrow lane that led to the footbridge over the river. The lane was hardly more than a narrow, rutted footpath, hedged in on both sides by bushes and briars. As I approached the bridge I heard the river and for a moment I imagined that I also heard someone gasping for breath. An image of Judith Kelly sprung to my mind, and though I knew that the sound was only my imagination, I still glanced over my shoulder as if I might see her ghost there in the darkness. But there was no ghost, only the tangle of bushes hemming me in on either side.

I reached the bridge, a steel structure built in place of the original wooden one which had been demolished after Judith Kelly was drowned. As a child I'd played here, had climbed the barriers which blocked off either end, to tip-toe along the rotting planks with the river visible and often seething in full flood below. It was here that Judith Kelly died, a waif-like creature with large brown eyes and arms and legs as thin and brittle as twigs. She'd been more daring than us boys – would run across the bridge, skipping from one precarious foothold to another, while the water waited for her far below.

The river had been patient, as if knowing all along that one day she'd miss her foothold. It was assumed that this was what had happened when she had taken a short cut across the river one October evening, fog already hanging over the water and shrouding the tops of the trees in Castlewood. The Gardaí found a piece of a broken plank still attached to a wooden cross member. She'd jumped the gap between two planks and, when she'd landed, the rotten timber had snapped and she'd fallen into the water, swollen by weeks of rain, and been swept downstream to the sea.

As I stood on the bridge and heard the rush of the water below me, I remembered that time as if it were yesterday. I remembered the funeral and how we schoolchildren had formed a guard of honour outside the church and at the grave-yard gates. I remembered how the other children had giggled when Judith's mother tried to throw herself into the open grave and, to their disappointment, was prevented from doing so by relatives. I had not laughed but had stood with my head downcast for fear anyone would see my face and decipher the secret I hid; or guess that in the hours after her disappearance, before the broken plank was discovered, I'd thought she might have suffered a different fate.

I remembered, too, the day following the funeral when the

bridge was demolished, and how as it collapsed into the water I'd felt a load being lifted from my shoulders. It was a piece of rotten timber which had led to the river's taking Judith Kelly's life, I told myself. I wasn't to blame.

Now there was another killer here, not inanimate like a bridge but a live, breathing man, maybe someone I knew, someone I'd gone to school with.

I was growing cold. The wind sweeping in off the sea seemed to have originated in the Arctic, and I wanted to get back to the hotel. I crossed the bridge and made my way out to Strand Street. As I emerged I glimpsed the moon before the clouds hid it again and darkened the roofs of the houses opposite. I crossed the street and walked back to the hotel, the stench again growing stronger.

As I entered the hotel I saw the vigilantes beyond the reception desk with glasses in their hands. I slipped into the self-service area and warmed myself at the fire. I saw them as they were about to leave again and the man who'd stared at me caught my eye. He spoke to Moran, who looked at me and then turned back towards reception. A moment later the receptionist stuck her head round the corner and looked at me too.

When they'd gone I went to the receptionist and asked her for the names of the two men with Moran. There might be a story in the vigilantes.

'Mr Bannon and Mr Devlin,' she said, and then in a whisper, added: 'He's the father of the missing girl.'

I thanked her, swearing under my breath. I'd hoped to visit the Devlins tomorrow and ferret out what I could, but what were the odds on my chances now? I swore again and headed down the foyer towards the stairs, wondering how I could have been so stupid.

It was then I saw McQuillan, seated in an armchair, hidden

from me until now by the reception desk. As I caught sight of her my first thought was to withdraw before she saw me, but I was too late. As our eyes met again, I had to make an effort not to swear aloud.

4

She didn't rise nor hold out her hand on this occasion, and I was relieved at that small mercy. 'You shouldn't have left like that,' she said. Her voice was light, but some deep emotion simmered below the surface.

'Callen didn't want me there,' I said. 'He made it quite plain.'

'Fuck him,' she said, no longer able to conceal her feelings, and I glimpsed in her eyes a darkness that made me want to run.

There was a time when I would have looked on the present encounter in a different light, when I would have gladly reciprocated her advances. I'd once thought that I'd lost most of my innocence beneath the bridge with Callen; had lost the remainder to the woman before me. Later I discovered that I'd discarded what remained bit by bit along a road which had lead me back to this place, where I'd thrown the first pieces away in an attempt to find a dream that eluded me – that dream, whatever it may be, that eludes us all. In the long years since then I'd seen too much, had too often betrayed myself and others, to now have a claim on innocence.

I thrust my thoughts away and asked her where Callen was, a reason to speak and nothing else. 'He's back at the pub,' she said. 'He'll be there for hours yet.'

'But what about closing time?'

'Don't you think the Gardaí have better things to be doing than to be bothering pubs about closing time? Sure there isn't a Guard to spare for anything since the murder. There'd be vandalism going on, too, if parents weren't keeping their children at home. Even the adulterers haven't had it easy.'

'Why's that?' I hadn't wanted to be drawn but my interest was roused. I'd been around newspapers long enough to know that it's the human interest story that sells them.

'Oh,' she said, 'you know...' She wanted to give the impression that she was a woman of the world but the effort was pathetic. The years she'd been away, far from giving her the gloss of sophistication, had only stamped her more indelibly as a loser. Paradoxically, she who hadn't been born here now belonged even more than the natives, belonged in this narrow world where the new-found freedoms – contraception, multi-channel television, the ability to live with a man without drawing down the wrath of the community – were for her not freedoms at all. She was trapped here – I could see it in her eyes – and I wondered what had drawn her back. But I didn't ask. To do so would have brought her life more in contact with my own, and after all, it's the small intimacies that damn and betray us.

'I don't know,' I said now. 'Perhaps you might enlighten me.'

She stared at me as if I were trying to make a fool of her. But I saw that she was frightened, too, that I'd go and leave her to crawl back to Callen, and she was willing to speak just to keep me there. 'Adultery's a secretive business,' she said, 'especially in a small place. Up to now the only one who might ask where you were or what you were doing was your wife or husband, but now suspicious Gardaí are asking questions and writing down the answers and checking up on them. Where were you at such a time? Who were you with? What were you doing? Who knows when another child might be killed and you'll have to account for your whereabouts? It's not just the children who can't go out to play anymore. So there might be a story in that for you, mightn't there? Callen tells me that you're writing a book about this. Well, I could let you have a little spice for it.'

She laughed as she had back at the pub, her features screwed up into a rictus that might have had its origins in pain, the sound itself with its tinkle of bitterness. Her face powder was flaking, and resembled the scales of skin my father used scrape from the soles of his feet with his cut-throat razor, the shiny blade flashing in the light, sending shivers down my spine.

She stopped laughing just as abruptly and looked at me, her face clouding over again with uncertainty. 'You are writing a book?' she said as if her whole future depended on it.

I nodded and she seemed impressed. She was like a symbol of the mess and failure I'd made of my own life and it was vanity that made me speak. 'There's almost certainly a book in this,' I said. 'I'm the ideal person to write it. After all, I know the area and the people.'

'And make money from it?'

'I don't write for anything else anymore.'

'You've been away too long,' she said. 'You're out of touch. Now I've been back a year. I know what goes on. I could help you.' She seemed eager, but I didn't want her help, repulsed as I was by the pathetic vulnerability I sensed hanging about her like a pall. Yet I asked her if she wanted a drink.

'I do,' she said, smiling now.

'Here?' I asked.

'Why not. I've never been here before.' She stood up and looked around as if to check on what she'd been missing – the dark oak-panelled dado, the pink embossed wallpaper, the paintings and the glass showcases of stuffed trout, the mahogany table with its vase of flowers – and seemed impressed by it all. We crossed to the bar, two large rooms linked by an arch. A gas fire, a poor imitation of the real thing, burned in the hearth; great black lumps of coal sat dead among the pale leaping flames. She asked for a Bacardi and coke, and, against my better judgement, I ordered a whiskey for myself.

I was aware of the interest in us, of the covert glances of people who were strangers to me. In the next room I glimpsed some journalists I knew. D'Arcy wasn't among them. I didn't want their false bonhomie just now, the raised eyes at my companion. 'We'll go back outside,' I said. 'At least we can sit down.'

She lead the way and I noted that she was heavier than I remembered, the legs thick and solid beneath the hem of the black skirt, the navy jacket a size sixteen at least. 'So,' she said, as she resumed her seat, 'it's been a long time.'

'A long time,' I agreed as I sat beside her.

'Don't you want to know what happened to me? What I've been doing for what... twenty-three years?'

'No,' I said. 'It's gone now. We can't have it back.'

I'd angered her, but she kept control. 'I often thought of you,' she said. 'Down through the years.' Her eyes sought mine and she willed me to believe her. But I didn't need to be willed. I knew she could never have forgotten me. I'd never forgotten her, and I had no wish to re-forge past links.

She hadn't been a virgin that first time – despite my inexperience I'd known that – and I'd been shocked. At that time I'd hardly had more than a kiss and a cuddle from a girl, and the tales of conquest we boys related among ourselves were just bravado. She'd denied that Callen had taken her virginity, and I remember wondering who else she could have known at fifteen. She'd told me she was fifteen, but I couldn't be certain if she lied or not. Yet what had I cared? In moments of passion the age or appearance of the object of that passion is immaterial. It's only afterwards, when the original desire seems no more than a memory, that we seek to question.

At the time I'd never questioned her motivation. It was enough to have the sex she gave so freely. It was only afterwards that I came to believe that she'd been trying to buy my co-operation. Now, with more practical experience of those matters, I believed that what she'd been doing then was venting her hatred and disgust, and anyone would have suited her purpose. She'd used me to try to exorcise her ghouls; had tried to trap me in her web of hatred and vengeance, and I'd come to hate her for it.

'You're living in Dublin these days?' she said, changing tack, setting aside the dangerous subjects for the moment.

'It's where you have to be in my line of work.'

'I used to like living in cities,' she said, 'but I was hopeless at finding my way about. I'd always be getting the wrong buses. I'd learn eventually, but then we'd move on and I'd have to start all over again. I thought coming back here was the answer, but it was a mistake.' Her voice rose on a note of bitterness. 'We should have gone to Dublin,' she added. 'At least I'd have a bit of life, a bit of excitement there.'

'One place is much like another,' I said. 'And I'd have thought there was enough excitement here just now.'

'The murder?' She looked at me as if there could be another source. 'I suppose it's brought excitement for some. But I'd swap it all right now for anything.' The earnestness in her voice surprised me and I thought of her earlier words about adulterers and the inconvenience caused them. Was she one of those inconvenienced? Didn't she want to reveal to the Gardaí where she'd been on a particular night? I thought of Callen's veiled threat in the toilet. Had he grounds for such suspicion?

Or reason to believe that she might turn to an old flame? If he had, then he must have known about us. I would have liked to have asked her, but to ask would be to share an intimacy.

'It's late,' I said, glancing at my watch. 'It's been a long day and I need to be out early.' Her eyes flashed anger, but beneath it her face seemed naked and vulnerable. I suppose it was pity – that most destructive of all emotions – that made me offer to have a drink with herself and Callen another night.

'Callen has his own cronies,' she said, dismissing him. 'Anyway he's not good company right now. He's sulking.' She spoke as if he were a child. 'His van broke down last Monday night and he had to pay out his drinking money to have it repaired. But we could have a drink – just ourselves...'

'I don't think he'd like it.'

'Fuck him,' she said as she had done earlier. This time her vehemence shook me. She picked up her drink and gulped it down and banged the glass back on the table.

'What is it you want?' I asked, committing myself.

'What?' She was flustered now.

'This isn't for old time's sake,' I said. 'I'm not a fool anymore.'

She flinched as if I'd struck her. 'Doesn't the past mean anything?'

'Does it mean anything to you?'

'You were the first. That always means something to a woman.'

Her audacity shocked me. She'd known, of course, that she was my first experience and maybe thought I'd been naive enough then not to know that she wasn't a virgin. But I'd had all of the theory if not the practice. That first magazine Callen had given me had contained an article on the art of love making. It was one of those articles in which everything was described in clinical terms with all the correct medical words. But despite that it had been thorough in its subject matter and treatment. So with all that theory under my belt so to speak, I'd known that she wasn't a virgin.

'You can't be serious,' I said when silence might have been the better option.

'I gave it to you willingly,' she said. 'That's the difference. But you let me down.'

'You can say that in all honesty. After what you did?'

'What would you know?' she said quietly. 'What would any man know?'

I'd expected anger again, maybe more recriminations, and her reaction surprised me. 'Maybe you're right,' I said. 'Who can say?' It was an end to it all and I made to get up.

'I only wanted to help you,' she said, speaking quickly as if she wanted to tether me there with words.

'By doing what you did?'

'Not then,' she said. 'I wanted to help you now. Maybe make up to you... I don't know.'

'How could you help me?'

'I know things,' she said.

'About the killing?' I leaned closer, my body tingling with that old familiar excitement.

'Maybe,' she said. 'One of the policemen who've been brought in – he told me things. But maybe you don't want to know.'

'There's no harm in knowing,' I said, wondering if she was leading me on. No Garda was going to go blabbing confidential information to her. Unless it was some form of payment for what she gave him in return – maybe things whispered in her ear in moments of passion to impress her. Hadn't I wanted to impress her? Though if it were so, she wasn't telling me because she wanted to make reparation for the past. What was her motive? At the moment I couldn't see one. 'So,' I added, 'are you going to tell me?'

'You won't tell anyone who told you? I don't want to get into bother.'

'I never reveal my sources,' I said.

She nodded as if satisfied with that. She glanced around and hesitated, and I thought it was all part of an act. 'You know,' she began, keeping her voice down and leaning towards me, 'that Majella Hawley disappeared this day week. She'd gone to a friend's house in town after school and apparently they had a row. Majella left the house before her father came for her. Someone saw her around seven heading for the footbridge. After that she was never seen alive again.'

'I've read all that,' I said. 'It's common knowledge.'

'But what isn't common knowledge is that she wasn't killed Monday night. She wasn't killed until Wednesday. Whoever kidnapped her kept her alive for two days.'

At first her revelation shocked me, but then my mind began to function again. There had been no hint from the Gardaí that what she'd told me was true, but it was the sort of information they might not wish to divulge. They might want the killer to think that they didn't know when the child was killed. Though to assume that the killer would believe that was surely a foolish thought. Perhaps the information was kept secret to prevent panic. If the public knew that the victim had been at the mercy of her killer for days, there was no knowing what the reaction might be. However, the most likely reason for their silence was that what McQuillan had told me wasn't true.

'You don't believe me?' she said, seeing the doubt on my face.

'It doesn't ring true,' I said. 'Why would someone abduct a child, keep her alive for two days and then kill her? It doesn't make sense.'

'Why would the policeman lie?'

'I don't know,' I said.

'You don't have to believe if you don't want to,' she said. 'There's others who'll believe me. And who'll pay.'

'So that's it,' I said. 'You're trying to sell information. And I thought this was all for me.'

'You're all the fucking same,' she said. 'Aren't you?' She didn't wait for an answer but got to her feet and walked out, and it was with relief I watched her go. I needed another whiskey but knew I'd pay dearly for it in the morning. I rose and made my way up to my room, putting McQuillan and her information out of my mind.

5

The next morning I met D'Arcy at breakfast, tucking into a bowl of porridge. If Jones's typical *Chronicle* reader was based on D'Arcy, then his market research was faulty. I'd be willing to swear that D'Arcy had never heard of muesli. As I crossed to his table he rose to greet me, holding out a brittle hand. 'Ah, William?' he said. 'You got here?'

I nodded. 'Mind if I join you?'

'Of course not.' He waited until I was seated before lowering his thin body back onto his own chair. He held the spoon poised and regarded me over the top of his steel-rimmed spectacles. The eyes were grey, like unpolished silver, and possessed a curious vitality which the man himself contradicted. I'd heard that he'd had talent and could have made it as a writer. He'd dropped out of Trinity amid rumours of an infatuation with an older woman who, as far as I knew, had never been seen by anyone. He'd drifted into journalism and, like most of us, never managed to escape the shackles.

'Jones has been in touch?' I said.

'Jones. Ah, yes.' He spooned porridge into his mouth, giving it all his attention.

'He's asked me to cover for him here,' I said. 'He now wants the human interest angle, the story behind the news – the sort of thing I do. I'm from here; I know the people involved. I can get him what he wants.'

'Yes?' D'Arcy wasn't happy about this. He was a good journalist. He reported facts and maybe interpreted them for his readers if he felt that was necessary, but he never allowed the human angle to intrude. For him it got in the way of truth. It was really surprising that a journalist like D'Arcy had lasted so long with the *Chronicle*.

'Jones wants you back in Dublin,' I said. 'There's this political row brewing.'

'Nothing will come of it, but I should be only too glad to get back.' He spoke with feeling. 'The weather's intolerable. And it's so backward!' He waved his spoon in the air like a conductor's baton. 'All these marvellous roads joining one horrible little town to another. Mind you the hotel's acceptable. It's clean, and the food's not too bad.'

'And porridge for breakfast.'

'Oh, it's just for me. I insisted. It lowers the cholesterol. Mind you, it's cooked in a microwave. Not like the proper thing at all.' He eyed me across the table as if I should make some derogatory remark. But as he sat there, with his sparse grey hair, thin figure and the veins bulging at his temples, I was reminded of my father. He too had eaten porridge, even up to the time when he'd been reduced by illness to little more than a shadow and could eat no more than the few spoonfuls my mother fed him.

He'd died at home, as had been my mother's wish, ageing twenty years in a few weeks, drifting off into a deep sleep one morning after the doctor had given him his painkilling injection, and never waking up again. I think she thought if she nursed him at home – let him die in his own bed – God would grant her her wish for a similar death sometime in the future.

I felt a stab of unease as I thought of them and I had to consciously push the thoughts away. Perhaps I should not have accepted Jones's offer. Indeed had I known that I'd meet

Callen and McQuillan, I would not have done so. But it was too late now for recriminations.

'So what's the latest on the killing?' I asked D'Arcy. 'You haven't heard a rumour that Majella Hawley was kept alive for two days – wasn't actually killed until Wednesday?' D'Arcy had spread marmalade on his toast and lifted the segment to his mouth, but now he put it back down on his plate untouched. Watching him I felt uneasy. It was no longer my father I saw in him but myself in twenty years, my life all but over, still chasing after the great story. I needed to get out of this business before it sucked me dry.

'In a matter like this,' D'Arcy said eventually, 'you have too many rumours. The skill is in separating out the truth. Tell me, where did you hear this ridiculous nonsense?'

'Pub gossip,' I said casually. 'Obviously you don't think it's true?'

'Pub gossip! Of course not. In my experience of these matters the victim is almost always abducted with sexual gratification in mind.' He wrinkled his face in distaste. 'It's not the sort of situation that lends itself to a meaningful relationship. A crazed sex-killer is hardly likely to keep a child alive in order to have someone to talk to.'

The man was priceless. No wonder Jones wanted him back and usually gave him politics to cover. However, he made sense.

A waitress took my order – orange juice and coffee with toast. It was the most a man could be expected to consume at this ungodly hour. The juice was from a carton and had a sharp bite. 'A black mark,' D'Arcy said.

'It is a bit sharp,' I said. 'Maybe we could get our restaurant critic down. She could deduct a star or two.' I laughed and stared at D'Arcy. 'Are you going back today?' I asked.

'Immediately after the press conference,' he said. 'I want to thank the Gardaí for their help.'

'What time's the conference?' I asked.

He stared at me, astonished that I'd not bothered to find out. 'The conference is at ten,' D'Arcy said. 'In the Town Hall.' He glanced at his watch. 'You've got an hour to prepare. Now if you'll excuse me.'

My coffee and toast arrived and the coffee was better than the juice. I'd just finished when Tommo breezed in, his bubbly personality much in evidence and just about concealing his manic-depressive tendencies. He was a photographer, more usually found chasing the beautiful people. 'Leitch,' he said, 'they've let you out. What brings you here?'

'My health,' I said. 'My doctor advised no excitement for a month.'

'Have you heard about the murder?' Tommo claimed that journalists as a rule were ill-informed and never missed an opportunity to rub it in.

'Murder! Do tell me.'

'Top secret,' he said. 'Mum's the word. Now, what's for breakfast?' I didn't ask him to join me and he moved away to a vacant table and sat there staring forlornly out the window. He was as much out of place as D'Arcy was, as I was myself. 'Your lot,' Jones had said, but we belonged nowhere.

I didn't wish to meet any other members of the travelling circus and I got up and made my way outside. It was fine, with that crispness in the air that's described as bracing. On the breeze there was only the faintest hint of a smell. I walked down Strand Street to the bridge, the town alive about me.

After the conference I'd visit the Hawley's to offer my condolences and ferret out what I could. I just needed a small bit of dirt and like God I could build a skeleton from that. Afterwards I'd flesh it out, breathe life into it, touch a raw emotion here and there. I'd need pictures too, ones readers could identify with – the child who was so much like their own.

A group of schoolchildren passed me by, that wild exuberance children display so well subdued. They were shepherded by three women whose faces showed strain. One of the shepherds stared at me, her face set against any threat I might offer her flock. As a child she would have been warned of the dangers posed by strange men, but now all men were suspect. She reminded me of the sheepdog bitch we'd got after my father died and how she'd snapped at me while I removed two of her puppies to drown them, weighing them down with a stone in a bag. They'd sunk into the black water of the boghole with agonising slowness despite the stone, and I'd stood to watch the air bubbles rise to the surface until something had snapped within me and I'd turned and run.

Had the killer carried out such a deed in his childhood? Had he stayed to watch and found that he obtained pleasure and power from his act? Sex crime had as much to do with power as with pleasure, and the ultimate power was to take another's life. Yet could there ever be a rational explanation for the killer's behaviour? Could we ever know what had made him what he was?

In the square a Garda stood at Whelan's corner. He paid me no heed as I passed up Main Street, and I assumed that he was a local who knew me for a stranger. As a stranger I was above suspicion. They were seeking one of their own, one who had walked this pavement, who possessed intimate knowledge of the town and surrounding area. Maybe as a boy like myself he'd searched the pools along the shore for crabs to race across the mud flats. Or had he pulled their claws off one by one, spurred on by a pleasure I could neither imagine nor understand?

I walked as far as the church, an impressive Gothic building dressed in limestone. The last time I'd been in the church had been for my mother's funeral mass, foolish old woman who'd expected so much from me. I thought of her now with sorrow, giving her a few moments of my time, something I had rarely done when she was alive. I thought of her during her final years when I was away at university and she found herself alone in a place that to her must have seemed cold and alien. I realised now that she must have endured the same isolation and loneliness she'd experienced when she lived in New York in those years before she met my father and married him.

I remembered her letters, the trivia of her life written down for me. The black cow calved and there was rain all week and Anthony Doran died. His daughter came from England in a fur jacket and a black skirt with a slit up to her arse, and a big flash car under her. The funeral wasn't as big as Daddy's though. She'd measured the esteem he'd been held in by the number of cars that followed the hearse that winter evening, telling me to count the lights of the vehicles as they came down the road from the house and swung left for Castleford – seventeen before a bend took them from my view.

I remembered her last letter, the blue-lined notepaper and the short paragraphs of news in her childish script. She'd sold the two big bullocks and the cows were in for the winter, and if it didn't snow before January she'd have enough hay to see her through. Danaher brought her five bags of coal and it would help to burn the wet turf and she had to rub Vick's on her chest because she got soaked when the polly cow broke out of the big meadow.

I hadn't read the letter immediately – I'd picked it up off the hall floor on my way out to college and stuffed it in my pocket. I'd forgotten about it until lunchtime, only taking it out then to read. Afterwards I'd crumpled up both paper and envelope and put them in the waste bin, unaware that she was dying – had been found unconscious at around the time I'd picked the letter off the hall floor.

'Chest bad,' the Chinese doctor told me that evening in the corridor of the hospital before I went in to see her. He kept nodding as if to ensure this important fact was properly emphasised. 'Lung collapsed. Most serious.' He spoke in two-word sentences as if he'd only mastered the stock phrases he needed.

With his warning echoing in my head, I entered the ward, a long room with tall narrow windows on one side, the curtains still open so that I could see the pinpricks of stars in the evening sky, their light sharpened by frost. She'd been a sturdy woman, capable of holding her own with any man, but when I saw her lying in the bed she seemed no bigger than a child. A green oxygen mask robbed her of identity and when I kissed her cheek it was cold and clammy.

The hand that pulled down the mask was as weatherbeaten as a man's. The skin was dry and wrinkled and veins stood out so prominently that they might have been piped blue icing. 'You came,' she said as if there might be a question of my not having done so.

'I came as quickly as I could. I only heard this afternoon.'

She nodded, holding the mask against the restraint of the elastic band about her head. Her hair was grey and stringy; the sickness had taken its lustre. Her chest heaved with each breath and I could hear the death-rattle deep in her lungs. I noticed she was wearing hospital pyjamas – regulation pink with thin white stripes – and it was then I felt the first pangs of remorse.

'You should take more care of yourself,' I said brusquely. 'You should sell the place and get yourself a flat in town.'

She stared at me and I knew I'd hurt her. 'I wanted to see you,' she said. 'I want you to know what my wishes are before I go.' It was an effort for her to speak and I suppose it was then I realised that she wasn't going to make it. Along the ward where the visitors gathered about the beds there was a sense of life. But here there was none.

'You should rest,' I said, as brusque as I'd been earlier. 'It's all you need.' The lie tripped easily from my tongue, an attribute which would prove so beneficial to me in my chosen career.

She held the oxygen mask in her left hand and reached out with her right to grip my arm, her fingers digging into my flesh with her last remnants of strength. 'Your father loved that land,' she said, 'and you want me to sell it?' She narrowed her eyes to watch me, to try and impose her will. 'You won't ever sell it,' she said. 'Promise me that.'

'Not while you live,' I said. 'If that's your wish.'

She wanted to say more, but the effort she'd already made had taken its toll. Sweat oozed from her forehead and the skin tightened about her lips. I took the oxygen mask from her hand and placed it back over her face. She sucked at it greedily.

She hadn't the strength to speak again and the remaining time passed in silence.

She'd been put on a boat for America when she was sixteen to earn money to send back home. Hardened to believe that she would never know affection for herself, she had lost her ability to show affection to anyone, even to my father, whom she had merely worshipped because he was a good man. I in my turn had become hard like her, hardening even more after the night with McQuillan. It was that which prevented me from telling her I loved her as I got up to go. 'Don't forget to feed the cattle, ' she said to me as I left. 'And don't let the fire go out.' These were the last words she ever spoke to me.

6

The Town Hall was a repository of memories. It was here I'd
come during the anguished, seemingly endless, years of
adolescence, seeking with the other boys what the songs
promised – pleasure, excitement, love, happiness – aware I
think that it was all a sad illusion. But still we sought it,
pretending – even believing – that the lust we felt for those
gyrating, mysterious bodies was love. It was here I'd first fallen
in love myself, certain then that this love would never die. But
in a few months it withered away to a bitter-sweet memory of
the smell of female flesh, the pressure of maturing breasts
against my chest and the warm moist feel of reluctant lips on
my own.

I'd come here with McQuillan, playing out the mating
ritual as all animals do before I took from her what I'd wanted.
I'd danced with her, the envy of all those who were desperate
for what she gave so willingly, thinking myself lucky.

It all came back to me as I entered, in spite of plywood
covering the cashier's hatch, the cloakroom door standing
open, rows of coat-hooks hanging empty. In the hall itself the
smell of decay and neglect hung in the stale air with the dust
which rose from the cracks between the floorboards.

Superintendent Halligan himself was on the stage, taking
centre place at a long table, flanked by two colleagues. Further
back two plainclothes detectives hovered. The stage was lit for

the television cameras and this created an artificial twilight in the cavernous hall. There were no windows and the lights still functioning only helped to emphasise the long years of accumulated gloom.

Inquiries were continuing, Halligan told us, and he was once again appealing to the public for help. 'Whatever information you have, however trivial it may seem to you, please let us have it,' he said. 'Let us be the judge of its worth.' He spoke directly into the television camera below him. 'Someone out there knows him. Perhaps they only suspect him. He may be a loved one – a husband or a father or a son; a brother, perhaps a neighbour. But your duty, whoever he may be, is to give whatever information you may have to the Gardaí. It will be treated in the strictest confidence. Remember,' Halligan added with more emphasis, 'that he has already killed at least once. There may have been a previous killing, though we're keeping an open mind on that. What is almost certain is that if he's not caught, he will kill again. If you have any information, you can call us in strict confidence, and with a guarantee of anonymity, on the telephone numbers the Inspector will now give you.'

There was going to be a reconstruction of Majella Hawley's last known movements this evening, Halligan told us. 'We're hoping that this may jog the memory of anyone who saw her last Monday, or indeed might have seen or noticed anything unusual that they feel would be of help to us,' he said. 'Now, have you any questions?'

There were numerous questions, and I left it to others to ask them, but the Gardaí were giving little away. 'I'm afraid that's confidential,' seemed to be the stock answer. For some reason best known to themselves, they were not divulging what information they had. This wasn't the time or place to pursue the information McQuillan had given me.

I turned to leave. As I slipped out I heard my name being called and turned back. The man who came towards me I'd last seen over twenty years before but I couldn't mistake him. 'Plodder' Doyle, as I'd known him when we were both school-boys, had hardly changed. He'd earned the nickname for his methodical attitude, and I could only think that he had taken up the correct profession when he joined the Gardaí. We shook hands and I felt the unease we all experience at unexpectedly meeting someone we once knew well and to whom we are beholden. 'You haven't changed, Willie,' he said when we'd exchanged the banal greetings. 'Life must be treating you well.'

'I could say the same,' I said.

He nodded. 'I suppose you're here for the same reason as myself. I'm a Detective Sergeant now. Can you believe it? They've brought me back because I know the area and the people. They thought it might be an advantage.'

'I'm here for much the same reason,' I said. 'I'm supposed to know the area and the people, too. Only sometimes I wonder...' I stared at him, trying to scale him down to the boy I'd once known. Was it possible that he'd been the only friend I'd ever had here, apart from Alec Whitley, owner and editor of *The Mayoman* newspaper? 'This business,' I said. 'Any ideas? Strictly off the record.'

It was his turn now to regard me – to try to picture the boy I'd once been – but I think he had no more success than myself. 'He's a local,' he said. 'Someone who knows the area. We probably know him. Had you thought of that?' He shook his head at the probability of it. 'We have to catch him,' he added, 'before he kills again.'

'You think he will?'

'He's killed twice already. He'll kill again if he isn't caught.'

'So you're convinced Jacinta Devlin is dead?'

'Where else could a ten-year-old child get to?'

I'd no answer to that so I asked him about Joe Hawley. He regarded me for a moment before replying. 'What can I say about him?' he said. 'I've got a daughter the same age.'

'I'm going out to see him,' I said.

'It's your job, I suppose,' he said, 'but go easy. After all, the past is past. We can't change it now.'

'I know,' I said. 'I'll be easy.'

He relaxed then, and after promising to arrange to meet him for a drink, I returned to the hotel.

The town was quiet again and seemed frighteningly normal as I headed for Hawley's. I wanted to get there while the other journalists were still at the conference. I drove out the Duagh Road, passing the bungalows that last night had been shadows in the darkness. As I passed the national school the children were out at play, unfettered by what had occurred here or by the future awaiting them. Did the death of their contemporary, even in its brutality, mean no more than a welcome diversion from the monotony of the classroom? Did they think of her as an angel in heaven, as I myself had once imagined a schoolfriend who'd died, an urchin with the wizened skin of a crab apple, whose each and every breath was an effort? I'd imagined his heaven as a place where he could at last breathe easily and where he would float on silver wings, his hand raised in blessing above us unfortunates who'd been damned with life and the unfathomable intricacies of long-division sums.

A teacher walked among the children, hands clasped behind his back, his head jerking here and there as he sought danger all about him; as if the killer might strike again in broad daylight. As the school slipped past, an ugly flat-roofed building in ash-coloured brick with large windows to taunt the inmates – teachers and children alike – with views of the world they'd temporarily relinquished, I realised with a shudder that I could so easily have been that man walking the yard with the children's cries echoing in my ears like the cries of gulls over the mud flats when the tide ebbed. As a boy I'd walked the flats barefooted, mud squelching between my toes, the roar of the ocean and the poetry of Yeats and Hopkins like a storm in my head, a dream clutched in my hands like a precious bird that would flit away if I eased my grip.

My father had always hoped that I'd be a teacher, having a faith in education that can only be had by one who'd experienced little of it. Had he lived would I now be a teacher, my life shrivelled up and the bird long since flown, the poetry no longer a pleasure but a damned imposition? He'd died before his influence could take effect and now I was like someone who's lost something yet still instinctively searches for it though he can no longer remember what it is he seeks.

I'd often thought of the accidents and chance encounters to which we owe our existence – what we are and what we become – and how a word or gesture or laugh could have changed it all. I often thought of the separate paths my parents took to a new world, separated in Ireland by a hundred miles, by ten years in their journeys across the Atlantic, by a few block in New York where, they told me, they'd even attended the same church without ever remembering seeing each other, until they met one evening in the porch of an apartment block where my father was the janitor and where my mother had taken shelter from the rain. Forever afterwards she was giving thanks to God for that meeting, for having answered her prayers and sent her a man to love her. She firmly believed that it was God who'd arranged it, who'd created the depression out in the Atlantic which had caused the downpour which in turn had forced her to seek shelter. But if God had arranged it, it was her loneliness that made her respond to my father's kind voice and to the offer of the umbrella he gave her in case the rain came again.

How many different strands had to come together for that to occur? How many more in the months that followed when my father courted her, as she'd also told me, in the only way he knew – with the kindness and affection he possessed for every living creature, which she took for love? How often in the year after they were married, and before I was conceived, did the sperm instinctively battle its way towards the egg, only to be thwarted? How often was my potential existence threatened by another's, which was destined never to be?

When I was born, the desire they'd had for a child now became a desire to return to Ireland, and in the property pages of a provincial paper they came on an ad for a small farm at Castleford in County Mayo. My father told me that he came to view it in May and that the weather exceeded the usual standards of an Irish summer. He told me how he turned onto the road I now turned onto and was won over by the trees which edged it, beech and sycamore weighed down with leaves, the ash still bare, clusters of pods just bursting open to betray the dark green heart of the uncurling leaves.

He decided then to buy the farm – the acres of cutaway bog and the scrawny hills and the dilapidated two storey farmhouse with its range of outbuildings – even before he'd seen it. On his decision that day my future was forged, because we are as much a part of our environment as we are of our childhood experiences and our parents' genes.

Had my parents not seen that ad; had it been wet the day my father came here; had the trees never been planted by a crazy Irishman who'd wanted to ape the English landlords he'd replaced... Had I never come to know Callen or McQuillan or Alec Whitley, who'd first instilled in me a love of books and poetry and the desire to be a writer... But to consider all that too closely could lead to madness – to my ending up drooling in a room with barred windows and the world locked away inside my head.

I crossed the railway bridge and passed the turn-off to my old home. I began to consider how I'd approach Joe Hawley: as the schoolfriend come to offer his sympathy, the past forgotten? Or as one seeking vengeance for the terror I'd suffered at his hands? Hawley had been two years older than me, a sly youth with a penchant for bullying. He'd been the leader of a gang of bullies, big lads like himself, brawn without brains, inheritors of a small part of the earth for that small part of their lives.

I was climbing now, low stone walls on either side, cattle grazing the thin grass in the roadside fields. There were few houses: the odd modern bungalow out of place in this all but barren landscape; a few abandoned cottages, the families driven out by poverty or restlessness of spirit. I reached the fork and took the narrow track leading down to Hawley's, the old farmhouse and outbuildings visible. I drove on through an avenue of bare poplars which dwarfed the young cypress trees growing in their shadow and only then glimpsed a new bungalow on my left, almost completely hidden from view by a privet hedge and shelter belt of conifers. A gateway gave access to a gravelled yard, and I drove in and parked beside a car with a trailer attached. A black mongrel slunk from a nearby shed to watch me and I made a mental note of its existence. It would add the right sort of touch – the faithful dog so beloved by the child, now pining for its mistress. It wasn't photogenic but that didn't matter. The reader's imagination would supply the picture.

As I switched off the ignition a woman came from the house – tall and slim with a boyish figure and long dark hair which she flung back over her shoulder with a twitch of her head. I assumed she was a relative. She was too old to be Majella's sister, and much too young to be her mother.

I wound down the window, determined not to be rebuffed. 'They don't want to talk to anyone,' she said as she bent down to look at me. Her denim jacket was open and the top buttons of her wine-red blouse undone. I had a glimpse of small childish breasts and the white edge of a brassiere before she self-consciously straightened up.

'I'm a neighbour,' I said. 'I went to school with Joe.'

'Oh, I'm sorry then,' she said. ''I suppose you'd best come in.' As I got out the dog slunk closer, its tail beating the gravel. 'Get out of it, Spot,' she scolded, but the dog only beat all the more vigorously.

I laughed and she turned to stare at me as if I'd sworn or made a lewd suggestion. 'Sorry,' I said. 'It's just the dog... He seems jet black to me.'

'Oh.' She turned to look at the mongrel. 'I never thought of that.' A smile lit up her features. She was young, eighteen at most.

'Are you a relative?' I asked as I closed the car door. She shook her head with a force that set her hair swinging, vitality in every rib.

'My father's helping them out with the farm,' she said. 'I came with him to see if I could do anything.'

I nodded, shivering, the warmth I'd soaked up on the drive seeping from my body. I followed the girl towards the house, watching the movement of her boyish buttocks in the skintight denims. Suddenly her presence touched something within me – that physical yearning of adolescence which one instinctively knew then could not be fulfilled – a yearning which had as much to do with curiosity and a need for knowledge as with pleasure, and which I'd thought I'd never experience again. The feeling disturbed me and I felt like a voyeur, like the killer who'd brought me here, and I imagined him following the girls around with the same adolescent longings, resorting to force in the end to take what he couldn't obtain by any other means.

I averted my eyes from her and gave my attention to my surroundings. The area to the rear of the house was concreted over and some black cast-iron cooking pots containing shrubs stood along the wall, relics from the past. I remembered my mother using one called an oven in which she baked soda bread, coals piled on the lid so that there was heat on top and bottom. It was a way of life lost forever as the world inevitably changed. Only our destructive desires remained constant.

The girl opened the door and we entered the kitchen, past the jetsam and flotsam which accumulates at the back door of any house: an old saucepan in which the dog was fed; a bucket and mop; a bag of coal; a couple of yellow gas cylinders. As I entered I fixed my mask in place – the mask we all wear to help us live from one day to the next – and silently told myself that I wouldn't leave until I'd got what I wanted.

7

It was the room I impressed on my memory – green emul-
sioned walls and a white ceiling darkened to a shade of ivory
above the cumbersome solid fuel cooker – as if it were less
painful to imprint it rather than the persons who occupied it:
the woman crouched in an armchair at the side of the Stanley,
wearing a threadbare dressing gown and tattered slippers, a
mug of tea in her hands; the man with the sandy hair who sat
at the table under the gable window along with two subdued
children – a girl of about fourteen and a boy of about ten.

They stared at me with varying degrees of curiosity and, if
I were not mistaken, resentment. The resentment, if it existed
(and how could I tell that it wasn't just my imagination?) was
not directed at me but at the life I represented. By coming
here I was flaunting it in the face of their loss.

The girl who'd come out to meet me (was it only when I
left the house that I learned her name was Lizzie O'Malley?)
closed the door and sat at the table, leaving me isolated. In my
nervous state it was the minor things I noticed: the Ninja
Turtle mugs they were drinking from; the clock on the wall
showing the incorrect time; the doors of the shabby kitchen
units hanging crookedly.

I thought of the other journalists who must have come here
– decent ones like D'Arcy, others like myself seeking only
sensation. But at least they would have been honest enough to

admit their motives, unlike me who'd slunk in like the mongrel might, and who was now willing to thump his tail on the imitation parquet vinyl.

Hawley stared at me, trying to put a name to the face. Once I would have shuddered before him, but he was the one who was helpless and frightened now. The skin of his face was pulled taut, as much by a lack of comprehension, I sensed, as by grief. There was bewilderment and anger in the eyes – that terrible need for vengeance which sometimes surfaces within us. I crossed to him and offered my hand and my sympathy, 'I'm sorry for your trouble,' the impotent words of the ritual we hide behind when faced with death.

'Thanks.' He mumbled the correct response and gripped my hand tightly, trying to take some of my strength for himself. I was aware of all the eyes watching me just like in those odd moments when we're alone and we feel ourselves under scrutiny. But when we turn to look over our shoulder there's no one there.

'It's Willie,' I said. 'The Yank's son.' It was a nickname they'd given me that I'd hated, but I used it to try to put him at his ease.

'I recognised you all right,' he said. 'After a minute.' He released my hand and I crossed to his wife and repeated the formula. She went through the ritual automatically. 'Willie Leitch,' I heard Hawley introduce me. 'The Yan...' He coughed to cover his embarrassment, and for a moment I felt a pang of genuine sympathy for him.

'Bobby and Maggie's son,' Hawley added, and I had the impression that he was talking to a disobedient child, was trying to humour it. But she never took her eyes from the mug, her fingers caressing the turtle, intent it seemed on broadening the smile of rapture on its face.

I was struck by her good looks – the evidence of fatigue and crying which gave her features the fixture of a grimace could-n't hide the fact that she was pretty. But for now she was changed to an older, more haggard version of the young girl, who even in the grainy newspaper blow-up I couldn't have mistaken for anyone but her daughter.

'Sit down,' Hawley said indicating the settee beneath the rear window. 'You'll have a cup of tea? Or something stronger?'

'It's a bit early,' I said, sitting down. 'Tea'll be fine.'

Lizzie got up and crossed in front of me. She bent down to search in the cupboard at the end of the settee and I was acutely aware of her closeness. I examined the bare patches on the vinyl to prevent my eyes being drawn to her, but I couldn't avoid her as she passed before me again, a mug in her hand. Hawley whispered to her and she left the mug on the table and crossed to the sink and filled the kettle and plugged it in. She returned to rummage again in the cupboard beside me, and this time I stared about me, impressing the room even more on my memory: the colour television in the corner; the net curtains, grubby at the edges; the framed photographs on the window-sill, the dead child conspicuous by her absence. They had removed her image as if that might dim their memory of her, erase from their minds what she must have endured. But despite their efforts, she was amongst us.

A chair leg squeaked as Hawley rose to his feet, the baggy jumper unable to conceal his flabby stomach. 'Right, kids,' he said. 'Off with you and find something to do.' They got up obediently and left the room. 'They've taken it bad,' he said to me, 'so we don't talk about it when they're around. The less they hear, the better.'

I nodded, watching him, a great brute of a man reduced to the pitiful state of a shambling clown who'd never forgive himself for what had happened to his daughter. He hadn't been there to protect her when she needed him, and he would carry that guilt with him to his grave.

He turned the chair about to face me and sat down. I noticed that his laces were undone and he was without socks. Lizzie eased by him carrying a cup and saucer and I had a reason now for the earlier whisper. As a guest I was entitled to something better than a mug and I was moved by the gesture, by the fact that he could still consider such niceties in the midst of the horror which had invaded his home.

'You still in Dublin?' he said now. 'Still with the papers?'

'Still there,' I said.

'This isn't a social call then? You didn't come all this way just to be offering your sympathy?'

'No.' I hadn't expected direct confrontation. I'd hoped to break the ice first, to establish some sort of rapport. 'The *Sunday Chronicle* wants your story,' I went on. 'Being as I knew you – that we'd been to school together – well, they thought you'd find it easier to talk to me.'

'We don't want anything to do with the papers.' It was Mrs Hawley who spoke. She hunched forward in the chair. 'We don't want anything to do with them. It's their sort of filth that... that...' She rose to her feet, the mug clutched in her hands.

'It's all right, Mary.' Hawley rose and took the mug from her. Left with nothing to occupy her hands she clutched her dressing gown. 'Come on,' he said gently, taking her arm. 'We'll go for a little lie-down.'

He lead her from the room, muttering endearments, reduced to this by the violence he'd once espoused. It made me uneasy. It was as if I'd just witnessed an intimacy which I'd tainted with my presence.

'She's not herself,' Lizzie said, turning to face me. 'Normally she'd have nothing but welcome for you.'

'I know.' It was something to say.

'I didn't know you were a reporter,' she accused. 'You didn't say. I think you should leave them be.' I knew myself that I should get up and go, but even the parasite has to live. I couldn't go without something to take away with me.

Hawley came back, blustering and apologetic. 'She's not herself,' he said. 'Look, you'll stay and have a cup anyway.' His eyes pleaded with me to stay, but he was giving me credit for far more decency than I possessed. 'You understand how it is?' he went on. 'We can't bring her back but we can't accept that she's gone either. We saw her off to school on Monday morning same as she went off every day. It was no different to any other day except that she didn't come home. Mary took away all the photos – she didn't want to be reminded – but you don't need a photo to remind you. During the week the Gardaí kept questioning us. What was she wearing? What state of mind was she in? Was she happy? And all the time we're hoping she'll come walking in the door just as she used to... I had to identify her. Someone has to, you see, formally identify...'

Mercifully at that moment Lizzie handed me my tea – country tea as my father used call it – lukewarm after the addition of too much milk and sickly sweet. Despite this I gulped some of it down, giving my attention to that, relieved that I didn't have to answer Hawley, or worse still look at him and see etched on his face what he'd suffered in that moment when the sheet was pulled back.

Years before, I'd got to know the morgue attendant at a Dublin hospital, and he'd shown me around one night to gather background material for a feature I proposed to write. Yet all I remembered afterwards was the chill of the place, the indifference of the attendant and the grey withered corpse of an old man who'd died just hours before in the geriatric ward. I remembered him because he reminded me of my dead father, though of course I'd never seen his naked corpse, only been aware from looking at the shape beneath the bedclothes that all that remained was skin and bones, and thinking of his kindness and his laughter and the day he carried me shoulder high across the top garden, and thinking too of what a pathetic embarrassing bundle we are all reduced to when the spirit's gone.

The proposed feature was never written. Maybe I hadn't the detachment necessary, even after all the years, to accept my father's death, and now the problem Hawley faced in relation to his daughter. He still saw her alive here in this house, in the faces of his wife and children. It wasn't his daughter he identified in the morgue – that living flame he'd known her life to be – but someone else. It was that someone else who'd suffered the terror, whose body would be cut up by the pathologist when he sought the secrets of her death.

'Is the tea all right?' Hawley asked, interrupting my thought. 'Maybe you'd like a bit to eat.'

'No. No thanks,' I said.

'Will you be staying in Castleford for long?'

'A few days I suppose. I haven't been back in years. I might have a look around. At the old place and that...'

'The Power lad was talking about doing it up when he got married, but he built a council house instead. They cleared some of the old fences, put a few fields together. You'd hardly know it, there've been so many changes.'

'We can't stand in the way of change,' I said.

'It isn't always for the best. If there hadn't been change, Majella... well, she'd still be alive, wouldn't she?'

'I don't understand.'

'Television. Books and magazines and that. Newspapers. They give this false idea about... you know... things...' He floundered helplessly, out of his depth. 'They put ideas in people's minds – bad ideas...'

'You feel strongly about it?'

'I didn't used to.'

'I could write about it,' I said. 'Make your views known.'

He eyed me with suspicion, having no reason to trust anymore. Despite the Garda claim that, without evidence to the contrary, they had to assume that the killer could be from anywhere, Hawley knew he was local. With that knowledge how could he trust again? 'I have to write something,' I said. 'Why not make it something you want people to know, a warning to others? You know that he'll strike again unless he's caught.'

'He's someone we know,' Hawley said, echoing my thoughts. 'We could've been at school with him. Why would he do this? The priest said it was God's will, but it wasn't his daughter that was taken and held for days...' He stopped abruptly and turned to stare out at the sky where dark clouds were beating towards us. As a consequence he didn't see my elation. I'd been prepared to dismiss what McQuillan had told me, but now I'd had it confirmed.

I took Hawley's statement and measured it for ambiguity, but there was none. I caught his eye as he turned back and I saw his unease before he turned away again. My sense of excitement increased. Already I was imagining the headlines. There would be repercussions, but I'd deal with them in due course. All I wanted now was definite confirmation. 'Did I hear you right?' I asked.

'What?' He feigned puzzlement but he was no actor.

'What you just said. About Majella being kept for days.'

'I don't know,' he said. 'I only meant that the Gardaí aren't certain. They don't know for sure when she died, not the exact time...'

I knew he was lying. I could scent success and wouldn't be thwarted. 'Don't you think you owe it to other parents?' I said.

'He has struck twice already. Do you want other parents to go through what you're going through? Think of your own wife and children...'

'What can it do? It can't bring her back? If it could, don't you think I'd do anything?' I'd touched too close to his loss, and anger made his face ugly and threatening.

'It can't bring her back,' I said, 'but it can prevent another death. If parents really knew the truth... it would make the Gardaí more vigilant. If there'd been a Garda presence on the streets after the disappearance of Jacinta Devlin, would your daughter be dead? Do you want another death on your conscience?'

I was brutal with him, but there would be time for shame afterwards. Now, like an animal scenting blood, I moved in for the kill. Had I been a stranger with no previous claim on him, I think that he would have thrown me out, but the past wouldn't allow him.

'I'll show you my milking parlour,' he said, indicating with a nod Lizzie who was washing up, the energy contained in her body like a coiled spring. He bent to tie his shoelaces and hesitated as he noticed that he wasn't wearing socks. He tied the laces, and I followed him outside and up the track between the poplars, avoiding the remnants of grey sky thrown in the puddles.

'Is your mother still alive?' I asked.

'She is,' he said. 'Though it might be better for her if she wasn't. This is no thing for her to be facing at this time of her life.'

'No.' I thought of Judith Kelly and the day we attended her funeral. Her grandmother had been there, dressed in black, her back rounded like a question mark from rheumatism. 'Why couldn't God have taken her?' I'd heard someone whisper as the old woman was linked to the graveside. Was that what Hawley thought? Why couldn't God have taken his mother and left him his daughter?

The milking parlour was a concrete building with a smell of cow and milk and disinfectant, a profusion of pipes and four milking attachments hanging from a rail. The unease between Hawley and myself persisted. 'Look,' I said, 'we couldn't really talk inside. So let's forget the past. We were just kids then. It was a part of growing up. I'm willing to forget it if you are.'

Hawley stared at me in horror. I think he might have run if I hadn't stuck out my hand. It was easier for him to take it and triumphantly I knew I had him. 'There was something you didn't want the girl to hear,' I hinted.

He nodded, staring out at the trees swaying in the wind, the rooks' nests like black growths on the bare branches. 'It's not easy to talk about it,' he said. 'It was the hardest thing to accept. It would have been easier if she'd died straight away.' I stared at him, wondering what was passing through his mind, elated at my good fortune, but also sickened by the implications of what he was saying. 'I asked the Gardaí to keep it to themselves,' he went on. 'I didn't want Mary or the children to know. They agreed – they seemed to think that it would help them. I shouldn't have let it slip. Now you have to give me your word that you won't write about it.'

'You're saying she was held somewhere for days?' I said, ignoring his plea. 'So when do the Gardaí say she was killed?'

'Not until Wednesday. I thought it might have been a mistake. But they can tell. From the digestion and that...'

'Jesus,' I said. 'I can't believe it. It should've been disclosed – you know that, don't you?'

'Why?' he said. 'So that Mary and the children could suffer more?'

'It'll all come out eventually,' I said, 'so they'll have to face it then.' It was a heartless thing to say, and I think at that moment he hated me. But I was merciless with him, probing now for details of the sexual assault perpetrated on his daughter. 'People have a right to know that, too,' I said. 'It's only fear that'll ensure they keep their children safe.'

He shook his head and I thought he was refusing to answer me and I pressed him even more. 'I don't know,' he said. 'I don't know. I asked them not to tell me. To think of her there with him for days, having to endure whatever it was...' He stared about him like a snared animal and caught sight of the mongrel which had slunk in to sit at our feet. His foot lashed out at the dog and it yelped and leapt away and cowered down at the door to watch us.

'I'm sorry,' I said. 'I won't ask you anything else. But maybe I could have some photographs taken. If you wouldn't mind, I'll arrange for someone from *The Mayoman* to call tomorrow. OK?'

He scuffed the floor with his boot and then coaxed the dog to him and stooped down to pat its head. I filed the moment away and asked him again about the photographs. He patted the dog a final time before straightening up. He looked at me with unblinking eyes and then nodded slowly. 'Tomorrow,' he said. 'But then we're quits. As you pointed out, it was a long time ago.'

He turned and walked back to the house and I followed him, keeping my distance like the dog. I watched him until he went inside and then I sat into my car. I grasped the steering wheel in both hands and sat staring through the windscreen at the house, thinking only of my story. Then the door opened and Lizzie emerged and came towards me.

8

With Lizzie beside me in the car, I was aware for the first time of her smell – the sweet-sour smell of body odour and the sweeter scent of some deodorant she must have applied before she ran out to ask me for a lift back to town. The smell was cloying, similar to the smell I'd experienced during childhood on damp Sundays in church, sitting with the huddle of humanity while the unwashed bodies and clothing steamed in the communal heat. Now I ignored the smell and glanced at her. She wasn't wearing her seat belt and I asked her to fasten it. Back at Hawley's I'd seen that boyishly thin body as an object from which I might take pleasure. Now, with her beside me, her aroma in my nostrils, she was no longer an object but a person, someone who sweated and didn't bathe too often or regularly change her underwear.

'That thing,' she said. 'It's always cutting into my chest. You should see the weals.' She looked at me with a disarming frankness while she fastened the belt, then hooked her thumb in the webbing and pulled it away from her. 'See,' she said, letting the webbing snap back against the swelling of the blouse. 'It'd choke the life out of you. Isn't it lucky I haven't a big chest?'

'There's a clip you can buy,' I said. 'It's supposed to help.' It was something to say while I tried to come to terms with this creature beside me. One moment I had the impression of a child and the next of some slut who would allow men to beat and abuse her. The image excited me, the thought of being one of those men made me shudder, and I imagined her naked on a bed surrounded by faceless men who held her down while I took whatever pleasure I wanted.

I was shamed by the thought and by the desire hardening within me. She was little more than a child, hardly more mature than Majella Hawley had been, she who'd paid the ultimate price in satisfying a man's murderous desires. Here was I fantasising about this odd creature beside me and I didn't even know her name.

'Elizabeth,' she said in answer to my question. 'But you can call me Lizzie if you like.' She laughed, throwing her head back in abandonment, her hair cascading down the rear of the seat like a cataract of black oil.

It was seeing her then – the sheer exuberance of youth, the dimple in her throat as she sucked in air, her face transformed into that of a child on Christmas morning at the sight of the presents under the tree – it was all of those things and none of those things that stirred my first feelings of tenderness for her. 'Lizzie it is,' I said. 'But haven't you another name?'

'O'Malley,' she said. 'Elizabeth Grace O'Malley.'

'You're kidding.' It was my turn to laugh. 'Grace O'Malley?'

'Please yourself,' she said. 'See if I care.' She turned to stare out of the window at the lines of hawthorn which ran beside the road like ravelled black blinds. Her hand beat time on her knee and I noticed that her nails were bitten down.

'I'm sorry,' I said. 'It's just, well, one automatically associates the name O'Malley with Grace, but you never expect to meet anyone who's actually called Grace.'

'It was my father's idea,' she said, turning back, 'to call me that stupid name. When I went to school and learned the Hail

Mary I thought it referred to me. Hail Mary, full of grace... I asked the teacher if it was me and they all laughed. After that they started calling me Grace, but I thumped them and they soon left me alone.' She laughed again, whatever slight I might have done her instantly forgotten. 'You're never to call me that name,' she added. 'Promise me that.'

I turned off the track onto the tarred road, the patchwork countryside spread out before me, the pewter grey sea visible in the distance out beyond Castlewood. Cloud was building up out to the west and I could tell from the movement of the hedges that the wind had freshened. It was exposed up here. The telegraph poles along the roadside leaned away from the prevailing winds.

'Do you live around here?' I asked.

'I wouldn't be coming into town with you if I did,' she said. 'Or are you thinking I just want to be in your company?'

'No. I'm just not thinking straight, that's all.'

'Am I having that effect on you?'

'No,' I spoke rather hastily and she laughed. I felt inadequate in her presence, like a man who's been trained for a particular situation and now finds the rules have changed.

'I have that effect on people,' she said. 'Especially men.' She waited for my reaction but I made none.

We'd dropped down now and were approaching the turn-off for my old home. 'Isn't this where you come from?' she asked. When I nodded she brightened as if a switch had been thrown. 'Let's go and have a look,' she said.

'I don't own it anymore,' I said. 'The Powers own it now.'

'They can't stop you from looking.'

'Maybe another time.' I wasn't ready yet to face that part of my past.

'Come on,' she said. 'Don't be a spoilsport. What harm's there in a look?' She stuck out her hand and playfully punched me on the shoulder, the first physical contact between us. It was like an electric shock and I grabbed the gear lever and changed down for the turn-off. As I swung onto the narrow tarmacadamed track I thought she'd clap her hands. 'You're not a spoilsport after all,' she said.

'There's some mightn't agree.'

'Who? Your wife?'

'I'm not married.'

She didn't speak again, and in the silence I had time to dwell on this unexpected journey back into a past I thought I'd left behind me. It was here that much of what I'd become had been decided, even as the blue of my eyes and the mousy texture and colour of my hair had been decided by the fusion of my parents' genes at the moment of conception. I might dye the hair a different hue, wear contact lenses to alter the colour of my eyes, yet nothing of what I was meant to be could be changed.

Whenever before I'd thought of returning, and there had been the odd time when I did so think, I'd imagined coming here with my family (there was a time too when I'd dreamed of having a family), taking them back to their roots and showing them the town which had dominated my childhood, the old building that housed *The Mayoman* in which my first poem was printed and Brogan's newsagents where I'd bought the paper that made me a writer.

Never was that moment to be savoured again with the same intensity – the opening of the paper, the search for page seven where in a box, framed with the same thick black lines which surrounded death notices, a single poem was printed. Mr Brogan, seeing my excitement, asked me what caused it and when I told him he picked up a paper, found page seven and read aloud my name beneath the fourteen lines of print.

Did I know then as I read the childish lines that what I was savouring was the pinnacle of success? Did I have an inkling in my moment of triumph of the waiting cup of failure, as later in the consummation of the act of love I was made aware of my own mortality? I do not know. All I know is that I would have told my family only of the good times which in moments of dark despair helped me carry on – the times before my father's death when I would have agreed to whatever he wanted for me.

When I thought of it now, back here where it had all begun, I realised with a sense of loss that all he'd have wanted for me was that I be happy, that I have the same security of a family that he himself had come to so late and which had been granted him for such a short time. He'd have wanted me to tell my family about him – about his scraggy grey moustache and his thin hair and his bushy black eyebrows which he told me were caterpillars, which like my belief in Santa Claus and God later became just another deceit and betrayal. But I couldn't blame him for that because I knew that if I had a family I too would pretend that Santa Claus existed. Maybe I'd even pretend to love them...

Lizzie must have sensed my morbidity and it made her sullen. 'If it was that bad,' she accused, 'maybe you should turn back.'

'It wasn't,' I said. 'I was happy here. Only I didn't know it then.'

As we breasted the hill I glimpsed the sea again, and Coogan's cottage, rooks circling the roofless building. Further along was Rooney's farmhouse with its outbuildings and a herd of cattle in a muddy field. Hawley's warning about the changes I'd encounter had prepared me, but it was still a shock to see the house up ahead naked to the elements. Not a single tree, the ash and beech and cypress my father had planted, remained. My immediate reaction was anger at the destruction, but the anger was short-lived. I'd no right to it, I who'd sold his dream for money. After all, what did the Powers care for his trees?

One of my most vivid memories was to see him walking along the lines of saplings on a summer's evening, testing for firmness the stakes which supported them, snipping off the bits of dead wood, patting each tree as he might pat the top of my head. I'd accompanied him on those walks, privileged to walk beside him, the man-of-the-house-to-be as he called me, to bask in the smell of cow and tobacco which were always a part of him, his sheepdog, Bran, at our heels, alert to the tone of his voice.

In the weeks following my father's death, Bran would sit by the gate, looking forlornly down the road as if at any moment he might hear the engine note of his master's car. Two months later he died, run over by a Castleford hackney cab. The dog had been asleep by the gate and was woken suddenly by the approaching car. In the muddled moments after waking up, he dashed out blindly to greet his master and ended up beneath the wheels. 'Isn't he the lucky one,' my mother said, but I'd no idea then what she meant. We buried him in a corner of the garden and oftentimes I'd found her down there, envying that dumb animal his peace.

As I drew near the house I saw that her garden had become part of the fields. The house itself stood with the farm buildings like an outcrop of rock in the sea, and seeing it I found myself wishing that I hadn't come here or that I'd come alone.

I pulled the car in off the road. I had no intention of getting out, but Lizzie unbuckled her seatbelt, opened the door and leapt out. 'Come on,' she mouthed through the window, beckoning me. At first I shook my head, but as she called more vehemently, I too got out.

'Come on,' she coaxed. 'We'll have a look now we're here.'

She placed her foot on the middle rail of the fence and swung herself over. Her jeans seemed to tighten even more against her flesh and it was impossible not to imagine what they concealed. I felt like a peeping-tom and I turned away with conflicting feelings of shame and desire.

Further along the track I saw the Powers' farmhouse, the new bungalow beside it. They'd been our nearest neighbour but they'd never accepted us, seeing us as the returned Yanks with money to burn. They could never have imagined how my parents had earned their few thousand dollars in savings, what hardship and loneliness they'd endured before fate threw them together.

'Well?' Lizzie said, and I turned back to her. She watched me with a mocking glint in eyes that were brown like the horse chestnuts with which I'd once played conkers. I couldn't be certain if I only imagined that knowing look she had – that look that women possess – as if the secret the serpent divulged to Eve in the Garden of Eden had never been passed on to us and we suffered from that lack. She knew I'd watched her as she climbed over the fence and she was pleased by her effect on me.

'Come on,' she said. 'Last one's a sissy.' She laughed and ran towards the house and she was a woman no longer, but a young girl playing hide and seek and excited at the prospect of being found, that excitement which is but the foretaste of sexual excitement itself.

She disappeared around the corner of the house towards the front where my mother's garden had been, a flowering cherry tree taking pride of place among the flowering currants and the fuchsia, whose fallen petals were like drops of blood on the ground. There in March the daffodils and narcissi were battered by the wind and in October the crab-apple tree shed its fruit which became homes for maggots. I shook my head and climbed over the rails and walked towards the gable, noting that the pebble-dash was crumbling away to reveal the stone underneath. As I walked the crumbling concrete foot-path to the door, I half expected to find it wide open and to hear the sound of the radio or the gramophone which my father listened to in the sitting-room on wet Sunday after-noons. But the door was closed, its Nile Green paintwork pitted and peeled by the elements to show the rotting timber beneath. Planks had been nailed across its width. Just then Lizzie came up behind me after circling the house. 'You can get in the back,' she said. 'It's not locked at all.'

'I don't want to go in,' I said. 'It's not mine anymore. I told you it belongs to the Powers.'

'It's your home,' she said. 'They didn't buy that from you.' It was another thing to surprise me. She was like a child, yet at times she seemed to possess the mind of one older and more mature.

'I don't want to see it,' I said. 'There's nothing here belong-ing to me now. It was all sold at the auction.'

'Well, that's where you're wrong,' she said.

'You went inside?'

'Didn't I tell you the door wasn't locked? I just looked into the kitchen. There's an old rusty range there.'

I turned from her. The kitchen had always been the heart of the house, cool in summer and warm in winter, the dog asleep at the side of the range, the cats beneath it playing with my shoelaces. I hesitated, and then there was no turning back. 'Come on,' she said. 'Don't be a spoilsport again.' She didn't give me time to refuse but hurried off, and it seemed as if I'd no choice but to follow her.

9

She was waiting for me by the back door. 'You have to go inside,' she said. 'It's bad luck if you don't.'

'What nonsense!' I said. I just wanted to go. My coming here had been a mistake. The house was devoid of any echo of the living. It could blow to the four winds for all I cared.

'Well, it should be bad luck, then,' Lizzie said, peeved, her shoulders hunched against the wind which had blown black clouds in off the Atlantic to form a dark canopy above us.

'It'll soon rain,' I said. 'We'll go before it does.'

'Please yourself,' she said. 'What do I care?'

Before I could speak again a man called to us from the road. 'You looking for something?' he said. His voice held no animosity – he was simply asking a question. Perhaps he thought we were Gardaí.

I turned and saw that he had the pinched face and red hair of the Powers. 'No,' I said, walking towards him. 'I'm Willie Leitch. I just stopped to take a look at the old place.' I blocked his view of Lizzie and he stepped aside so that he could see by me.

'Willie Leitch?' he said, looking only at Lizzie. 'This was your place before my father bought it?'

I nodded. 'I thought I'd take a quick look as I was passing.'

'Sure, go ahead,' he said. 'That your daughter that's with you?'

She laughed and I turned to look at her, needing the

moment to recover. She leaned against the wall and for a moment I saw her as the daughter I might have had if life had been different. She would have been my future as I'd been my parent's future once. 'No,' I said, turning back to him. 'I'm just giving her a lift.'

'It's Lizzie O'Malley,' he said. 'J.P.'s daughter. I didn't recognise her for a minute. Howya, Lizzie?' he called, and if she'd been my daughter I'd have been offended by the sexual innuendo he managed to convey in two words. She wasn't my daughter but the daughter of another I'd once feared. J.P. O'Malley had been one of those bullies Hawley had commanded.

Lizzie laughed again and called a greeting to him, and I felt as if I were a child in the midst of adult banter. 'Well, go on,' he said. 'Ye may as well have a look around now ye're here.'

I nodded and walked back to Lizzie before she could come to join us. 'He's a terror,' she said. 'Maybe it's the air up here. Sure you might be a terror too for all I know. Would I be safe now going in there with you?'

'You don't have to,' I snapped, as memories spewed up my throat like bile. 'I didn't want to come here anyway.'

'It was just a joke,' she said. 'Surely you can take a joke. Look, I'm sorry.' She caught my arm and pulled me about to face her. 'I won't joke again. OK?' Her eyes looked as if they'd been polished and the cold had brought colour to her cheeks. It was the closest I'd been to her and I just wanted to reach out and touch her. I felt conscious of Power watching us, but when I turned to check there was no one there.

The movement broke the spell and she released my arm. 'Come on,' she said. 'I have to be back for when my sister, Bridie, comes from school. I have to watch out for her after what's happened.' She glanced at me, pushing the door fully open.

I followed her into the hall, which divided the house in two. Here there were smells of must and decay and a sense of abandonment. Above my head the ceiling was cracked and, like the walls, was the colour of faded newspaper. I hesitated on the threshold, certain that ghosts would emerge as the vermin did when darkness fell when I was a child, cockroaches and woodlice and the mice my father caught in the traps my mother insisted he set. In my mind I saw him now as I'd seen him so often then, sneaking outside with the traps and their dead burdens, trying to shield me from it all, maybe pretending to himself that the world wouldn't hurt me some day in the future when he'd no longer be there to protect me. Now the mice had free run here and he and she were gone.

Lizzie walked into the kitchen and I watched her from the doorway. The range was still there as she'd said, pocked with rust, and the old sink unit remained under the window. 'It won't bite you,' she said, but I didn't want to enter. If I did so I knew that I'd see my father and Alec Whitley sitting before the range, the fire door open and myself gazing into their faces, hanging onto their every word.

I turned away and walked down the hall past the stairs. The door on my left was open and I looked in: the room was bare and empty, the old black fire-grate filled with bits of sticks. Enclosed by years of dust and cobwebs they resembled a bundle of old brown bones in a string bag. It was here my father had spent his final days. It was here he had died, shrivelling up like a plastic doll that's been left too close to the fire. It was here he had called me to him the day he came from the hospital, all hope gone, though I didn't know that then. Sitting up in the bed facing the window, his face the colour and texture of an old potato, he'd clutched my hand and made me promise to take care of my mother. 'You'll have to take my place now,' he'd said. 'Promise me you'll do that before I go.'

'Where are you going?' I'd asked. 'Are you going to hospital again?'

'No,' he'd said. 'I won't ever go to hospital again.'

I'd realised then that he was going to die. It was my second betrayal. I'd learned the previous Christmas that there was no Santa Claus, but now I discovered that there was no God. If God had existed He would have answered my prayers and given my father back his health.

Over the weeks he'd repeated his plea that I take his place, while all the time the doll shrank more and more. Towards the end he'd had the bed turned round so that he could avoid looking into the summer sun he imagined shining in his eyes through the black blinds my mother hung over the curtain on the window, and which were hardly needed to block out what little light there was in the short dark February days.

I took his words literally and when he was dead I let her take me into her bed. Hadn't I promised him that I'd take his place, avoiding his eyes in which I might have glimpsed the twin reflections of myself, avoiding his ravaged face where I might have seen the image of my own death? Hadn't I been afraid to sleep alone in my room, frightened that he'd come tapping at the window with skeletal fingers as Marty Coogan's father was said to have come one dark winter's night, wanting to be let in out of the snow? Yet when the fears were replaced by revulsion for the cloying warmth and smell of that body that had given me life, I still kept my promise. I remained in her bed, lying in the hollow of the mattress my father's body had pressed out, my own body as stiff as a corpse with rigor mortis while her arms held me tight, pulled me close to the yielding flesh of breasts and belly. Four long years I suffered that nightly horror. Until the day I went under the bridge with Callen.

That night I screamed at her that I would sleep with her no longer and steeled myself against the loneliness and rejection

I saw like a shadow on her face. From then on she deterio-
rated, and the madness I'd glimpsed before began to manifest
itself. She took to wandering the house at night, coming down
to this room where she tried, I am sure, to commune with the
ghosts of my father and the people who'd been part of her life
before she left Ireland: her parents and family; her brother
who'd died of meningitis and whom I was named after, her
wish in giving me his name that I should not only be her
future but the future of a child who'd died long before I was
ever born.

It disturbed me now and I was glad of Lizzie's presence as
she emerged just then from the kitchen, a young girl as my
mother had once been in the pictures I'd seen of her – her slim
firm body, her long dark hair, her eyes which were a washed
blue and which surely were the only part of her I'd inherited.
I looked at Lizzie and saw my mother in her, saw her destined
to grow old and lonely and afraid and disillusioned.

'You look like you've seen a ghost,' she said, attuned to my
mood. She peered into the room and dismissed it. 'Nothing
to be scared of there,' she said, and I envied her her youth and
her certainty.

She crossed the hall and flung open the door of the front
room. I felt that I should hear the music from the radio or the
gramophone and my father call me, his voice filled with longing, for what I never knew. Had he foreseen the future even
then, foreseen this day when I'd return more of a stranger than
he'd been the first time he came? Had he foreseen that I'd be
frightened of the past and of his ghost – he who'd loved me
and only wanted me to have the best?

'Hey,' Lizzie called, dispelling these thoughts for the
present. 'There are pictures here. Is this you?' She came and
caught my arm and dragged me with her. I could picture my
father in the armchair at the far side of the fireplace, but when

I shut my eyes and opened them there was nothing there but the empty room and that dull flat echo such rooms possess. 'Here,' Lizzie said with the infectious enthusiasm of a child. 'Is it really you?'

She dragged me across to the alcove on the far side of the fireplace where I confronted my own image, taken at my first communion. My innocent face stared at me from behind grimed glass, the picture faded, blistering from age and damp. It was an image of what I'd once been, and of what I'd discarded. And if I were asked what it was I'd now become, what could I answer? What remained of that child who'd stood to attention for the photographer more than thirty years ago?

'It's cute,' Lizzie said with that inflection in her voice that most women possess for the young. 'But weren't you terrible to leave it here like that. And all those other ones as well.'

'I thought the Powers might have thrown them out,' I said.

She stared at me and I knew that she detected the lie. 'Well you can take them with you now,' she said. 'The Powers won't mind. Are these your parents?' she added, crossing over to another picture which hung opposite the fireplace.

I joined her and we stood together to look at a picture of my parents taken in New York before they were married. My mother clutched my father's arm and faced the camera with the self-satisfied look of possession which comes from knowing you're loved. He seemed younger than his fifty years, as if beside her he'd re-captured some of his youth. There were other pictures, too, one of my father which she'd hung after his death in the other alcove where prior to that a holy image had hung of the Virgin and Child. I remembered often finding her in here, staring at the picture as if trying to remember whose image was locked behind the glass. Or had she been praying to him instead of to the Virgin, praying for what she'd lost and could never have again?

'Wasn't it lucky that you came?' Lizzie said now.

I nodded because it was easiest to do. What had I to gain by telling her that I didn't care – that the pictures were only images on paper which would hang here after I'd gone again, that if they were taken down from the walls, hands other than mine would remove them. 'We'll go,' I said instead. I wanted to get back to town and have something to eat and contact Jones with the latest developments. The future was all I possessed now. This house filled with the detritus of memories, the good ones sullied by the later ones, was but an empty shell – the body that remains when the spirit's gone. And I could no more love a shell than I could a bundle of old bones.

'I want to take a look upstairs,' Lizzie said. 'Can we? Just a quick look before we go?'

'OK,' I said.

She skipped from the room and I followed her upstairs. The third step from the top creaked; it had always done so, and during my childhood, when fear threatened to overwhelm me, I'd lie in bed at night and listen for the twin creaks that assured me that my parents had come up and that all was well and no demons would emerge from the darkened corners of the room that night.

Lizzie entered my parents' room and stood at the window looking out. I don't know what it was – the way she stood? the potency of the memories? – that made me want to cross the room and hold her. The need persisted for a moment before my eyes were drawn to the rusting iron bedstead I'd shared with my mother, and I thought to everything there's a beginning and an end. It was the only object in the room. Everything else had been plundered for the auction. But no one had taken the bed, as if they'd sensed what it had been responsible for – nothing in a way, and yet everything.

It takes only a moment to blight a life and how can we ever know what hell we leave in our wake? What hell might I now leave if I gave way to my desires and crossed the room and crushed Lizzie to me, flesh against flesh as once I'd been pressed to my mother's body in that bed rusting in the dampness? I didn't speak but turned away and walked down the hall to my own room to find that nothing remained to remind me that it had been my world once, that it was here the dreams had been born.

Under the window a table had stood with a shelf on which I could rest my feet. The table had been covered with a dimpled green oilcloth cut into rectangles by thin white lines. It was at that table I'd first started to write in a red hardbacked copy. Outside the window my tree had stood, a beech planted by my father. 'So that you can climb up to your room when you've been out late at night with the girls and you don't want us to know what earthly hour you returned,' he'd laughed on the day he'd planted it. I'd never used it to climb back up, because by the time I went out with girls he was dead and my mother no longer cared whether I returned or not.

Long nights I'd sat there at the window with only the moon for light, the branches of the beech waving in the wind and creating patterns of shadow on the lined paper and the black squiggles which were a desperate attempt to bring the words in my teeming brain to some sort of order. Later, when doubts plagued me, I'd lie awake watching the shadows of the waving branches create patterns on the wall, sickened by the bile of failure, wanting an end to it, because surely no dream was worth such pain.

I walked to the window now and looked out, the sea a grey streak on the horizon. Below me was where my mother's vegetable garden had been and where after my father's death she'd spent her every spare moment, rooting in the soil with arthritic fingers which came in time to resemble the gnarled roots of a tree. How often had I watched her from here, her body bent over, her hands scrabbling in the earth, trying to commune with the dust my father had become, envying the old sheepdog his peace?

I was so engrossed in the past that I didn't hear Lizzie cross the room. She tipped me on the shoulder and for one illogical moment I was a child again, the ghosts and demons who'd always hovered behind me taking form and reaching out to touch me. I experienced a feeling of pure terror and swung wildly about to face them, but it was Lizzie's face which loomed in my vision, her look of mischief quickly turning to apprehension. 'Jesus,' she said, taking a step backwards.

We stood with our eyes locked together, no past and no future existing for us, only this present moment. I could hear our breaths, harsh and quick, and even, I swear, the beat of our separate pulses. As Lizzie's apprehension eased her face softened and I reached out to her. I took her hands in mine, registering the fact that they were cold as I drew her to me, wrapping my arms around that pitifully thin trembling body.

I'd no thought then for anything other than her comforting presence. It was the same need that had driven my mother to take me into her bed, that emptiness each one of us carries within and that needs someone else to fill. I held her face against my shoulder, her sweet-sour smell repulsing me even as the firmness of her breasts against my chest urged me to consume her. I don't know how long we stood like that, silent and still, before she pressed her thigh against the stiffening in my trousers.

Over her shoulder I could see the fireplace, soot stains on the wall above it like dried blood. In the winter a fire had burned there in the evenings, and often I had sat in the dark with the flame shadows cavorting on the walls and my body craving to hold a woman. Yet with Lizzie now in my arms the need was for a future where I would no longer have to search.

We can never know what our actions may lead to, otherwise we would be forever inhibited, locked away in darkness, frightened of venturing out. If we lived like that I wouldn't have allowed my hands to slide down her body and cup her bottom, while she in turn moved her hands from the small of my back to clasp my head and pull it towards her. Then her lips were on mine and her tongue was like a warm animal in my mouth. I looked at her, her eyes clenched shut, her skin crinkled as she screwed up her features in a frenzy of passion that was frightening and exhilarating and, somewhere in a part of me still functioning normally despite my desire to possess her, disturbing.

I took a hand from her bottom and with it unbuttoned her blouse, one red button at a time. She opened her eyes to look at me and I could have sworn that I saw fear behind the black dilated pupils and the brown pigment of the irises which glowed like polished rosewood. I stopped, expecting her to protest or plead. Had she done so – had she spoken a single word, made a single gesture – I would have let her be. But she didn't speak or make a sign.

I opened the last button and when my fingers touched her bare flesh she trembled. She wore a white bra and I fumbled it up to expose one of her breasts which I cupped in my hand. She drew breath, shuddering, as if a knife had penetrated her. She clasped a hand over mine and pressed more firmly, and as my fingers dug into her flesh, there was no mistaking her whimper of pain.

Within all of us there's a need to have power over others, to conquer and possess them. When we truly love another person we sublimate this need as best we can and only sometimes in the act of sex do we give it rein. I do know that at that moment I'd no love for Lizzie. Her age I didn't know. Was it possible that she might be no more than sixteen? But I didn't care. At that moment there was only the uncontrollable urge to possess her, to make her whimper again. There's a moment too in the sexual act when we no longer have control over our actions – that moment one hears so much of in cases of rape, that moment when the woman says 'no' and the man takes her by force because by then language no longer exists. Even with the dogs in the street, there's a moment of no return, and surely it's in the throes of the act of sex, just as in the acts of birth and death, that we come closest to the animal?

That moment came now and from then on what happened was inevitable. I can't recall the sequence of events – whose hands fumbled at whose clothing – as we stumbled about in the movement of some new erotic dance. I bent to kiss her breasts, and with my face pressed to her skin, her smell was much more potent. Now it was an aphrodisiac. I wanted to suck the sweat from her pores.

Her jeans and panties were pulled down and I cupped my hand between her legs and felt hair and wetness and warmth, as if her sex were a new-born animal drenched in the mucus of its birth. Her hands were in my trousers, gripping me with a deftness and sureness of touch which was not accidental. The dance continued and we stumbled across the room until her back rammed up against the wall, forcing an agonised moan from her.

'Turn around,' I ordered in a voice so thickened with lust that I couldn't believe it belonged to me. She didn't seem to understand and I spoke again, this time with more urgency. Her eyes showed fear but, more potent still, they showed mute submission, and exalted I grabbed her and turned her to face the wall, dehumanising her. She was just an anonymous body now, created only for my gratification. I put my hands on her shoulders and pushed her forward, and as if she'd done this before she bent over, submitting herself to whatever it was I wished to do with her.

I drew breath sharply as I entered her, my drawn out moan of pleasure like the keening of the ghosts who'd once crouched hidden in the darkened corners here, fashioned from light and shadow and the stirrings of my own imagination. Her hair hung down both sides of her face like screens, dehumanising her even more. I reached for her breasts, but now couldn't thrust into her with any force so I released them. Instead I caught her round the middle with both hands and, pulling her towards me, began to thrust with more urgency, wanting to hurt her, to bury myself deep within her and then withdraw, tearing her as if I were fitted with barbs.

We moaned and whimpered together and now she grabbed at her breasts, intent it seemed on drawing blood. Each fibre and nerve and sinew in my body was stretched to breaking point and when I thought I could take no more my body arched as I pumped into her – a Francis Bacon figure caught in what might have been a rictus of agony.

As the pleasure subsided I slumped forward on her body, my face coming to rest on her back, the nodules of her spine hard beneath my cheek. It was the moment to whisper something, even speak her name, to honour her as every man should honour the woman who gives her body to him. But I didn't speak. I was spent now, that wild crazy urge to possess gone as if it'd never been.

I drew away and saw my limp thing hanging down like a piece of excess flesh drenched in our juices. I hurriedly bent down and pulled up my underpants and trousers and tucked in my shirt. As I did so she bent down to pull up her own clothing and I turned away from what moments before I'd looked on with lust. When I turned back she was dressed and had that look on her face that women from time immemorial have had, the look that doesn't so much ask for love in return for what they've given, as demand it.

I walked over to the window and stared out, the grey streak which had been the sea darkening in those few moments – how long had it been, five minutes from start to finish? I turned back and saw her eyes were once again dark with apprehension. She was frightened that I'd reject her, wanted the reassurances of love. It seemed a small thing to give her just then, and I held out my hands to her and she came to me like a child.

I should have said: 'Let's go.' It would have been the decent thing to do, an end once and for all to everything. But I didn't. Instead I took her hands in mine, aware that I was giving her the impression that what had happened in this room had significance beyond the act itself. I saw the apprehension drain from her eyes, and what I might have taken to be hope flood in to take its place. 'Do you like me?' she asked. 'Tell me you like me a little.' The apprehension hadn't gone. It was there crouched behind her eyes.

Maybe it was that more than anything else that made me nod, made me cup her face in my hands and kiss her. 'I like you,' I said, pulling her gently towards me, passion spent. 'You're beautiful,' I told her, which was the truth.

'Did you like it?' she asked and I nodded and her arms tightened about me and I thought I heard her murmur: 'I'm glad.' I wanted to go, but to stand there while she held me was a small price to pay for what she'd given me. I don't know how long we remained clutched together. I remember looking out of the window and noticing that clouds had darkened the sky, and though there was no longer any sunshine, they seemed to cast shadows on the earth.

We separated as if by mutual consent and stood for a moment at arm's length. 'We'll go,' I said, and she nodded, still obedient. She held onto my hand as we walked down-stairs, leaving the other rooms as I'd left them long before, closed and empty.

10

She released my hand as we emerged and I pulled the back door tight shut. It was colder now and I saw her shiver. In the car she put on her seat belt without demur.

'What time is it?' she asked. 'It's not three yet, is it?'

'No,' I said, 'it's just gone two. Are you in a hurry somewhere?'

She shook her head. 'I have to be home for when my sister Bridie comes from school.'

'Won't your mother be there?' I asked.

'She's dead,' she said. 'She died three years ago.'

'I'm sorry. I didn't know.' I glanced at her and she turned to look at me. She was beautiful, but a wistful sadness hung about her, as if it were now, and not three years ago, that death had come into her life.

I wanted to reach the town and let her out of the car, be free of any reminders of what we'd done. Or rather what I'd done, because at any time I could have stopped, and she would have accepted that just as she had accepted everything else. It was with relief I saw the school up ahead, no children at play now, no teacher walking the yard to remind me of what might have been. Earlier I'd seen him as a prisoner, but wasn't I a prisoner myself – in a different prison perhaps but I'd face the selfsame death in the end? The teacher might envy the opportunity just presented to me and taken without question. But he would be foolish to do so. I was the one who should have the envy – I who was without roots anywhere.

I tried to imagine what it would be like to be settled down, even with Lizzie, coming home to her at the end of the day. We'd eat together – one of the communal sharings which, like sleep and love, make us human – but never again would she bend over submissively, never again would we capture that wild abandonment. There was a price to pay for everything.

She asked me to drop her in the square and when I stopped the car she unfastened her seatbelt and opened the door. She hesitated, then turned towards me. Her face might have belonged to a child but the eyes betrayed knowledge.

'Will I see you again?' I asked. 'Maybe this evening?'

She laughed and she was someone else now, someone I hadn't seen before or maybe hadn't wanted to see. 'If you want to,' she said. 'I usually babysit for the Keoghs, my neighbours, but I can make other arrangements. You can call out to the house this evening. I'll be there on my own after seven.'

'Is that your father's old farm off the Dublin Road?'

'You'll have to be finding that out for yourself,' she said, 'if you want to see me again. For all I know you might only be interested in my body. Isn't that right now?'

'Maybe.'

'You're a terrible man,' she said. 'No one'd be safe with you.' She got out and stared in at me, and now I wondered which of us had been used.

'You'd never be safe with me,' I said. 'So where's the house?'

She laughed again and slammed the door shut, and I watched her in the mirror walk back up Main Street and enter Burke's pub. She did not look back once. I grabbed the wheel and swore under my breath and drove to the hotel. I'd get my feature sorted out in the next few days and then go. I'd had my pleasure here.

After a late lunch I phoned Jones, and his unmistakable Dublin voice in my ear was like a breath of normality. He was a man of few words – the mark of the true journalist. Years before I'd read some of his work and admired it, but like all of us he'd sold his soul for money. 'Well?' he said, never a man for pleasantries.

I told him what I'd learned and he listened without interruption. He had the ability to see the worth of a story or spot potential flaws while another would be trying to grasp the details. 'You think there's any truth in this?' he asked.

'It's true,' I said. 'Why would the Gardaí tell Hawley something like that?' I'd taken care not to mention McQuillan.

'You don't think he made it up? He was talking to a journalist.'

'No. No. He's had enough sensation. My hunch tells me it's true. I'm going to pursue it. I just wanted to sound you out first.'

'Carry on,' he said. 'But why would the Gardaí agree to suppress such information?'

'It's something I've been trying to figure out,' I said. 'Maybe they just don't want to alert the killer to what they know? But I can't see him falling for that. Maybe they know something else they haven't divulged. They sometimes suppress details to prevent copy-cat killings. They haven't released details of the sexual assault either. Then there's the question of panic. People are frightened. There are vigilantes on the streets, led by a local councillor. You make it public knowledge that the killer keeps his victims alive for days, add to that the rumours circulating that the girl was tortured and mutilated, and you've got a serious situation on your hands.'

'Maybe,' Jones said. 'So why tell the father then?'

'Halligan knew the truth would emerge eventually and I think he wanted to spare the Hawleys from finding out later, maybe in the papers. So he simply told Hawley, and it was only when Hawley suggested that they suppress the information to protect his wife and family that Halligan decided to do so. Perhaps he did it simply for the Hawleys' sake.'

'Maybe,' Jones said again, careful not to touch on my implications. If we published the story it'd bring more pain to the family. 'Tell me,' he added, 'is there any word of that other missing girl? Do the police think there's a possibility she's still alive and that's why they've not released the details?'

'It's possible,' I said. 'But I think they know in their hearts she's dead. They've searched the area thoroughly over the past few months. If she were alive they'd have found her.'

'How come they didn't find this Hawley girl then? They searched for her, didn't they? I can't believe that her killer abducted her, took her away with him, kept her for two days, killed her, and then brought her body back so he could bury it in the woods. Why take that risk when he could have buried her near where he'd kept her? Or have taken her further away.'

'You've a point,' I said. 'Perhaps the killer comes from outside the area. He dumped her body back here to centre suspicion in Castleford. He needn't be a total stranger. He could be from here originally. Personally I believe he's a local and he simply buried her near by. After all, the woods are extensive. It was only by chance she was found.'

'Maybe.' It seemed to be Jones' favourite word. 'Look,' he added, 'see what you can turn up. If you can confirm the details we'll run it.'

When Jones rang off I had another thought. Had the Gardaí suppressed the information because they knew the killer would strike again? If they knew he'd kept Majella Hawley alive for two days, did they conclude that they'd have a chance of finding the next victim before she was killed? If this was so and we ran the story, would the killer dare keep his next victim alive? The thought disturbed me and I thrust it away. If I allowed my feelings to intrude, I'd be as well to pack up and go home.

Rousing myself I rang the Garda station and spoke to Doyle. I told him I had some information that might be of interest and he agreed to meet me in half an hour. I then rang *The Mayoman* to arrange to have a photographer call to Hawley's. I asked to speak with Alec Whitley, my knuckles white from my grip on the handset, but I was told he wasn't there and I promised to ring back later. I decided that tomorrow I'd see the Devlins and ferret out whatever I could, despite last night's incident. Then it was a matter of hammering it all out, faxing if off to Jones, and getting the hell out of here.

That's what I told myself, but I didn't want to go. I wanted to savour again what I'd had this morning. I wanted to see that body bent over in submission, offering me my desires. I wanted this morning's episode repeated endlessly – the empty room, the coldness and the anonymity, the vulnerable bare back and buttocks, the certainty of triumph and then the whole world dissolving, everything shrinking to insignificance in that final moment of abandonment, that moment when we promise anything that might be demanded; when we whisper love and mean lust; pledge faith and mean betrayal. That moment when we might even kill for what we craved.

From the street below came the faint voices of children and I walked to the window and watched them go past, shepherded again by adults. What fear drove those adults to think that the killer might strike on the few hundred yards walk from the school in the gathering dusk of a November evening? I'd once thought that it was only in childhood that we experienced fear: the bogey man who'd come for us if we were bold; the witch who hid in the wardrobe; the moon-cast shadows of the branches of a tree; the moan of the wind in the chimney. It was only as I grew older and saw those fears for what they were that I learned there were worse fears: the possibility of failure; the pain of loneliness; the inevitability of death.

I turned back from the window and already the dusk seemed to have thickened. I glanced at my watch and saw it was time to go down to meet Doyle. At reception I enquired for the O'Malley's and discovered that J.P. had inherited the farm. Now that I knew for certain where Lizzie lived it was an extra link between us. The thought of seeing her again gave rise to feelings I hadn't experienced in years – the urgency of the chase and the inevitable pleasure.

I was thinking of this when Doyle arrived. He took a table in the self-service restaurant while I got coffee and cream cakes. 'Shouldn't really,' he said, taking an eclair. Cream squashed out as he ate and he licked his fingers. He chewed slowly and methodically and drank some coffee. 'So,' he said. 'You've something for me?'

'I saw Joe Hawley,' I said, not wanting to probe him yet. 'He's pretty cut up. Though I suppose it's only to be expected.'

'Children are the worst,' he said. 'You can't help blaming yourself.'

'Maybe if he was caught,' I said, 'it'd help. Knowing he's out there, still free, must be almost too much to bear.'

'It must be a living death,' he said. 'If there is a hell – and I don't say that there isn't – I think of it as one that's personal to each of us, that changes with circumstances. Once yours was what Hawley and his cronies did to you. Back then you couldn't have imagined a worse one.'

I nodded, but he was wrong. My worst hell hadn't been created by Hawley. Instead it had been to sleep in my mother's bed with the smell of her sweat in my nostrils and her hands wrapped tightly about my body. Later it was to relive those hours after Judith Kelly went missing, before they discovered the broken plank on the footbridge and I knew that she hadn't given herself up to the river. Looking back, it seemed ridiculous to have thought like that. But at fourteen, with the interminable span of a life stretched out before me, it had been easy to think that she might have drowned herself rather than endure what she'd been subjected to. That had been my personal hell then, and I suppose I thought that there could never be a more terrible one.

'When I was talking with Joe Hawley,' I said now to Doyle, wanting to kill the memories, 'he gave me some information.' I waited for him to be drawn but he didn't rise to the bait. 'He told me,' I said, 'that his daughter was in the hands of her killer for two days. Is that right?'

He stared at me across the table, then picked up the remainder of the eclair and put it in his mouth. He chewed and swallowed it and washed it down with coffee. 'Superintendent Halligan's the man you want,' he said.

'Come on, Plod,' I said. 'I just need a yes or no.' But he wouldn't be drawn. 'So what is it?' I pressed him. 'You can't, or you won't, tell me?'

'You think it's that simple?' he demanded. 'You got kids of your own?'

'No. I'm not married.'

'When did that ever stop anyone?' He didn't look at me. The jibe, if that's what it was, wasn't aimed at me. 'I got two myself. A boy and a girl. I think I can imagine what it's like to lose a daughter. Or a son for that matter. To go into the morgue and look at them dead and know you're alive. There's a man's hell. Now why would you or I want to add to it?'

'I don't want to add to it,' I said. 'I only want the truth. People have a right to know.'

'Do they? I see your papers every day with their banner

headlines about the foibles of this person or that, their sins, as it were, held up in public. They have families too – wives, children... Weeks later I see a paragraph hidden away on an inside page apologising for errors. Lies, if you want to give them a precise name. Yet you call it truth.'

'There are always casualties.'

'See Halligan,' he said. 'And let me give you some advice. I wouldn't print that information, even if it were true. There's a killer out there, if you don't already know. He's killed twice. He'll kill again if he isn't caught. He's got a taste for it now. My job's to help catch him. Anyone who hinders me will be as guilty as the killer when the next victim is found.'

'You think that concealing that information is going to help you? You can't imagine that you're dealing with a fool – that he's going to keep his next victim alive for days while you're scouring the countryside for her?'

Doyle didn't rise to the bait now either. 'We're not dealing with a normal person,' he said. 'We're dealing with a sick mind, with someone who has no conscience, no normal human feelings. He thinks everyone else except himself is a fool. Even the Gardaí. He's abducted and murdered two children without being caught. For all we know there might have been others elsewhere. Now he thinks he can abduct and kill at will. If he wants to keep his victims alive for days, he can do so. But if you plaster that fact all over the papers... Personally I think he'll strike again. But as you say, he's no fool. He's cunning and clever and knows when the odds are against him. He won't take risks. Self-preservation's a strong instinct, even in psychopaths.'

'You're admitting Majella was held for two days?' I said, certain now.

'I'm admitting nothing. I'm giving you advice. The death of anyone, but especially a child, must be a terrible thing to have on your conscience. Think about that.'

'But supposing a child dies because information was suppressed and parents weren't adequately warned...'

'Willie,' he said, as if speaking to a child, 'if they're not vigilant now, then nothing will make them so.'

'Maybe,' I said, 'but I think people have a right to know.'

'Is that your real motive?' he asked. 'Ask yourself if a child's life is worth a story in the paper, when the next day someone will light the fire with it.'

'I have a job to do too,' I said.

'It's your conscience,' he said, 'but revenge is never sweet.'

'You can't believe that,' I said angrily.

'I'm sorry,' he said. 'It was uncalled for. We've been under a lot of strain. Look, do what's right, Willie. There'll be other stories.' He rose to his feet, the sturdy schoolboy grown into a sturdy man. I remembered that day in secondary school when Hawley and O'Malley cornered me in the shed and ordered two of their cronies to grab my sidelocks and lift me off the ground. As I stood on tip-toe someone pushed through the laughing mocking throng that had gathered to gloat at my humiliation. 'Leave him alone,' Doyle said, and when the two torturers hesitated, he struck one and both of them yelped and let me go. 'The next time fight back,' he said to me, standing beside me until my tormenters slunk away.

I looked at him now and envied him, as I'd envied him then, but I knew that I'd never swap my life for his. I walked with him to the entrance where he turned to me again. 'Do what's right,' he repeated, and this time it was a warning.

I watched him walk up Strand Street into the gathering darkness, each streetlight he passed under giving him the ethereal substance of a ghost. I was sorry that I hadn't pressed him further. But at least my information had been confirmed, and I could always get more details from McQuillan.

As I turned away I knew that tonight I'd go to Lizzie. I'd take what was offered and to hell with the doubts Doyle had stirred up. What did I care anyway? There was no one I loved, nothing I cared for except this body within which I existed like a snail in its shell. If the snail remained hidden, then life couldn't touch it.

11

I was preparing to go and see Lizzie when reception buzzed to inform me that a Mr Alec Whitley would like to see me. Until then I'd been like a love-sick teenager preparing for his first date, except that lust-sick might be the more appropriate term to describe me. Now I had to prepare myself to meet an old man who'd been my friend and mentor. It was twenty years since I'd seen him – a handshake at my mother's graveside and an invitation to come and visit him and Alice afterwards, the sum total of that meeting.

He was at reception when I came down, his back towards me, and I saw that he was as erect as ever. He was in his seventies, but I'd learned in a recent issue of *The Mayoman* that Alec was still managing editor.

If I'd ever had affection for anyone other than my parents, it was for Alec. It was he who'd introduced me to the world of books and poetry – Yeats, Hopkins, Dylan Thomas, Patrick Kavanagh. If he hadn't ignited my desire to be a writer, then he had certainly encouraged it, yet when he'd first suggested I become a trainee reporter on the paper, I'd said no. I hadn't seen myself as a journalist then. I'd wanted to live as Kavanagh lived, to suffer for my art.

A myriad of regrets crossed my mind as I walked towards him. 'Alec,' I said, and he turned and fixed his eyes on me, those eyes which as a boy I was certain could read my innermost thoughts.

'Willie.' He took my hand and clasped it tight. His eyes I noticed had lost their vivid blueness; they seemed greyer now, as if covered with a thin membrane, yet the intensity of his gaze had not diminished. Maybe the vividness of the blue I remembered was only in my imagination. 'I didn't know what to expect,' he added, 'but you've hardly changed.'

'I could say the same.' I pulled my hand away, having the impression that if I didn't, he would have held it all night.

'Go on with you,' he said. It was his pet phrase, only ever spoken to those he regarded with affection. When my father was alive and Alec would call of a winter's evening and they'd sit talking in the dark kitchen with the glow from the Stanley's firebox the only thing to penetrate the murk, I'd hear that phrase repeated over and over like a prayer. When he would recite bits of poetry his face seemed to take on the fire's reflection. After my father's death, which surely had been as much of a blow to Alec as to myself or my mother, he'd never called alone to the house again. Not only because my father wasn't there to chat with him, but because in his opinion, to call on my mother in my father's absence would have been the height of impropriety. Instead I made his house a second home, going away after each visit with the books he gave me, unaware then that he loved them as if they were his children.

'You're looking well,' I said.

'Alice'll be glad to hear it. She thinks this... this sad business has taken its toll on me.'

'She's well?'

He nodded and the old face lit up for a moment like a child's. Along with my parents, they were the only other couple I ever thought were happy. 'She still talks about you,' he said. 'She can hardly wait to meet you. "Go and see him, Alec," she said to me today. "Invite him to dinner." He'll be busy, I said to her, but she wouldn't listen. So here I am with the invitation, if you'll accept.'

I was tempted to refuse. I had another invitation after all, and though I'd had a great affection for them once, they were now no more than people who'd touched my life years before. Lizzie was awaiting me and why should I sacrifice what she had to give me for an evening with an old couple? I would have refused but for the longing on Alec's face, his certainty that I wouldn't accept, and the intolerable burden it would be for him to have to inform his beloved Alice that he'd failed her. So certain was he that I was going to refuse him, that my acceptance was not only a surprise but a source of pleasure. 'She'll be delighted,' he said, as if his request and my agreement were for her benefit alone. 'She was in at the butcher today for his best leg of lamb, and she told me to tell you that she's doing creamed carrots and parsnips.'

'She shouldn't have bothered,' I said, embarrassed, and chastened that she should remember, after all this time, the preferences of childhood.

'It pleases her,' he said, 'and what harm is that? What does it cost us to indulge someone now and again?'

'Nothing,' I said. 'Nothing.'

He shuffled from one foot to the other and rubbed his thigh and it struck me that he was an old man and that I shouldn't have kept him here talking. 'A drink?' I suggested.

'I'm afraid not. Doctor's orders.'

'You pay heed to them?'

'Alice ensures that I do. Though I haven't lost the will for living yet. Maybe it's because this present life is the only existence I'm ever likely to enjoy.'

'I hadn't meant...' I said.

He waved my explanations away. 'No offence meant and no offence taken. It's just that I find it difficult to stand for any long period. That's one of my many afflictions, but I promise not to bore you with them. Anyway, I'd best be getting back. Alice'll be apprehensive. I think she was afraid you mightn't come. "Bring him back with you," she said, as if I could drag you back by force. She'll be so glad now to hear you're coming. You won't change your mind, will you?' It seemed to have just struck him that I might do so. 'I'll call,' I'd promised him that day at the graveyard, though it was a promise I'd never intended keeping.

'Did you walk?' I asked. 'If you did, I'll drop you back.'

'I walked,' he said. 'I don't drive anymore. Alice takes care of all that.' He was like a big child dependent on its mother, and proud of it. They'd had no family and Alice had made her husband and lover in the image of the son she'd always wanted, as my own mother had tried to make me in the image of the husband and lover she'd lost.

'Let me drive you,' I said.

'Maybe we'll walk. More doctor's orders, but I can easily abide that one. Unless of course you're doing anything yourself.'

'I was going to the reconstruction,' I lied.

'Nothing of importance will happen there,' he said. 'Anyway, one of my lads is covering it and I can let you have the details. You could come back with me now if you like.' He couldn't hide the fear he had that I wouldn't come and it showed on his face like an affliction.

'I'll walk back with you,' I said and it was worth acquiescing just to see his pleasure.

Night was drawing in as we walked down by the river, the water black as oil. The cannons were cold to my touch as I passed, brush of my hand against the killing metal. Mist hung above the river and the detritus of the day lay in the gutters. An old woman emerged from the supermarket on the corner. She looked about her anxiously and then scuttled down

Strand Street, her fear palpable. 'You'd imagine,' I said, 'it was old women who were being murdered.'

'Fear isn't a rational thing,' Alec said. 'Even Alice is afraid to go out alone at night. We've known fear here since Jacinta went missing. No one dares to trust anymore. Even an old man like myself is suspect. People use their own experiences to judge. You look closely at your own life, or at the lives of the people you know, and you begin to realise what one is capable of. After that it's easy to fear.'

'You're surely not implying that anyone is capable of killing a child?'

'I think we're all capable of anything,' he said. 'Can any of us say, hand on heart, that we wouldn't do such or such a thing given a particular set of circumstances? What happens in a sexual situation when at a crucial point the woman says no? Or the child?'

'You're not saying that a child would have a choice?'

'No. I'm just making a point. What if the child says she'll tell?' He looked at me as if he could have known about the past, which common sense told me that he couldn't. 'The instinct for self-preservation is terribly strong. One might not intend to kill, but be driven to do so by fear. Why do I pay heed to a doctor's orders? Isn't it because I'm afraid?'

'You said you wanted to live.'

'I know, but isn't it the same thing? We give ourselves motives and we pick the one that suits us. It's easier to say I want to live than admit I'm frightened of dying. I'm not frightened of death. But the dying... that's another thing entirely – the sickness, the pain, the humiliation. It's why I doubt that there's a God – a benevolent God, that is. There's a God, all right, but He's indifferent. We're just His playthings like a child's toys. Only the child has outgrown the toys.' He stopped and looked over the stone wall at the river where the lights had punched holes in the blackness. 'He's out there,' he said suddenly. 'That's the sort of power God possesses. He could point him out if He wanted.'

'You don't believe that,' I said. 'That some god should put a black mark on his forehead?'

'Someone knows,' he said. 'Someone knows or suspects.'

The stone of the wall was cold and damp beneath my hands and there was a stench from the water. Further upstream the lights lay shattered in a million bits in the swirls and eddies of the river.

'I can't imagine anyone would hide something like that,' I said. 'Why would they?'

'Fear? Loyalty?' He turned and walked on and I fell into step beside him. Strand Street became a terrace of houses, the doors opening onto the pavement. The terrace gave way to a few cottages and bungalows and the hospital built in the grounds of the former workhouse. Beyond that the bulk of the electronics factory loomed against the darkening sky. His house was beyond the hospital on the opposite side of the road, set behind the inevitable shelter belt of pine and cypress. It was a two-storey dwelling which had belonged in the family for three generations. The paper Alec's grandfather had founded no longer belonged exclusively to the family – there had been need for outside investment – but I felt certain Alec still held control.

He pushed open the gate, leading me inside the encircling trees which created a box of darkness punctured by the porch lantern. The gravel on the drive crunched beneath our shoes as we walked up to the house, dark windows like so many blind eyes staring out of the ivy. I was aware of the expanse of lawn at the front and the closeness of the woods at the rear, ten acres of broadleafed trees planted by his grandfather, where once I'd collected acorns. Alec rang the bell and while we waited he tried to hide his nervousness. We heard Alice's footsteps in the hall, and when she opened the door I saw his own pleasure reflected in her face.

'Willie!' I held out my hand but she ignored it and opened her arms to me. Her body felt thin and brittle beneath the blue wool dress, and yet I was surprised by the power of her embrace. Her lips were dry on my cheek, but I could have sworn I felt dampness before she let me go and stepped back to look at me and see what changes the years had wrought.

'Well, Alice?' Alec closed out the door and stood behind me, the child waiting for the thanks that would make his achievement worthwhile.

'I knew you'd come,' she said. 'I can't tell you how happy it makes us to see you. We talk of you all the time.' She spoke as if I'd been away but a few weeks, as if it were not twenty-three years ago since she'd tried to persuade me to defer university and accept Alec's offer to work on the paper. 'Why not take the job?' she'd asked, the hurt that my refusal had caused Alec visible in her eyes. 'You know how Alec believes in you. Give it a year, Willie. If it's not for you, then do what you think is right. You're young. University can wait. And your mother needs someone with her.' She played her last card. 'You're all she's got now.' But I'd shaken my head, unable to explain to her why I couldn't stay.

'Come on,' she urged us now. 'It's too cold to be standing here in the hall. There's a fire in the study. You two go in there while I get on with the cooking.' She spoke to us like children.

She ushered us into the study with its bookshelves and desk and the leather armchairs on either side of the coal fire, the only light that from a standard lamp which stood behind the door. Once this room had been my sanctuary. It was here for a little while that I had been able to banish Callen and Sissy

Bradley and Judith Kelly from my mind and it was here I should have come when I ran that night from McQuillan.

'A drink?' Alec suggested as I sat in one of the armchairs, the years peeling back with the smell of leather and burning coal, and as I'd always once felt, the smell of printer's ink that hung about him.

'No thanks,' I said. 'I don't bother with it much.' That wasn't strictly true.

'Have you spoken to Willie?' Alice asked.

'Not yet,' Alec said. He avoided my eyes as he took the seat opposite me and gingerly lowered himself onto it.

'You'll have a chance to talk now,' she said. 'Dinner won't be for an hour.' She hesitated at the door, then closed it behind her.

'You want to talk to me about something?' I asked Alec, conscious that he was reluctant to speak.

He nodded and stretched his feet out to the fire, the glow reflected in the polished leather of his shoes. 'We've been talking about you,' he said, 'since we heard you were here. We wondered if you'd ever considered coming back?'

'Here? I hadn't really thought about it. Why do you ask?'

'It's your home. I always imagine that people must yearn to return.'

'Like the salmon? Don't they come home to breed and die?' In my mind I saw them as I'd seen them long ago, thrusting up river against the current, the instinct to perpetuate themselves greater at that moment than any other.

'So they do,' he said. 'And why shouldn't we be like the salmon? Why wouldn't we want to return?'

'I don't know,' I said. 'Maybe I don't want to breed. Or I don't want to die.'

'None of us want to die.' There was a reprimand in his voice.

'I'm sorry,' I said. 'I didn't mean anything. Look, why did you ask?'

'My retirement's overdue,' he said. 'By rights I should have given it up years ago, but to tell you the truth I didn't want to. It's been my life... the paper. Now it's inevitable. Doctor's orders and Alice's insistence. I've promised them both I'll retire. My present editor will take over my position which leaves a vacancy...' He looked at me across the fews yards of space, across the years, and now there might have never been that break.

'Are you offering me a job?' I asked in amazement.

'That's the idea.'

'Do you have a sense of *déja vu?*'

'Life's a wheel,' he said. 'It revolves endlessly. Only we can make different choices the second time around.'

'I can give you a dozen reasons for refusing,' I said. 'And that's outside any personal motives for so doing.'

'I know all the reasons,' he said. 'I've already considered them. But they're not insurmountable. I know you only did two years on a provincial paper and that was ages ago. I know that you've little editing experience, but who has to begin with? Anyway I'd stay on for a while. You'd learn all you need to know from me. Outside of those reasons, your refusal would have to be based on those personal motives you speak of.' He kept his eyes on my face. 'Why wouldn't you come back, Willie? You must realise by now that what drove you away doesn't matter now. I'm sure you must often wonder why you ever ran in the first place.'

It suddenly seemed hot in the room and I wished that I'd taken a drink. But slowly the fear subsided and common sense came to my aid. He couldn't have known. I'd never spoken of it to anyone and surely neither had McQuillan. 'What do you mean?' I asked, my voice under control. 'Whatever drove me away? I don't understand.'

'Whatever made you run? I knew you wanted to go – that you saw this place as a prison – but I've often wondered what it was that actually made you go in the end. And I've wondered too if I could have done anything.'

'You think something made me run away?'

'I know something made you run. It also destroyed your talent.'

'It's the poetry you regret,' I said in a flash of intuition. 'I was your protégé and never fulfilled the promise. Don't you think that maybe I didn't have what it takes? We're not all born to pluck the sword from the stone.'

'There's few of us born for that,' he said, 'but we can't know until we try. You can't classify yourself as a failure at seventeen.'

'And you think that if I come back here I'll fulfil my promise? What if there's no promise? What if one is destined to be third rate?'

'All we can do is work within our capabilities. If your poetry is the best that you can do, then it's every bit as valid as anyone else's. Once I thought you had the makings of a poet – maybe even a good one. I want to give you back that chance.'

'That's your only motive?'

'Why would I lie to you? Alice'd love to have you back. She sees in you the son we never had. I shouldn't say these things, but you want the truth. Now, you know it's your decision. I don't want an immediate answer – go away and think about it. I'll give you a couple of months. After that I have to make a decision. I can't be fairer than that, can I?'

'No,' I said. 'You can't.'

'That's all I ask. That you think about it. Now we won't talk about it anymore.'

He was as good as his word and the subject wasn't mentioned again. But I knew from Alice's good humour during dinner that he'd told her of our talk and my promise to consider what he'd said. We talked instead of old times and of my parents and of the world we knew then. It was a pleasant evening. Not once was the horror which had brought us together mentioned.

At times Lizzie loomed large in my mind and I was tempted to bring the evening to a close and go to her. But for too long I'd been alone, shut off from everyday civility and decency and values of life. So I stayed a little longer, as if some of those values might rub off on me.

When I did leave they came with me to the door where Alice embraced me. Alec walked me down to the gate, the fog which had gathered through the evening muffling our footsteps. I asked him if he'd arrange for some photographs to be taken and he told me to call him in the morning. We parted without any reference to what we'd spoken of earlier, but I knew that it was uppermost in both our minds.

I walked back by the river and a Garda car slowed while its occupants checked me over. Seemingly satisfied they drove on but took away with them some of the goodness of the evening. I thought about Alec's offer and what it would mean if I accepted it. For years I'd been my own man, answerable to no one. If I returned there would be rules I'd have to abide by. I would have to live here and answer for my actions.

Back at the hotel there was a message from McQuillan to say that she wanted to see me. She and Callen were another factor to be considered in any decision I might make. Lizzie was a factor too.

I screwed up the message and threw it in the waste bin, casting away the final remnants of the pleasure of the evening. But I'd another pleasure now, the thought of seeing Lizzie again. I hadn't gone to see her tonight but there was always tomorrow, and it was a thought to keep me warm through the dark cold hours.

12

Cloud had blown in off the Atlantic during the night and next morning it hung above the town like a shroud. It pressed about the car as I drove out into the countryside, hemming in the tension that gripped me with vice-like jaws. It was partly due to a restless night in which my dreams had been taken over by formless monsters and partly due to my desperate need to see Lizzie again.

It was in an effort to ease the tension that I drove out to her home after breakfast, but as I stopped by the gable I knew there was no one there. Despite this I got out of the car and went in through the gateway, blocked by a rusted iron gate. I knocked, not knowing what I'd say if someone other than Lizzie herself answered, but no one did.

The overgrown garden was split in two by a cracked concrete path. The surrounding hedge had not been trimmed in years. The cottage was old-fashioned, with small square windows and pebble-dashed walls. It hadn't been painted in a long time and the original pebble dash showed through in places like reflected splotches of the overcast sky.

I returned to the car, the tension unabated. I could hear the wind moaning in the ragged pine trees on the opposite side of the road; further on a few sycamores were silhouetted against the grey-black sky. The scene, the rural equivalent of an urban slum, should have depressed me, yet I felt only the excitement that comes from the promise of the forbidden. I wanted Lizzie again. It was a need that drove me to crave her body, to do with it whatever I wished.

I wondered where Lizzie might be. If she wasn't here, wasn't it likely that she was out at Hawley's? I'd earlier made arrangements with Alec to have some pictures taken and it gave me an excuse for calling there. I knew I should be calling on the Devlins – I'd already got what I needed from the Hawleys – but my craving to see Lizzie had taken possession of me.

I drove back to town and out past the school, all doubts banished by my wanting. When I parked in the yard only the mongrel ventured out to meet me. I got out of the car and crossed to the house.

'Photographs?' Hawley said at the door, frowning as if it were a word he didn't understand. I craned my neck to look into the kitchen, but there was no one there and the stab of disappointment was acute. 'You'd best come in, I suppose,' he added, convention still binding him.

'I won't,' I said. 'I only called to let you know the photographer'll call this afternoon.'

He nodded and I turned away and walked back to the car. Seated behind the wheel I regretted not having asked him about Lizzie. I looked back at the house before starting the engine but he'd gone inside. The door was closed and it was like a sign. I put the gear lever in reverse and let out the clutch, and as I swung about I saw her run from the house, her hand waving frantically. If I wanted another sign, surely this was it. But there was no more thought of symbols as I stopped the car and she opened the door and jumped in with a flurry of hair and limbs and that laugh I wanted to hear. 'God, am I glad to see you,' she said.

'Well, I'm glad that you're glad to see me,' I said, driving off. I couldn't hide my pleasure and she sensed it immediately.

'It's not you I'm pleased to see,' she said. 'I'm just relieved to get away. I don't know why you'd think I'd be pleased to see you anyway.'

'No?' I laughed. Anger showed as two red spots on her cheeks and I was triumphant. 'You must have a bad memory.'

'It's you who's got the bad memory,' she said.

'Look, I couldn't get out last night. Something came up. I'm working, you know. I can't neglect my work just like that.'

'I was waiting for hours,' she said. 'I was watching for the lights of your car, but you never came.'

'I'll come tonight. How about that?'

She ignored me and I glanced at her. She wore the jeans and jacket from yesterday but the blouse was different, cream in colour and buttoned to the neck. With her beside me, my obsession to see her eased and I could just take pleasure in her presence. To have her here was sufficient for now. I drove on and as we approached the turn-off for my old place I slowed down. 'Will we stop?' I said, smiling to show her I spoke in jest.

'What do you think I am?' she accused. 'I just want a lift to town. If you're wanting payment I can give you money. Will that do you?'

'I'm sorry about last night,' I said. 'It couldn't be helped. But I did call to the house this morning. Only you weren't there.'

'You're expecting me to believe that, are you?'

'I can describe the house for you.'

'Go on then.'

'You don't believe me?'

'Describe it. I'll tell you then.'

I described it for her, the rusting gate, the blue paint peeling from the door, and I knew that it was my first capitulation. 'Well?' I said. 'Will that do you?'

'You called. So what?'

'I wanted to see you again.'

'You're seeing me now, aren't you?'

I nodded. 'But... You know what I mean?'

She didn't speak but began to hum some tuneless ditty. Like a salesman she'd given me a sample of her wares yesterday. Now she wanted payment for them before she'd let me have any more. And this time there would be a price demanded. This time I'd have to give her my soul.

As we approached the town I thought of Alec Whitley's offer. Could I return to live here, accept the monotony and narrowness of small town life? Would it be made more bearable with Lizzie beside me, the empty future which beckoned me banished? Could I live here and raise a family because that too was part of the price she'd demand? Could I bear to grow old and die here and be buried beside my parents in the graveyard where the yews were stunted by the salt wind off the sea?

All I knew now was that I wanted Lizzie again. She was hardly more than a child, less than half my age, and I'd only to see her beside me with her soiled clothing, and smell her unwashed body, to know I was a fool. But I wanted her, and what did I care about the consequences? In a few days I'd be gone. But before that I had to have her and I had the means to persuade her to acquiesce. Why not use them?

'I've got some news that might interest you,' I said. 'I may be coming back here yet.'

'Here?' I had her interest now. 'Sure, why would you come back here?'

'To work,' I said. 'Alec Whitley's offered me a job.'

'At the paper?' She turned to look at me, but I avoided her eyes.

'I haven't decided yet. It's a big decision to make. So what do you think of that?'

'It's mighty.' She thumped me playfully on the arm and laughed. I felt a surge of hope and desire and wondered what it would be like to spend my life with her – to sleep with her after love-making and to wake in the morning with her beside me and reach out and touch her...

'Will I take you home?' I asked, confident now.

'I've got to get some bread first,' she said. 'If you drop me in the square, I won't be a minute.'

'I'll take you home then?'

'If you like.'

I stopped the car and she got out and I watched, imagining her naked. Even her grubby clothes and her smell were part of the desire. She turned to look at me before closing the door and I could have sworn I saw submission in her eyes. 'Not a word about what I've told you,' I said.

She nodded, serious, and then her eyes twinkled and I felt the stir of something that had nothing to do with my craving for possession. I wanted to hold her now, nothing more. I watched her run to the supermarket, the jeans tight to her buttocks and the tenderness died in me and desire flushed my body with heat.

I watched the entrance to the supermarket, waiting for her to re-emerge, so I didn't see Callen approach until his face loomed at the window. As I wound down the window, I caught the stale smell of cigarette smoke and bad breath. 'The weather's a bit cooler,' he said, clearly ill at ease.

'It's cool all right,' I said, drifting into the banalities of a hedged-in life. At every turn there seemed to be not only reminders of the past but also of what life might be like here now. Could any woman's body, any fantasy fulfilled, make up for what I would have to accept?

'You'll be going soon?' he said, eyeing me with a mixture of suspicion and worry. Again I couldn't figure out why he should react to me like that. I wasn't likely to divulge his secrets. After all, they'd tarnish me too. Or was it that he knew McQuillan had been to see me? Was he frightened that I might take her from him and leave him to the selfsame loneliness I myself endured?

'I'll probably be gone by Saturday,' I said but it didn't seem to ease whatever was bothering him.

He nodded and I felt he was about to speak again when Lizzie emerged from the shop and walked towards us. Callen's eyes narrowed and I saw there what I took to be puzzlement and then relief. 'Hello, Lizzie,' he said, and I saw her reaction to him on his own face, the eyes tightening and the lips coming together.

'Hello,' she said, no warmth in her voice. 'Can we go, Willie?' she added to me, and I thought that it was the first time she'd spoken my name.

'I'll be seeing you,' I said to Callen and wound up the window.

'Him,' Lizzie said, shuddering as I pulled away. 'Him and McQuillan – they're well matched.' She clutched the carrier bag to her and said no more. It was only as we turned off the bypass that she spoke again. 'That's where I mind the children,' she said, and I saw a bungalow concealed behind a shelter belt of palm trees.

'I thought you said you waited for me last night?'

'I did, too.'

'But weren't you there?' I nodded at the bungalow.

'Bridie went instead.'

'Send her again tonight,' I said.

'That's supposed to make it all right, is it?'

'Last night couldn't be helped. If I take the job I'll be here all the time. What about that?' She didn't reply, but I felt her attitude change. Already she was looking to the future. It was the moment to temper her hope, but I didn't do so. As I stopped by the gate she opened the door and I felt diminished already by the threat of her absence. 'Aren't you going to ask me in?' I said.

'Not now.' She got out of the car, the bag still clutched to her body. Again I wanted to hold her, to go into the cottage with her and watch her make tea and butter bread for me and eat and drink with her there beside me. Maybe she saw my disappointment because her face softened. 'Call tonight,' she said. She smiled and slammed the door shut.

I drove back to Castleford, and after lunch I decided to call on the Devlins. It was raining now and the countryside was bleak and dismal, the sea thrashing itself in a frenzy. As I drew near my destination, apprehension surfaced and I was tempted to turn back, but I drove on to the house. Whether it was the rain or the awful sense of desolation about me – the dilapidated farm buildings and house, the rusting abandoned machinery, the scrawny trees – it depressed me. One can tell whether a place is happy, whether it's loved, and I sensed that there was no love or happiness here.

Devlin answered my knock, peering out from deep gloom within. 'Willie Leitch,' I said to him. 'We met the other night.'

'You'd best come in out of the rain,' he said and stood aside to let me enter. We made our way into a large kitchen. 'Sit down,' he said, pulling a chair out from the table in the centre of the floor. Just then a woman came into the room rearranging a cardigan about her shoulders. 'Willie Leitch,' he said to her. 'The Yank's son.'

She shook hands with me, a tiny hand that might have belonged to her daughter. 'I came...,' I faltered. 'If there's anything I can do to help...'

'Like what?' There was no animosity in Devlin's voice, no hope either.

'I could make an appeal in Sunday's paper,' I said. 'Being as I'm from here – that I'm known to the people about... If someone is holding your daughter it might make them think again. Or if someone knows who's done this thing. Someone must know. If you just knew that she was OK...'

'Anything,' the woman said, turning to me, the anguish on her face frightening to behold. 'We'd do anything just to know...'

'It might work,' I said, aware that no appeal was ever going to move whoever had taken the child. He was beyond normal human emotions – couldn't comprehend what it was to have regret or compassion. But there was nothing to be gained by admitting that.

'Can you make that appeal?' Devlin asked, and it was then I detected the first seeds of hope.

'I can,' I said. 'It'd get prominence in the paper. If I could have some pictures, too, and some words from yourself to go with them, it'd have even more impact.'

'We went on the television,' Devlin said. 'That didn't do any good.'

'He might not have seen it,' I said. 'Even if he did, he could have put it out of his mind straight away. But with the paper... He could re-read it over and over... It might make him realise what he's done.'

'You think she's still alive?' It was Devlin again.

'I think so,' I lied. 'Otherwise there'd be no point in doing this.'

'She has to be alive.' Mrs Devlin stared at me as if I were the one responsible for her anguish. 'It's all we've got – that hope.'

'Maybe you'd tell me about her,' I said. 'What she liked... likes doing. School, friends, that sort of thing.'

They told me everything – how she'd been ill with flu just before she disappeared, how she went into Castleford that

Saturday evening to visit a friend and never got there. They made her seem perfect, belying the hints I'd read in other reports that she'd been troublesome, and had been constantly missing school. I wrote down what they told me – I didn't need to because it was common knowledge now – but I needed photographs. Once they'd committed themselves to helping, they'd find it more difficult to refuse what I asked.

This would be so much better than any piece on Majella Hawley. Majella was dead. There was no drama there anymore. But with the disclosure that she hadn't been murdered immediately and hints that Jacinta Devlin might possibly still be alive – the rumour of what the killer had done to Majella Hawley adding its own prurient horror – I'd have my story. With some hints as to why the Gardaí might have suppressed the information and with the implication that perhaps it had been irresponsible to do so, I'd add a little bit of controversy. What more could Jones want?

When they'd given me the information, Mrs Devlin made tea. There were broken biscuits in a battered tin and I ate a few bits out of courtesy. Devlin even apologised to me for the incident that first night. 'Councillor Moran's helped us with some grants,' he said. 'When he asked me to become a vigilante I couldn't refuse. I thought we were doing some good.'

'You want me to write about that?'

'Oh, no!' He almost jumped up from his chair. 'You mustn't mention it.'

'You have my word,' I said and he gave me a grateful look. 'If I could have some photographs though,' I added, seizing my chance.

'I suppose we could let you have some,' he said, glancing at his wife who didn't oppose his suggestion. 'Mind you, they're only snaps.'

'I'll have some taken,' I said. 'The photographer from *The*

Mayoman'll do them for me. Maybe some of yourselves with the other children. We'll include them with the picture of Jacinta you're going to give me.'

'Oh, yes,' he said. 'Will you get it, Mary?'

She went away and returned with an album which she placed beside me. Photographs of the children – christenings and birthdays, first day at school, first communion, in Jacinta's case a record from birth to death. Mrs Devlin stopped turning the pages and I saw she was crying. I stared at the album while I waited for the emotion to subside, impatient to have my picture and go. I began to leaf through the pages myself, mostly snaps as Devlin had said. I'd have to make do with one of the professional photographs of her first communion.

I felt their reluctance when I asked if I could have the photograph, posed beneath a flowering cherry in the church grounds. 'It'll come to no harm,' I promised. 'You'll have it back in a few days.' I looked at them both and Devlin nodded, but I sensed that they loathed me. I slipped my pad and pen and the photograph into my pocket and got up to go.

Devlin came to the door and we shook hands, formal to the end. 'I'll keep Councillor Moran out of it,' I said as a parting threat. 'And I'll get the photographer to call. Who knows but Jacinta might be back home again in a few days.'

He said nothing and I turned away and walked to the car. He was still in the doorway as I drove off, and though I raised my hand to him, he didn't acknowledge me. Perhaps he'd known all along that I'd been lying.

13

It was raining again as I drove out to Lizzie's, the headlamps transforming the drizzle into a fine black dust which seemed to be the main constituent of the darkness pressing about me. I had with me a basket of sandwiches made up at the hotel, and a bottle of wine, and despite the ravages of the years, I might have been the boy I'd once been on my first date – that boy who'd cycled into Castleford one autumn evening with fallen leaves fringing the roadsides and the brittle smoke of a bonfire in his nostrils. She had been older than me, and apart from the fact that her breath had smelled when I kissed her, there was little else I now remembered. She might have been part of a dream, one of those creatures who have substance only in our dreams and who flit away like wraiths when we awake.

It was the same expectation I experienced now as I'd experienced then, but what was good and natural for the boy seemed obscene in a man nearing the watershed of middle age. It was a thought to make me stop – to turn about and go back to the hotel and join my colleagues.

I could have done so and suffered hours of torment before bedtime – and then endured the further torment of imagining what it would be like to have Lizzie beside me in the bed. But I didn't turn about. I could claim that it was desire that drove me, but was that all? Did the fact that she was J.P.

O'Malley's daughter have anything to do with my obsession? The thought was uncomfortable.

The road here was edged by hedgerows which seemed to give solidity to the darkness the headlamp beams shovelled up on either side. Some creature scuttled across my path and further on I saw a cat poised on a bank, so entranced in watching its prey that it ignored, or else was unaware of, the car.

The light from Lizzie's was a welcoming beacon. A lamp, fixed on the gable, cast a triangle of illumination and the black shadow of the gate on road. I noticed light from the windows, and as I swung through the farm gate further on, a floodlight lit up the yard.

As I got out of the car, she came hurrying towards me. She'd discarded the jeans and jacket and wore a red dress which flounced about her calves. She was like an apparition in the light, the shimmering drizzle falling all around her but seemingly not touching her. The dress was buttoned to the neck with long sleeves and a belt which emphasised her slim body. In the thrill of seeing her – of having her there before me – I forgot everything except the wonder of her presence.

'You came,' she said, looking at me as if she couldn't quite believe that I was here.

'You didn't doubt that I would?' I asked.

'No.' She shook her head, but her doubt was in that single word, hidden beneath her pleasure and relief.

'I brought some wine and sandwiches,' I said, holding them out to her.

'Are you going to make me drunk and take advantage of me?'

I ignored her teasing, flushed with the hope that I'd do just that. 'It's raining,' I said instead. 'Aren't you going to invite me in?'

'Maybe I shouldn't,' she still teased, 'but this is the only decent dress I've got. If it gets much wetter I'll have to be taking it off.' She waited for a response, but when I didn't speak she came and possessively took my arm and led me to the cottage. 'Not a word in front of Bridie,' she warned. 'She has these funny ideas about love.' She spoke as if she herself were a mature woman, knowledgeable in the ways of love's pleasures and betrayals. 'She asked me just now if I was going to let you kiss me. Can you believe that? But then, she's only twelve.'

'And are you?' It was easier to joke than to consider what she said. For a moment faces loomed out of the drizzle – Sissy Bradley's and Judith Kelly's frighteningly clear; Jacinta Devlin's and Majella Hawley's blurred as if by the rain. None of them older than Bridie...

'Only if you behave.' Lizzie's words brought me back to the present where it was still easier to joke than to think of the suck and pull of the water which had taken Judith Kelly, her screams which surely no one could have heard above the howling of the wind and the roar of the river before she was dragged under for the last time. Easier to joke than think of Majella Hawley alive for days with her killer, subjected to what horrors before he put his hands about her throat and choked the life out of her... 'Are you going to behave?' Lizzie added, squeezing my arm.

'I don't know,' I said, never more glad of her presence.

'You're awful,' she said, letting go my arm and turning into the cottage. The front door led directly into the living-room, a door to the kitchen directly opposite. The room was lit by a lamp which stood on the television, and by the leaping flames of a peat fire. The place was shabby with its battered armchairs and a settee, and a long dark cabinet, its top cluttered with the bits and pieces any family accumulates – photographs in cheap plastic frames, ornaments, bric-a-brac, papers and letters – yet the light and the fire gave it warmth. A young girl, a clone of Lizzie, sat in one of the armchairs, watching television.

'This is Bridie,' Lizzie said taking the wine and sandwiches. 'TV's greatest fan. She never misses *Home and Away.* She's terribly interested in all the romance.' She winked at me, linking us together as if we'd been old lovers.

'No, I'm not,' Bridie protested, turning her head to look at us. I saw her appraising me before she turned back to the television.

Lizzie laughed and winked at me again. 'Sit down,' she said. 'I'll be back in a minute.'

I sat on the couch, drawn to the television, the Australian accents as alien to me as the young people portrayed. 'Do you like serials?' I asked Bridie.

She nodded and looked at me, her eyes bright with enthusiasm. 'I like the American ones best,' she said.

She glanced at me and she seemed so much like her sister that I imagined that it was the child before me whom I'd penetrated yesterday with the urge to hurt and conquer, and it scared me.

Just then music blared from the television to signify the end of the episode and Bridie got to her feet and switched off. The real world now had a claim on her. 'I have to go,' she said. 'It's nearly seven.'

'Will I take you?' I asked.

'She always takes her bike,' Lizzie said, returning as if on cue. Her words implied that there had been other occasions when Bridie had been sent in her place, and the thought stirred something within me. The first stirring of jealousy, I realised with a shock.

They left the room and I heard their voices like bird-song from the kitchen. I heard a door slam and Lizzie returned and crossed to the window and pulled the curtain aside. She stared out, seeing, I was certain, only her own ghostly reflection. 'Aren't you worried about her?' I asked.

She nodded and turned back, allowing the curtain fall into place. 'I worry all the time,' she said. 'It's like having a daughter of my own.'

'Shouldn't you have gone with her?' I said. 'It's dark outside.'

'She has a light,' she said. 'And I can see the house from the top room. When she gets there she switches on the outside light and I know then she's OK.' She went out through the door by the side of the chimney breast and after a couple of minutes returned and sat beside me. 'She got there,' she said, 'so now you can relax.'

I shrugged and looked at her face, innocence hidden beneath make-up which only served to emphasise her youth. The dress was made of a man-made fibre and cheaply finished, yet she endowed it with a vitality and freshness it didn't merit. 'She likes you, you know,' she said, taking me by surprise.

'Bridie?'

'Who else?' She laughed, the worries of a few moments ago forgotten. That's what it meant to be young. I would have given anything then to have a little of her youth for myself. As if I might filch some of it, I held out my hand to her. She grasped it and I was surprised at how cold her hands were and how large my own hand appeared in comparison.

'But do you like me?' I asked.

'I might,' she said, 'now that Bridie's given you the all clear. She said it would be OK to kiss you.'

'So what are you waiting for?' I asked.

'Maybe I'm old-fashioned,' she said.

I pulled her to me and she came without resistance, and I

felt the dampness of her dress as my arms encircled her. There was the taste of lipstick off her lips as her body shifted on the couch and strained against me. I took an arm from around her and touched her breast, the nipple hard beneath my fingers. She moaned, and as her teeth ground against my lips, I slipped my hand down to her knee; but as I attempted to thrust it beneath her dress, her thighs convulsively clenched together, preventing me.

I didn't try to force the issue but instead stroked her knee while my other hand stroked her back, her shoulder-blade solid to my touch. I don't know how long we remained like that, maybe it was but a few moments, before she relaxed. When she did so, she took my hand from her knee and, as her thighs parted, pushed it upwards.

I felt dampness and heat and, as my fingers wormed their way inside her panties, the crinkly texture of pubic hair. She took her mouth from mine and I could see her face now, her eyes inflamed, the brown irises hardly more than a ring of colour surrounding the black dilated pupils. 'Do you like me?' she asked in a harsh whisper. 'Tell me you do.'

I nodded, not trusting my voice, and she clutched my lapel, pulling it so firmly that I felt certain she would rip it. 'Tell me,' she ordered. 'Tell me you care just a little.'

'I do care,' I said. 'I've never seen anyone so beautiful.' Just then I'd have said anything, promised her anything. Like Faust, I'd have sold my soul. But she needed no promises and I watched as she began to undo the buttons on the bodice of her dress. Slowly she opened each one, her eyes never leaving mine. As she opened the last button I let my hand slide down from her shoulder towards her breasts, but she caught it and gently thrust it away. 'Wait,' she said, only it wasn't a command but a promise.

She crossed to the front door and I heard the rattle of the

bolt being shot home. She came back and switched off the lamp, plunging the room into deep gloom. 'Leave it on,' I said, a rasp in my voice, but she ignored me.

In the firelight the dress appeared colourless, but when she moved it seemed aflame. She came and stood before me, and close up the dress took on the colour of congealed blood. It rustled as she moved and the noises of the night outside, the wind gusting in the chimney, the banging of an outhouse door, were banished, became part of a world I never wanted to inhabit again. I watched as she eased off one shoe and then the other and kicked them away from her. She stooped to catch the hem of the dress with her fingers and she slowly pulled it up to reveal first her knees and then her thighs, where I could see the shape of her bones, and then the white triangle of her panties. She stood motionless and then her hands seemed to do a trick like a conjuror and the dress slipped to the floor where it lay like the bloodied pelt of an animal about her feet.

Naked she looked more boyish than ever. As she stood before me I was acutely aware of her vulnerability, of the terrible burden a woman carries – the need she has to be loved and the sacrifices she's willing to make to claim that love and hold it. We were the fortunate sex. Maybe at times I might wonder why we were damned with the demon that is desire, that possesses and drives us and whose power and passion no woman can ever comprehend. It's the demon that drives us to rape and kill – to abuse a child, to hold it in terror for days before tightening the tourniquet of death about the neck.

I reached out and took her hand, still cold in contrast to her body which had been so hot beneath the dress. I pulled her to me and she came obediently to kneel on the vinyl, her head coming down to lie in my lap, iron of my erection against her cheek. I touched her face with my fingers, and bent down to kiss her cheek and her earlobe and her hair, the scent of her perfume mingled with the scent of our passion.

'Love me,' she said, and it was like a plea for help. She pulled away and moved to the rug by the fire and knelt again, the flames giving her body the sheen of white marble, the same cold marble whiteness a corpse possesses. The thought touched me as I got to my feet and began to undress. I couldn't see her eyes – they were just pools of darkness – but I felt her watch me.

I undressed to my underpants and knelt beside her. We kissed and then divested ourselves of our last pieces of clothing. We stretched out on the rug, side by side, the floor hard beneath us. Yesterday might have never been, for now she seemed as demure as a virgin. I wanted more and I tried to turn her over on her face – some crazy idea possessed me that if I had her in a similiar position to what she'd been in yesterday, I'd recapture that same passion and excitement. But she pushed herself down tight against the rug and pleaded with me: 'No,' she said. 'Please... no.'

As I reared over that thin body with those dark pleading eyes staring into mine and the firelight glinting on each strand of her hair, I was reminded again of what a terrible world it was in which to be a woman with her whole life open to use and abuse by men, and I let her be. It was with gentleness I penetrated her, no desire within me now to hurt her or to make her cry out. As I moved within her, she closed her eyes and arched her body as if to escape the hardness of the floor.

We didn't speak. We could have murmured the word love but there was no need of it. If love existed then this was a manifestation of it, the whole mystery of life caught in this communion of bodies. There was nothing ugly or dirty or obscene in the room, nothing but that thinking might make it so.

My face hung above hers and I kissed her cheeks and the tip of her nose and her forehead and lips. She cupped my face in her hands; when she briefly opened her eyes I thought I saw reflected there all the terror and pleasure the human race has ever endured and momentarily I was afraid. But what it was I was afraid of, I could not say. Then she clenched her eyes shut and banished the fear and only the two of us existed now, the sound of our breathing and our sighs of pleasure and the quickening movement of our bodies and that catch in her voice when she called out a litany of no's, the words rising into the air like startled birds, their wings beating about the room with the wind in the chimney and the rattle of a door somewhere caught in a draught. And then she was arching her body higher and I was thrusting into her with urgency, just the centre of the pleasure there now, rising to that moment when we possess the world – earth and trees and grass, the air we breathe and the water we drink – we embrace it all, wrap our arms tightly about it, rich beyond our wildest dreams, never ever to be so rich again. Afterwards there is that moment of satiation when we wonder how we could ever again want what we'd just had, that moment when we're reborn and die, caught in the relentless cycle of such moments from womb to grave.

Her nails dug into my back but I welcomed the discomfort. Now I honoured Lizzie, lying there close to her, my arms about her, the embodiment of those words: With my body I thee worship. For what else was I doing if not worshipping that body beside me, breathing as I breathed, pleasured as I was pleasured, satisfied as I was satisfied, maybe grateful as I was grateful. Her face was flushed with passion, or the heat from the fire. I kissed her cheek, hot and with a taste of make-up, tasting it now as if my senses had been heightened and were making the physical world more real for me.

'Tell me things,' she said, her voice languid.

'What will I tell you?'

'Anything. Tell me lies. I don't care.'

'You're beautiful,' I said and she stiffened and withdrew from me as if I'd struck her. 'Did I say something wrong?' I murmured.

'You don't love me,' she said. 'I can tell that you don't. You just want sex like all men.'

'It's not like that,' I said.

'Isn't it? What about yesterday? Was that love? Turning me about like that... Like you tried just now. Is there something else you want from me? Is that it?' She stared at me but I had no answer. 'What about protection? Did you think of that? I could get pregnant or catch a disease!' She moved away from me and sat up, the small breasts forming under their own weight, the nipples dark. She seemed so much older and more mature now and I felt an awful sense of sadness. Here was a moment I might never again experience – here was the dream my parents had sought, that I myself was surely seeking but which day by day was receding from me. Yet right now it was there for me, and I'd only to reach out and take it.

I reached behind me and picked up my jacket and placed it about her shoulders. I let my arms linger and I told her that I loved her and would always love her. What made me speak – pity, shame, guilt, fear? I could never know. But with the words she opened herself up to me again like a flower.

I don't know how long we lay there afterwards as the fire burned down. All I know is that I never wanted it to end. Maybe it was then, too, in those moments following the act of love, that I began to think that I could have the dream after all.

It grew cold and, as we rose and dressed, I felt the damp of our juices on the rug beneath my feet. She told me to put turf on the fire and I did so, stoking up the embers so that sparks flew up into the black maw of the chimney, dying in the suck of the draught. She brought in the wine and sandwiches and we pulled the couch across the fire and placed cushions on the floor and sat side by side staring into the kindling peat, maybe trying to see our future there.

The wine was warm and we drank from tiny glasses which contained but a mouthful. There were sandwiches of ham and chicken and beef and we ate, hardly speaking. Outside the wind was becoming blustery and rain beat in flurries against the window. It felt good to be inside with the fire and the wine warming me and every hope I might possess for the future right there beside me. 'Have you ever thought of leaving here?' I asked, thinking to myself that if I didn't come back then maybe she'd come to Dublin and share my life there.

'Sometimes,' she said. 'But I can't go yet.'

'Why not?'

'I have to take care of Bridie.'

'Hasn't she her father?'

'What sort of life would she have with him?'

'But you can't be expected to sacrifice your own life.'

'I'm not,' she said. 'I'm only seventeen. In a few years Bridie'll be able to look after herself.'

Seventeen. She was younger than half my age. But hadn't I known it? To be just seventeen and have so much knowl-edge... I reached out to her and she came obediently into my arms. She could be my daughter and I knew that if she were, I'd never be more protective of her than I was at that moment.

How long did we sit there staring into the fire? I know the rain died out though the wind seemed to blow much stronger before we roused ourselves. Had we been more comfortable we'd have fallen asleep, and I promised myself then that I would sleep with her before I went away.

'I'll have to be getting Bridie,' she said eventually. 'She has to be up for school in the morning.'

'I know.' I still held her, never wanting to let her go, but the real world awaited us. With the realisation of that, apprehension surged through me, but now it wasn't for myself. 'How will you get back?' I asked.

The anxiety in my voice touched her and she drew her head back so that she could look at me. 'I'll walk,' she said. 'How else?'

'It's not safe,' I said, 'to be out on your own.'

She laughed and in her laughter I detected the certainty all youth possesses that they will never die, and it separated us all the more. I had come to a time in my life when death had to be considered. Only recently a friend had said that between forty and sixty were the dangerous years. For a moment the possibility of separation struck me like a blow. Were we doomed to have no future beyond what we had now? The thought made me pull her to me and I kissed her and tightened my arms about her. 'Don't walk back alone anymore,' I said. 'Promise me that you won't.'

'No harm'll come to me,' she said, laughing at my foolishness.

'Don't laugh,' I said, gripping her shoulders, digging my fingers into her flesh until I could feel the bone. 'Promise,' I urged until she whimpered. 'Promise me now that you'll never go out alone again until this killer is caught.'

'I promise,' she said, and behind the firelight reflected in her eyes I saw the glimmering of fear.

My fingers relaxed and I drew her to me. 'I'm sorry,' I whispered in her ear, her hair against my lips. 'But I don't want to lose you.'

She nodded, her face bumping my shoulder. I felt the warmth of her body, and was again taken with a terrible apprehension for which there was no logical explanation. It was love, I told myself, a sense of great joy mingled with fear. After the searching and the disappointment and the seeming inevitability of facing the future alone, I had at last, like my father before me, found love.

I thought now of what Alec Whitley had said to me – about the hope he had that I might return and fulfil the promise I'd shown. The past was dead and buried. I'd taken no real part in what Callen or McQuillan had done. I was innocent. The realisation came to me with another surge of joy – with a breaking of the bonds that had held me for so long. I'd been given a chance of a new future. It was up to me to take it. For all I knew it might be the last chance I'd ever have.

We left then and I dropped Lizzie at the gate to the bungalow and, with a final farewell kiss and a promise to call again the following evening, I drove away. As I came into Castleford I felt the loneliness of the coming night descend on me as it had done so often before, but now I was able to put it to one side and look to the future.

14

The next morning the town was shrouded in black sheets of rain. After breakfast I attended a Garda press conference, but there was nothing new. There had been a positive response to the reconstruction and all leads were being followed up. I asked no questions and left before the conference was over.

As I walked out I saw Doyle, and though he returned my greeting, there was a barrier between us now. Through the years I'd been away, whenever I'd thought of him or of the people who'd touched my life while I'd lived here, I'd always seen them as permanent, unchanging, never escaping the chains I'd cast off. Now I wondered which of us had cast off our chains.

When I emerged the town was bleak and miserable in the rain. It should have been enough to depress me, but instead I felt elated. Last night with Lizzie was so vivid in my mind that already I was looking forward to tonight.

I drove to the premises of *The Mayoman*, a two-storey block at the end of Station Road. Alec was there and I had a coffee with him in his office. 'I'm considering your offer,' I told him.

'We were worried that you might not accept,' he said. 'Alice has sort of set her heart on it.'

'There's nothing definite,' I put in quickly, not wishing to get his hopes too high.

'Oh, that's understood,' he said. He watched me across his

desk, the mug of coffee held in his hands. I asked him if his photographer could take some pictures of the Devlins this afternoon and he agreed, but his expression was troubled. 'I hope you know what you're doing,' he said. 'There's been a lot of grief here. We're a small community – we've all suffered.'

'I've got a job to do,' I said, defensively. 'You, better than anyone, knows how it is. People want the truth. They have a right to it.'

'I sometimes wonder,' he said. 'Many years ago, a man came into my office one day. I'd never met him before, though I'd seen him about the town. He'd been summonsed for having faulty stoplights on his car. The thing was, you see, he didn't know the lights were faulty, but he was pleading guilty anyway, and he'd called to ask me not to report the case. He wanted to know what good it'd do apart from causing his family distress. His son especially would be upset. I told him I couldn't help him and went ahead and reported the case. I thought the world deserved even that small truth. Though we became friends afterwards, he never agreed with what I'd done.'

'What's the point of all this, Alec?' I asked.

'I don't know anymore which of us was right. A newspaper is a powerful medium. Used fairly it's invaluable, but you and I know it's not always used fairly. Where the powerful are concerned we tread warily, but with the weak and the defence-less... Have you never twisted the truth, never slanted it for your own benefit?' He stared at me, unaware of how close he'd come to detailing the very attributes I possessed. 'What would you say to that man if he walked in now?' he continued. 'You're the editor. It's your decision.'

'I'd refuse, of course.'

'And if he's your most valued advertiser, a powerful man with the right connections who might influence others in the town against you? It's a small town remember.'

I laughed. 'OK,' I said. 'I get your point.'

'I don't think you do,' he said. He put down his cup and looked at me. 'What if he's a relative? When that man came into my office that day, he was a stranger, but he was some-one's father. Maybe even yours...'

'Mine?' I'd never known how Alec and my father had become friends.

'"I'm Bob Leitch,"' he said to me. '"I want a favour,"' Alec shook his head. 'Do you know the word decent?' he contin-ued. 'It's a word that's lost meaning, like so many others, but it meant something once. It described your father, Willie. Maybe the reason I've offered you the job is because you're his son.'

I felt uncomfortable under his gaze, certain he would see through me. He might think of me as my father's son but I didn't possess his decency. 'Don't mind me,' Alec said now. 'I'll get your photographs for you. On condition that you visit us again soon.'

'Maybe over the weekend,' I said. 'I'll give you a ring.'

'I'll tell Alice,' he said.

I left him and returned to the hotel. For the remainder of the morning I worked on my article, using the very attributes Alec had spoken of, elaborating, hinting, slanting the truth to obtain the effects I wanted. I lunched alone, and the thought of returning to my room afterwards depressed me. I consid-ered calling on Lizzie but instead decided to do some research. I'd go out to Castlewood and see for myself where Majella Hawley had been buried – get a feel for the place.

I drove there and parked my car by the gateway that gave access to the woods. I climbed over the wooden stile and walked along the track which lead deep into the wood. There was a rank smell of decay all about me, a contrast to the smell I remembered from summers long gone. I knew that I was probably treading on the footsteps of the killer of Majella Hawley and I wondered if he'd dragged her here, not only with the smell of decay in her nostrils, but with the suffocating stench of fear and death, too. Or had he carried her body here, stumbling under the burden?

Her grave had been scooped out of rotting leaves and pine needles and soft tilth about fifty feet off the track, and I found it without difficulty, lead there by the path others had made before me. There was a simple wooden cross stuck in the ground and the trampled area was strewn with flowers.

I closed my eyes but there was only darkness: no flash of inspiration; no vision of a male face; no glimpse of the vehicle he must have used and which must have been parked by the stile. How long would it all have taken – half an hour or more? No one had reported seeing a vehicle parked there on any night during that week, yet the only convenient access point to the woods was from the main road. It was a busy road, yet no one had seen anything. Or had people seen something but been too scared to speak, perhaps because the person they'd seen was someone who was highly respected or maybe feared?

I suspected that this wasn't original thinking on my part. No doubt the Gardaí had already considered these points. So had the killer been on foot? Had he accosted Majella Hawley as she walked from town? It was a possibility despite the fact that no one had claimed to have seen her walking along the road. It was almost a mile from the footbridge to the entrance to the woods. It would have taken her a minimum of fifteen minutes, maybe nearer twenty, to walk that distance. Surely someone should have seen her?

But even assuming she'd walked here and had met her killer – that it was an opportunistic crime – where did that leave my information that she'd been held alive for two days? If it were correct, and I was convinced it was, Majella Hawley had not been killed until Wednesday. Surely her killer hadn't left her alive here in the woods where there was a possibility of her being found? Indeed she would have been found, for I knew that the woods had been searched on Tuesday. Everyone assumed that the grave hadn't been located then because at that time the searchers had been looking for a live person, but of course the grave had not been found for the simple reason that it hadn't been there. I began to see a reason why the killer had brought the body to be buried here. He'd known about the woods being searched and calculated that they wouldn't be searched a second time. He hadn't taken into consideration the chance of a man out walking his dog coming across the grave when the dog began to dig in the soft earth.

Was Jacinta Devlin also buried somewhere here? So far the Gardaí had not committed themselves on that point. I knew that over the weekend they'd used sniffer dogs here without success, but to search the woods thoroughly for a grave would take immense manpower and time. Halligan had hinted that he would do so eventually if they didn't make progress, but I thought that he hoped to find the killer first and let him lead them to the body.

But where did that leave me? Majella had disappeared on the Monday evening somewhere between the footbridge and her home. For the next two days she'd been held a prisoner. Then sometime on Wednesday she'd been killed and her body dumped here. But how had the killer avoided detection? Where had he kept her those two days? And why had he kept her alive? Surely it was a risk to have done so. If it was a sex crime, and according to the Gardaí it was, then why didn't he kill her immediately after gratifying whatever lust drove him to take her in the first place? But there seemed no logical answer to any of it.

I scuffed the ground and stood a moment in silence. The dead, unlike the living, belong to all of us, and there on that patch of ground that had been forever violated, I felt a kinship with the child and was shamed. I was using her for my own ends too. I thought of my article – of what Alec Whitley had just said – what Plod Doyle had said. What would I achieve? The world wouldn't change and only a fool would think that it might.

I returned to the car and drove on. I found myself stopping at the railway bridge where it had all begun long years before, the day Callen had been waiting for me as I came from school and asked if I wanted to see the treasure which his uncle had given him.

I was fourteen then and he must have been seventeen, a shambling boy in whom the man was waiting to burst out. I knew he'd been in trouble with the Gardaí on numerous occasions, had hardly ever attended school regularly, and had spent six months in a reform school. He lived most of the year with his uncle in Duagh but returned home when that relative was away in Wales. What I also knew was that I should not have anything to do with him.

I would never have gone beneath the bridge with him if he hadn't given me a glimpse of the treasure – that pile of magazines whose names escape me now – which he kept hidden behind a loose stone. Even yet I vividly remember the pictures: the wonder of breasts which surely in reality were never as wondrous again; the curve of belly and buttock; the thighs between which lay the secret place, always hidden, imagination trying desperately to give it substance.

It all seemed a long time ago now as I got out of the car and climbed over the stone wall, topped with a single strand of barbed wire. I scrambled down the steep bank onto the line where the rails lay buried beneath grass and nettles and weeds.

I stood under the arch of the bridge, where I'd pored over the pictures that day, my eyes feasting on a surfeit of naked flesh, an ache of pleasure rising in me that I'd never before experienced. Overhead I heard a lorry go by, drawing gravel from the sandpit, its vibrations as it passed filtering down. I'd wanted to remain there and forever gaze on one picture of a woman on all fours, the camera angle giving the merest hint of the shadow created by the cleft between her buttocks, the small pointed breasts drooping under their own weight, the nipples which even to my inexperienced eyes seemed too large, pointing to either side. Her face was turned back to the camera so that her eyes looked directly at me. Her mouth was open and the tip of her tongue rested invitingly on her lower lip. I'd heard of French kissing, had laughed with false bravado and an aching longing at a description of it I'd heard in the school toilets, a concrete urinal with earth closets which steamed oppressively in the summer, and where in winter the urine froze in the blocked trough.

Like most of the other lads I'd learned the facts of life from Jimmy Manahan who, when he left school at fifteen, could neither read nor write. He'd described for us the pleasures to be had so that oftentimes while awake in the darkness of the night with my mother snoring beside me, I'd found myself burrowing my face in the pillow which smelled of Sunlight soap, sucking at the cloth until the taste of the ticking and the feather stuffing forced me to stop.

It was the same excitement I'd experienced that day on seeing the picture. I'd wanted to press my lips to her lips, to force my tongue into her mouth. I'd wanted to fondle her breasts, to slide my hand between her legs and feel the hair which hid her mystery. I'd known that there would be questions and recriminations from my mother for being late – but I didn't want to leave.

I put the magazine in my schoolbag, and it was like a promise against my back on the journey home. That evening I hid it beneath my jacket and retreated to the hayshed. It was October and the evening light was fading. In the distance a cow lowed and I heard the noise of a tractor engine.

The hay was yielding to lie on, like I imagined the body of the woman in the picture to be. The yeast-like scent of the hay was her perfume in my nostrils as I opened my fly and pushed down my trousers and underpants to grind my bare belly and the sore-hard iron of my developing manhood into the hay, imagining it to be the pubic hair which hid her womanhood from my greedy eyes.

It was my first never-to-be-forgotten experience of orgasm, the seed pumping and my face buried in the hay, my lips sucking at the wisps of dried grass which I had saved in the fields that summer, one hand violently burrowing in the hay while the other rubbed my belly and thighs, avoiding the thing which was beginning to go limp between my legs, sticky with the residue of the semen now soaking down through the hay.

I lay spent, my face still buried, and a few moments later the hay made me sneeze. I clamped a hand over my nose and mouth to muffle the sound, my heart beating from excitement and the terror of being found and the guilt which was crawling into me like the death maggot, the pleasure now seeming of little consequence when measured against the threat of damnation.

But it had only been a beginning. How often over that winter and the following spring had I crouched down here with Callen and waited for Sissy Bradley to join us? Here for the reward of a sweet or a piece of chewing gum, or indeed at times for nothing at all, she'd do what Callen wanted. He took me to Duagh with him when his uncle returned from Wales, and there I heard stories of that man's sexual exploits. I remembered him laughing as he told us about some old ugly whore with withered breasts who was a favourite of his because she had false teeth. And then laughing at me because I didn't understand what he meant.

That summer Sissy Bradley was taken into care, but Callen said that it didn't matter. She was getting to the stage where soon she'd have been of no use to him. I didn't really understand what he meant. I'd imagined Sissy Bradley telling the authorities about us and the Gardaí taking me away in handcuffs. I stopped going beneath the bridge, but as the weeks passed desire drew me back, and one evening I found Callen there with Judith Kelly. Sissy Bradley had been eleven, but Judith Kelly was not yet ten. Compared with Sissy she seemed a mere child, and even then I must have been receptive to innocence. 'Run,' I'd said to her. 'Run. Don't ever let him touch you again. If he does, tell your parents.'

I'd faced Callen's wrath to save her, or so I'd thought then. But that autumn she drowned, her death a catalyst in my own life, and no matter how tempted I'd been afterwards, I'd never gone under the bridge again until today.

Now I reached out to touch the blocks of stone, green with slime. I thought of childhood, that time of innocence, that time we squander and can never have back. I thought of the past and of Lizzie and of returning here, of putting what had happened behind me. The past was gone now like the trains that once had run beneath this arch, like the magazines that had tempted me all those years ago. I left it then, climbed back up onto the road, and drove back to Castleford.

15

As I emerged from the alley at the side of the hotel I saw McQuillan. She was walking towards me. Her timing was such that we would meet by the entrance, and I knew she'd arranged it so. She wore jeans in which her thighs bulged and beneath her open jacket a white blouse moulded itself to her breasts and protruding stomach. She had a shoulder-slung handbag, one hand gripping the strap so tightly that her knuckles showed white.

'You don't seem pleased to see me,' she accused, seeing in my face an annoyance I didn't bother to conceal.

'I'm busy,' I told her. 'This isn't some pleasure trip.'

'That's not what I've been hearing.' Now her eyes were like searchlights probing my face, and I turned away to stare into the hotel. A man emerged and I heard a rumble of voices and a woman's laugh before the closing door abruptly cut it off. 'Anyway I didn't ask if you were busy,' she added. 'I said you don't seem pleased to see me.'

'I have things on my mind,' I said.

'Like Lizzie O'Malley?' she laughed.

It was my turn to stare at her, at the face which like the rest of her body was already showing signs of middle age. 'Callen should mind his own business,' I said.

'You think he told me?'

'He saw Lizzie in the car with me, didn't he?'

'But did he see her out at your house?' She watched me closely and I saw her eyes narrow at my reaction. The scene in that room flashed before me and a horror gripped me that someone had watched us – a face pressed to the window-pane like the grinning face of the bogey man I'd imagined as a child. Illogical: we'd been on the first floor. Power must have told someone that I was there with Lizzie. I should have known that something like this would not remain secret.

'It's cold,' McQuillan said when I didn't speak. 'I need a drink.'

'I've things to do,' I said. 'I'm busy right now.'

'With Lizzie?' She tried to sound flippant but it was bitterness that filtered through.

'I have to go,' I said. 'What's past is past. It was all a long time ago. We can't change it now.'

'But I have to talk to you,' she said. 'You owe me that.'

'There's nothing to talk about.' I spoke firmly.

'Tonight,' she said as if I'd not spoken. 'I want to talk tonight.' It was a demand.

'I can't see you tonight,' I said angrily.

'It's her, isn't it?' she said. 'You're seeing her tonight?'

'You're not telling me you're jealous?' It was absurd.

'Why do you think that you're so important?' She watched me with those sick eyes, her face the colour of old newspaper. 'I don't care what you do. You go and fuck Lizzie if you want to. She's only paying for what she wants like all of us. With this.' She gestured at her body, her fingers curled like talons. 'But I've already paid. Now I'm here to collect what's owing to me.'

I laughed then, easier to laugh than deal with the chill that touched me. There was a finality about her words I couldn't ignore. She was fermenting with old memories and bad experiences and my instinct was to run as I'd run long ago – run from the darkness which suddenly seemed to have thickened about us.

As if sensing my urge to run she let go the strap of her bag and grabbed my arm. 'Do you think I gave you what I did out of love? Remember that last night? That's all I wanted – a helping hand. That's what I paid you for.' Her eyes held mine. 'Well the debt is still owed,' she went on. 'So we meet and talk and agree to what I want. Otherwise I'll have a chat with Lizzie. And what will your love think of you then? Or the Gardaí? I could have a chat with them, too.'

'Chat away,' I said. 'It's your funeral.'

'That's where you're wrong,' she said. 'I want to get away from here. You're the one who wants to return. I saw Lizzie today,' she went on. 'I bumped into her accidently. She's in love – did you know that? I told her you'd run away, but she wouldn't believe me. She never knew we'd been friends. It surprised her – loosened her tongue it did. She told me you're coming back to work on *The Mayoman* so that you can be together. When I heard it I couldn't believe my luck.'

'So what if it's true?'

'You've everything to lose. Once I was the one in that position. That night when I thought I was making sure of holding on to it all, I was really losing everything. Now I want another chance.'

'And you think you can force me to help you with whatever crazy idea you've got in mind this time? You think I'll help you if you threaten to tell Lizzie or the Gardaí about what happened that night?'

'You've got it all wrong,' she said. 'I wasn't thinking of that. Do you remember Sissy Bradley?' she asked, changing tack. 'Do you? Poor silly Sissy. Wasn't that what you boys called her?'

'It was pretty harmless,' I said. 'Didn't everyone have a

nickname?' Fear made me talkative. Surely Callen hadn't told her? But it was the kind of thing he might boast about.

'Oh, the name was harmless enough,' she said, 'but what about all the other things?'

'What things? I don't know what you're talking about.' I turned away as if to escape. A few cars passed. A man went by on a bicycle and I followed the ticking of the freewheel until he turned into Bridge Street. I could hear the river across the street.

'Don't you?' she said. 'Don't you remember? Would it help you if we went into the bar and I asked you there? Or will I ask you out here? I could shout it out if you like.'

'What do you want?' I asked. I felt tight with fear.

'To talk,' she said. 'Is that too much to ask?'

'No. If you want to talk, that's all right with me.'

'I know about Sissy,' she said. 'About you and Callen and Judith Kelly – what you used to do. Poor Sissy. Did you know she spent years in a mental hospital? She chopped off her hair and kept scrubbing her scalp until it was raw and bleeding. Scrubbing and scrubbing to try and clean off the the dirt...' Her fingers tightened their grip. 'What would Lizzie think of that? Or Alice and Alec Whitley?'

I didn't answer her. I just needed to get away. I needed a drink too. A couple came out of the hotel, normal people, part of a world I no longer inhabited. They stared at us. I realised that others in the hotel were watching us. 'Will we have that drink?' I asked, desperate to get out of the street.

'I don't want a drink anymore,' she said. 'I've got to go.'

Threatened with her going, I was now the one who didn't want her to leave. While she was beside me I could control her. She must have been aware of this because she let go my arm. 'I saw Sissy recently,' she said. 'She doesn't live too far away.'

'What is it you want?' I asked.

'Not a lot. I should be looking for more but, as you said, the past is past. We can't have it back. All that's left us is the future. If you want to spend the future with Lizzie, what do I care, providing my future's secure? Ever since I can remember I've been used. Maybe even beyond my memory, for all I know. But this is the end of it. I'm going to run once more and you're my ticket. After that you'll never hear from me again. I'm giving you your future back in return for mine.'

'I don't love Lizzie,' I lied.

'What's love?' she asked. 'You want to fuck her. Isn't that enough?'

'But you seem to think that telling Lizzie about the past is going to make a difference.'

'But I wouldn't be just telling Lizzie,' she said. 'I'd have to give the information to the Gardaí. Now wouldn't they be interested?'

'In what kids did more than twenty years ago? And what about Callen?'

'You're forgetting what's happened here recently. They'd be interested all right. Of course there wouldn't be any real danger for either of you. You weren't here when the girls went missing and Callen was with me on both occasions. It'll be inconvenient for him, but what do I care. You're the one with everything to lose. Do you think Alec Whitley would have you work for him? Or that Lizzie would have anything to do with you?'

She had it all worked out. I wanted to tell her to go to hell but then I thought of what she'd said, 'Lizzie loves you,' and I didn't. 'Where will I meet you?' I asked instead.

My capitulation brought her a look of triumph. She'd waited a long time for this moment. 'I'll meet you here,' she said.

'When?'

'I wouldn't want to spoil your evening, so I'll give you enough time. A few hours should do, don't you think? Especially when you're in love. They say men don't want to do it that much when they're in love. So we'll make it ten o'clock.'

'I'll meet you here,' I said. I turned to go into the hotel but her voice stilled me.

'Ten o'clock,' she said. 'Be here.'

I didn't answer but walked into the hotel. I needed a drink but I knew that if I went into the bar I'd remain there all night. So instead I retreated to my room.

For a while I stood at the window as twilight softened the hard edges of the buildings across the river and the street-lights, which had just come on, absorbed the last shreds of daylight and turned everything to sepia. I thought of packing up and heading for Dublin, but I knew that I wouldn't get ten miles before I turned the car about and came back. My future, whatever it might be, was here. Even the reminders of the past couldn't kill my desire for some stability and permanency. I'd found a means of having both and surely for a little while I could be happy. I wasn't so much of a fool as to imagine that I could be happy forever.

I left my post at the window when the bells from the church chimed out the Angelus and buried myself in my work, able to lock out the world for an hour. I gave no thought to the rights or wrongs of what I was doing but did my job to the best of my ability.

I left for Lizzie's after seven and on the journey I tried to banish the past and McQuillan from my mind, but they hung about me like old smells. I bore no gifts, unless the tenderness I felt for Lizzie was a gift I'd been given and which I could give to her in turn.

As I drove up to the cottage I met Bridie on her bicycle and I stopped to speak with her. She was the image of Lizzie as she must have been at that age, and I wanted to fold the child in my arms as a father might. She chatted about what she'd just been watching on television and then told me Lizzie was in a bad mood, her face stark in the glow from the dashboard lights. 'You'd best not be standing on her toes,' she said seriously.

'I'll be careful of her corns,' I said conspiratorily and she laughed and I was aware that I was in the presence of innocence. The past loomed in my mind again and I had an image of Sissy Bradley scrubbing her scalp. But surely Sissy Bradley had never been innocent?

I said goodbye to Bridie and continued on up to the cottage. I parked in the yard, but no one came to meet me and I had to knock before Lizzie answered the door. As I held out my arms to her I noted that she wore jeans and a knitted jumper. She didn't resist my embrace, but her heart wasn't in it. I pushed her to arms length and looked in her eyes. 'I met her in town,' I said. 'She told me she talked to you.'

'How could you?' she said. 'With... with her?'

'We were kids. It's what... nearly twenty-five years ago. She didn't mean anything to me. You can't imagine that she means anything now?'

'Why did she tell me then? If it didn't mean anything she wouldn't have told me.'

'I don't know,' I said. Maybe I should have sat her down then and told her the truth about the past, but I was too frightened of losing her. Instead I told her what she wanted to hear – that she was beautiful and desirable and that I loved her – and though it was true, she would have believed it even if it were not.

After we'd made love and lay entangled, I asked her if she'd come away with me for the weekend. She made excuses at first but eventually agreed. Bridie could stay with friends in town and she'd tell her father that she was going to visit her mother's sister in Galway. 'He never has anything to do with her,' she said, 'so he'll never know.' I nodded, aware that here was yet another betrayal. Was our relationship to be founded on nothing else? Or was it that in the nature of human love, betrayal was the norm?

I thought of what McQuillan would demand from me for her silence. But *would* she remain silent? Wouldn't her threat always be there as the past had been? If the dream I had of returning and sharing my life with Lizzie came to fruition, I'd be even more vulnerable. But there was little I could do until I knew what she wanted.

'I have to be back by ten,' I told Lizzie. 'I'm expecting a call.' It was another lie but what did one more matter? I peered at her – we were side by side on the couch – and I saw that she believed me. We'd just made love and I hadn't made demands on her, hadn't tried to turn her over, and she was incapable of thinking that I might ever betray her. For now I was made perfect in her image of what she wanted me to be.

'I'll make some coffee so,' Lizzie said and she disentangled her limbs from mine and stood up. The light had been left on and I saw her body clearly. Her skin was taut about her ribs and when she stooped to pick up her underclothes from the floor her vertebrae stood out like knots on a rope. I watched without desire as she got dressed and then she came and kissed me and brushed me with her fingers and my breath caught. She laughed and I knew McQuillan didn't matter to her anymore.

While she made coffee I dressed and then we sat by the fire and drank the coffee. We talked of our proposed weekend away – we'd go away tomorrow afternoon and return on Sunday evening – wherever it was she wanted to go. 'We might as well go to Galway,' she said. 'That's where I'm supposed to be going, isn't it?'

'That's fine with me,' I agreed, thinking that when it came down to it we were both well versed in the art of deception. Maybe that was what the success or failure of a human relationship depended on, how well one could deceive and pretend. So we made our arrangements for deceit and I wondered if it crossed Lizzie's mind, as it did my own, that if we could deceive her father now, who might we deceive in the future? Perhaps even each other.

I left her at a quarter to ten. She would relieve Bridie a little later. I think she wanted time alone to savour what she'd just had and to dream of what was to come.

McQuillan was in my mind as I drove back to town, the moon hanging amongst the clouds like a hole punched in the night. As I entered the avenue of beech trees, the bare branches seemed to close above my head and I had the illogical feeling that I was in a dark tunnel from which I might never emerge.

16

McQuillan was waiting in the lobby, and couldn't conceal her relief. 'Where will we talk?' I asked, and she suggested we go to the Point, in my youth a favoured haunt of courting couples. Indeed myself and McQuillan had once made use of its seclusion.

'You'll be safe there,' she said. 'There won't be anyone to tell Lizzie except me. And I shouldn't have reason to tell after tonight. Isn't that right?'

I knew then that I should walk away from her, but I didn't have the courage or the conviction for that. When I'd run all those years ago, fear and horror had given me the impetus. Now I'd committed myself. If I ran I would have so much to lose. Twenty years ago I'd had hopes and dreams and youth to take away with me. Now there was only disillusionment, approaching middle age, the knowledge that the dreams were but dreams after all.

'We'll go,' I said and she followed me outside. She was silent as I drove up Strand Street and turned left at the bridge. We passed the ruins of the castle which gave the town part of its name and I was reminded of the transient nature of life. We live and we die and the world lives and dies with us.

Farmland gave way to open shore land where grass grew tough and spiky and yellow with wind-burn. Though the windows were closed I could smell the sea, visible on my left, aglow in the moonlight, a fringe of foam on the shoreline. I turned onto the track leading down to the beach and saw the ocean now before me.

I parked, facing the ocean, and shut off the engine. McQuillan spoke for the first time since we'd left the hotel. 'Leave it on,' she said. 'I feel cold.' I restarted the engine and switched on the fan. She stared out through the windscreen. 'I've never been back,' she said. 'I expected to find it all changed.'

'Only people change,' I said.

'Do they?' she said. 'I don't think they do. They just learn to hide what they really are. You'll never tell Lizzie what you are. She'll see what you show her and what she wants to see. That's all.'

'It's just a way of coping with the world,' I said. 'How long do you think we could live with each other if we knew what we really were?'

'Some of us have to do that,' she said. 'It's the price we pay for not being alone. Only sometimes the price is too much.'

'Is it too much for you?'

'It was always too much,' she said. She turned towards me. Her face was taut as if the skin had shrunk and was stretched tightly over her bones. 'Do you remember the last time I ever saw you?' she asked.

I nodded. 'It's not something I'm likely to forget, is it?'

'I don't mean that,' she said angrily. 'I mean the night itself. There was a dance in the Town Hall but you wouldn't take me. You didn't want to have anything to do with me anymore. It was August – the festival dance was on. You must remember that.'

'Sort of,' I said. In reality everything was frozen in my memory.

'I still remember it vividly,' she said. 'I don't know why I went, but I did. And you were there. You were dancing with that Clancy one...'

I couldn't quite believe this. What was it now? Twenty-three years ago, and she could tell me who I'd danced with.

'You don't remember,' she accused. 'I asked you to dance and afterwards we went out to the car. You'd no driving licence or insurance and you used that as an excuse not to take me here. Yet it had never stopped you before. It was cold for August and there was something wrong with the car and you couldn't leave the engine running.'

'I remember that,' I said, thinking it strange how selective memory could be, and hoping that in recalling something I might please her.

'I bet you do,' she said bitterly. 'But you don't remember what's important. Why would you?'

'Maybe if you told me what it is I'm supposed to remember.'

'It was what you said. Don't you even remember that?'

'No.' I shook my head. 'It was a long time ago. We were only kids.'

'Kids!' She laughed. 'I remember,' she said bitterly.

'I'm sure I didn't mean it,' I said. 'We all say things we don't mean.'

'Oh, you meant it all right.

I shrugged. I wanted an end to this. 'Look,' I said, 'we'll have to go soon, so can you tell what me this is all about.'

'You took me out here eventually,' she said, 'after a lot of coaxing. But you just sat and stared out the window. I asked you if it was all over and you shrugged. It wasn't important. You were going to be a writer. You were off to university. Why would you be bothered with someone like me?'

She had it all wrong but I didn't correct her. I had dreamed of being a writer but hadn't intended going to university, at least not then. 'We were young,' I said now. 'What did you expect? That we'd get married? Is that it?'

'I wasn't a fool,' she said, 'whatever you might think. I didn't want to marry anyone. Why would I? I wanted freedom, the right to my own life. I saw you as someone who might be useful to me. Just like Callen. Only he'd been stupid enough to get himself put away. When I met you, I saw you as his replacement. Whatever I gave you was payment for what I wanted.' She spoke with vehemence, trying to convince herself that it had been so, but her voice was laced with the bitterness of rejection. She'd loved then, whatever love may have meant to her.

'So we used each other,' I said. 'But it was all a long time ago. It's so much water under the bridge.'

She laughed then and I stared at her, but there was no hint of what she wanted in those eyes which seemed to be dark cavities below the fringe of hair. She stared back and I could see wry amusement on her face, but it was only a mask. She waited for me to speak, but there was nothing more to say. 'We'll have to go,' I said again. 'So you'd best tell me what it is you want.'

'I'll tell you,' she said, 'in my own good time. I want you to know everything first. I want you to know why I did what I did – what it was like when you ran away. I needed you and you ran. I want you to know what the price is now. That's why you're here – to pay for what you've had and for what you said to me that night. Only you don't remember.'

'No doubt you'll enlighten me,' I said, stung to retaliate.

'I asked you what I'd done wrong,' she continued as if I'd not spoken. 'Why you didn't want me anymore. You wouldn't say, but I pressed you and must have touched a raw nerve. You told me that you couldn't have anything to do with a girl who gave herself so freely to everyone.' She laughed again but it couldn't hide her anguish. 'How could you think I gave myself freely to anyone?' she demanded, each word oozing bitterness. 'What did you know of it?'

'Nothing,' I said, resigned to this. 'But you'd been with Callen...'

'Had I?' she said. 'What do you know of that either?'

'He was obsessed with sex. I can't imagine he made do with a cuddle.'

'He wouldn't make do with that,' she said. 'No one should know that better than you. But it wasn't him. There was someone else. Long before that, there was someone else. But that fucker's dead now, isn't he?'

Her words didn't register with me at first, and then I didn't want to believe what she was telling me.

'I was seven,' she went on, 'when my grandmother died. My mother came to the funeral and I thought she'd take me away with her to Birmingham, but she still wanted nothing to do with me. Her husband wasn't my father – he'd only agreed to marry her when she'd sent me to Ireland to my grandparents. I was only four then and I hadn't wanted to go, but when I came to Ireland I found that my grandmother was kind to me and I came to love her. She was the only one I ever really loved. When she died I didn't really understand it – I kept thinking she'd come back. But the first night my grandfather took me into his bed and started kissing and feeling... I knew then she was never coming back...'

She stopped. In the silence I heard the whirr of the fan and the hum of the engine and farther off I imagined I could hear the ebb and flow of the sea. I couldn't bear to look at her and I stared out through the windscreen.

'That's all he wanted at first,' she continued. 'But then one night he turned me over on my face and did it. I still remember it – the pain and the terror. It seemed to go on for ever –

this thrusting and the pain and his weight crushing me. I could feel his hot breath on my neck and his hands underneath me pawing... I begged him to stop. I was crying and pleading, but he...'

She stopped to draw breath and the silence seemed to intensify about me. 'I don't think he came,' she went on. 'I only remember that the thrusting stopped and he rolled off me. He fell asleep and later I heard him snoring. I wanted to get out of the bed but I was frightened of waking him up and having to endure it all again. I couldn't sleep. The pain was too bad and I was frightened by the wetness between my legs. I thought I'd wet the bed. But next morning I saw that it was blood. It was caked on my thighs and there was a red stain on the sheet. I thought I was going to die, that I'd be put in a box like my grandmother and then put in a hole in the ground. I woke him up and asked him if I'd die and he laughed. He told me that I'd only die if I told anyone what had happened. It was our secret. I'd to get up then and make him tea before I went to school. I remember being terrified that the teacher would know – that it wouldn't be a secret anymore and I'd die. But no one ever found out. I never told a soul until I told Callen.'

I didn't know what to say. How often had I wondered why she'd committed that terrible deed? Well, I had my answer now, but maybe I'd be better off if I'd never known.

'You've nothing to say?' she said when my silence went on and on.

'What is there to say? Maybe if I'd known what you suffered...'

'Suffered?' she snorted. 'What would you know about it? What would any man know. Can you imagine what it was like? To be helpless – unable to do anything. To have that night after night throughout your childhood, and everyone telling you how lucky you were to have a good grandad.' She stopped again. 'He didn't come often. He was virtually impotent. So he'd try until he went limp – he always had me turned over on my stomach. I think I resembled my mother and he couldn't bear to look at me while he was doing it. It's what I think but I could be wrong. Maybe it was just a kink – I don't know. He'd thrust and paw me and mutter endearments and curses, the dribble from his mouth dripping on my back. One night he pulled out abruptly and I thought it was over, but it was only beginning. He grabbed my head and forced me down under the bedclothes. He was wearing long-johns – he always wore them – yellow from age and stinking of stale sweat and piss. But worst of all was the way the crotch hung loosely between his legs like a sac. He was fumbling at it and then he forced my face down and his thing was all limp and wet and stinking against my cheek. I remember retching and having the taste of bile in my mouth and his thing pressed against my clenched lips. I wouldn't open my mouth but he grabbed my hair and pulled it until I did. I could taste the piss and the salt and I thought I was going to be sick. I tried to pull away, but the pain from my hair being pulled was excruciating. And when you're only seven or eight years old...'

She stopped again and I knew that she was reliving that experience once more. We are our childhoods. All our lives we're governed by the events and memories from then. For the woman beside me this was an expurgation of everything that had made her what she was. But surely it had come a lifetime too late?

'A few weeks later,' she said, 'I'd do it without protest. I'd go under the bedclothes before he even started. Anything to keep him off me – not to have to endure his weight and the thrusting, his hands pawing me and the slobber of his mouth and the stench of whiskey and tobacco... I found out too that I held power over him. I could get money off him for sweets and later for cigarettes. Yet all the time I hated him and wanted an end to it all.'

My stomach felt queasy – the same sickness I'd experienced that night I'd run from her. But all the time I'd been running in a circle, ending up back where I'd started from. In a moment she'd make demands and what could I answer? How could I deny her? I glanced at her but her face seemed hewn from rock and I knew she was still in the past, a child again beside the sleeping man she'd shown me one night out at her house, a wizened face above the threadbare, soiled quilt. I thought of her as the child she'd been then – the girl I remembered from school who had always been in trouble. I thought too of Sissy Bradley and Judith Kelly. I wondered who else Callen had taken under the bridge. Had he taken McQuillan – was that where she'd got to know him? Or had they gravitated inevitably together, drawn to each other because they were both damned?

'You see now,' she said, 'why I did what I did? Who would have given me justice? For years and years I never slept alone. They taught me at school that hell was a place of punishment – that the wicked are punished there by fire. Maybe that's why my hands were burnt. That was my punishment. Or was it just a taste of what I might expect when I die? Is that it?'

'I don't know,' I said.

'Feel my hands,' she said suddenly, thrusting them at me. 'You can still feel the scars.'

I couldn't bring myself to touch her.

'He had this oil lamp,' she said now, but she was no longer talking to me. She was confessing and I was the surrogate priest who'd intercede for her. 'He'd become afraid of the dark – maybe it was hell he was frightened of, or that his Aggie would come back to haunt him. Whatever it was, he kept this lamp lit beside the bed. He smoked in bed, mostly his pipe but now and then a cigarette. He always lit the pipe with a match, but for the cigarette he used the lamp, turning up the wick until the flame leapt to the top of the globe. I'd watch him, hoping that he'd drop the lamp and set fire to the bed. I imagined him burning – burning now and burning forever in hell.'

She laughed. I supposed that it was easier than crying. 'He was sick, that summer when I met you, and had the doctor. I listened at the door. I hoped the doctor would send him to hospital. Or tell him he was dying. Instead he scolded him for smoking in bed. He was always dropping ash and there were burn holes in the bedclothes. "You'll burn the house down," the doctor said, "with yourself and the child in it." It was like a revelation. I could kill him and no one'd know. I spoke to the doctor. I told him that he was smoking in bed and using the oil lamp to light his cigarettes and I was worried he'd burn himself. "I've warned him about it," the doctor said, never suspecting what I was at.

'It was then I planned it. He was on tablets that made him sleepy and he was getting feeble and infirm. I knew he wouldn't be able to get out of the bed that quick. If I could make sure that the fire got a good grip first... Only I wanted to be certain that no suspicion fell on me. I needed a witness to back up my story. I knew Callen and we planned it together – the idea of seeing someone burn appealed to him – but he got caught breaking into shops in town and was put away. I thought then that was the end of my idea – till the night I met you.'

Her words dropped into my consciousness like lead and I didn't want to hear anymore.

'If only you'd cared,' she said, 'even a little, I might have accepted everything. But all my life I'd been used. I'd been conceived out of a man's need. I'd been sent away for a man's need. My grandfather had used me for his own perversions. Callen was no different. He'd his perversions too. But you were different. You were a poet, and strange as it may seem, poetry was one of the few things I liked at school. I never told you though. I thought you'd laugh at me. All my life I'd been put down. What could I know about poetry? I dreamed that maybe you'd write a poem about me – that I'd see it in a book one day with a dedication…'

She made a sound that might have been a laugh. 'But you were like all the rest. You only wanted one thing. Maybe I could have accepted that, but that last night we came here – when you said… I knew then I couldn't take anymore. So I persuaded you to take me home and to come in. I… I wanted you there. You'd be my witness, and if it went wrong, you'd be in trouble too. I'd tell the Guards we planned it together. You didn't want to come in but I said what was the harm in doing it once more for old time's sake?'

'You came in and I went into the bedroom to check on him and shut out the door so you wouldn't see anything. He was asleep and I tucked in the blankets so's he wouldn't be able to get out in a hurry. I didn't want to make a mess of it. There was a can of paraffin kept in the room for filling the lamp and I spilt half of it on the quilt and on the pillow each side of his head. I lit it with a match and then threw the lamp on the bed. It blazed up straight away and I could smell burning hair. I watched and some seconds passed before he became aware of the fire. He opened his eyes and stared up at me, bewildered and frightened. That was the best moment of it all – when he knew that I'd done it. He knew why he was burning – that it was a foretaste of hell. I'd waited years for it, and when he spoke my name I spat on him. I turned away and came back out, opening and closing the door quickly again so that you still wouldn't see. The rest you know.'

It was claustrophobic in the car and I had a terrible feeling that I was her next victim. I needed to get away – to escape from the reminders of that night which had been made so vivid again for me with her recalling of it. I could see her in my mind as she came out of the room and closed the door behind her. It was warped and had to be pulled shut. I'd thought that she'd closed the door so that the old man wouldn't hear us. It excited me, for at that moment, before the extent of the horror was revealed to me, I'd wanted her one last time.

I opened the car door and stepped out into the night and banged the door closed behind me, shutting her in with the memories. But they followed me – were out here now with the cold and the wind off the sea. I could hear the noise of the car engine and the water sucking at the shingle on the shore and in my imagination the screams of an old man.

It was from the room the screams had come – high-pitched nightmarish screams of terror and agony – such terror and agony as I'd not heard before and could never wish to hear again. I'd been sitting in the armchair by the dead fire and had leapt to my feet at that awful sound which reverberated through the house.

'He's paying,' she'd said to me, standing by the door. I'd stared at her, stricken with paralysis, while the screams went on and on. I don't know how long it was, a few seconds only, but it was sufficient time for him to get out of the bed and cross to the door and pull it open.

It was then I saw him. He was burning. His vest and long-johns were on fire. I saw what remained of his face, the skin hideously blistered and beginning to peel away, the mouth opening and closing like a landed fish, not a mouth at all but a gaping hole which emitted those awful screams. He was beating at the fire with hands which resembled charred wood and from which shreds of flesh flapped about like bits of rag. I still couldn't move. Only my senses of hearing and sight and smell functioned. The stench of burning flesh and hair was overpowering and I gagged. I thought she was trying to kill the fire when she started to beat at him with her fists. She seemed oblivious to pain and it took a moment to realise that she was trying to beat him back into the room where the flames from the burning bed were leaping about like demented demons from hell.

I screamed at her and realised in that moment that I was the only one now making a sound. His screams had ceased, and in the silent struggle taking place before me, I heard the roar of the fire. Maybe he stumbled, maybe his strength failed him, maybe her efforts were successful. Whatever it was he took a step back into the room and she pushed him and he went sprawling, a grotesque effigy of a human being, the flames dying out as the clothing was burnt from his body. She pulled the door shut and held the knob so that it couldn't be opened again. He must have had a remnant of his instinct for self-preservation left because he made a last desperate effort to pull the door open. She held tight for the few seconds his attempt lasted, before he realised that it was over and gave himself up to the fire, falling back into the burning room where his body was later discovered.

It was only then I noticed that her hands were burnt and I finally broke and ran. I somehow opened the front door, and as I did so, she tried to grab me. Her touch only gave me more impetus and I ran blindly across the yard while her pleas followed me. The car was parked beyond the gate and somehow I reached it. As I sped away I saw flames pouring from the window of the room.

I shivered now in the cold, reliving that night as I'd done so often in nightmare. In the nightmare it is I who calls for help, but no one comes. In the nightmare I experience what it must have been like for him, the fire all about him as he must have imagined hell to be. I sit up in bed, terror giving movement to my limbs, and I throw the burning bedclothes from my body and swing my legs out as the fire catches hold. I feel my hair alight, but there's no pain. I don't endure the agony he must have endured as he staggered to the door of the room, screaming for help. For some years now the nightmares had not plagued my sleeping hours, only my waking ones.

I heard a movement behind me and I knew McQuillan had got out of the car. I heard her slam the door shut and then the sound of her footsteps as she came towards me, magnified by my heightened senses. I didn't turn my head to look at her, but instead stared out at the leaden sea.

'You never forget,' she said. 'You never forget the smell or the way the skin swells up and bursts – the way the charred flesh hangs like strips of torn clothes.'

'What is it you want?' I asked, angry and bitter.

'I want to get away from here,' she said. 'Away from Callen... I did what I did to escape then, but I just ended up in another prison. When I left hospital in Dublin and went to Birmingham to my mother, Callen followed me when he was released. He knew what I'd done and he knew how to use that knowledge. As well as that my grandfather had left me everything in his will. As if he could buy... Callen knew about that, too, and demanded a share if he was to keep quiet. And I was lonely in Birmingham. I knew no one and my mother and her husband didn't want me. Callen seemed a godsend... Since then we've been tied together by what we've known about each other.'

'If you want to go,' I said, 'why don't you? No one can punish you now for what happened then.'

'I've nothing to go with,' she said. 'He never did give me

157

any money. This time I want a clean break. I don't want him to find me. I want to escape and have a new life for myself.'

'And you think I can help you?'

'I'm not asking for charity. You're writing a book about all this. I'll help you. I know things. I can tell you so much. About other men who liked children. You don't think that Callen... that he was the only one?'

'You should go to the police,' I said, 'if you've got information.'

'I couldn't go if I had to stay here afterwards. But with the book... You'd get money. You could pay me for what I'd tell you. I wouldn't give it to anyone else. It's my price for not telling about the past. If you don't do as I ask, you lose Lizzie and everything, just as I lost everything. And there'll be someone else to pay for what I know. And if you think I won't go to the Guards, then think again. If I could do what I did all those years ago...'

I didn't know which way to turn. I could call her bluff, but what if she did as she threatened? How badly did I want Lizzie and a future?

'I need time,' I said. 'You can give me that, can't you? I can't do anything at the weekend anyway. And you might as well know there's nothing definite about a book. It's only a possibility – a slim one at that.'

'But you told Callen...'

'It was only talk,' I said. My voice was hollow.

'You're lying,' she said. 'I know it. I'll give you till tomorrow. I want an answer then. I want five thousand pounds.'

'You're mad,' I said. 'I don't even have five thousand pence.'

'You can get it,' she said. 'You've no choice but to get it. I know what you want. You're frightened of the future. You don't want to face it alone. We're alike and different. I'm frightened of the future, too, but I want to face it alone. This is my chance to have that. I'll give you till tomorrow. After that I'll tell Lizzie, and if I have to I'll go to the Gardaí. Once I tell them what I know there'll be plenty of others looking for my story and willing to pay. So it's up to you. My way you get Lizzie and a story. The other way you get nothing.' Abruptly she turned away and walked back to the car.

I stood staring out over the water. The sea looked cold and hostile, and I imagined the seabed littered with the bones of dead men. I shivered and returned to the car and started the engine. We didn't speak again on the way back to town. I dropped her in the square, no thought now for who might see us.

'I'll be at the hotel tomorrow evening,' she said. 'Be there.' She slammed the door and I watched her walk down Market Street towards Dempsey's. Was it only four nights ago that I'd met her and Callen there? Four nights in which I'd found a future and now was threatened with the possibility of losing it. I watched her until she entered the pub and then I drove on to the hotel. I was tempted to ask the night porter to get me a bottle of whiskey, but I knew I'd some thinking to do and I needed a clear head.

In my room I sat in darkness by the window. The river was black and treacherous and shone like molten tar in the sporadic moonlight. Chaotic thoughts trampled through my head. I grew cold with the night but only roused myself when I started to shiver. I took a shower and then crept between the cold sheets and lay there in the gloom, resisting sleep, I was in abject terror of sleep and of the nightmares that had once been a part of my life. It was to quell them that I'd once turned to whiskey, drinking it down like water to keep out the ghost who came in the night to my window, tapping on the glass to be let in. Yet it wasn't the ghost of McQuillan's grandfather who came; nor the ghost of Judith Kelly. It was my father I saw at the window – and it was from him I recoiled. Now too it was his ghost I feared as I held on to reality. Even reality was preferable to the world that would come into being if I slept.

17

No nightmares came, however, to haunt my sleep, and I began to nurture hope again. Over breakfast I dwelt on the coming weekend with Lizzie, and afterwards work took priority. I saw Tommo, who was returning to Dublin in the afternoon, and he agreed to take the photographs and my article to Jones. I rang Alec Whitley, who wasn't in his office and whom I caught at home. Alice answered the phone and invited me to lunch. I'd arranged to meet Lizzie at four and it would help pass the time until then.

Alec promised to have the photographs delivered to me within the hour and they arrived as I was giving the article a final polish. I entrusted the lot to Tommo and left for lunch. I walked down by the river and stopped at the bridge to look over the parapet at the water seething and boiling below me. It seemed dirtier than it used to be. Along the banks where the water flowed more sedately, the flotsam and jetsam of a careless world bobbed on the eddies. Eventually the litter would be swept out to sea, but the sea would cast it back, as it had the body of Judith Kelly. I thought of Sissy Bradley and wondered if it would have been better for her if she'd died – had suffered a few minutes of agony and terror and then had peace?

I left the river and walked on. When I reached Alec's I stopped at the gate to look at the woods behind the house, the trees black and bare in the sunshine, and remembering the summers I'd played there, I knew I wanted to come home.

Alice answered the door and it was as it had always been when I'd come here as a child. There were smells of beeswax and baking bread and meat roasting, and it set me looking forward to the day when I'd wait in my study for Lizzie to show in a favoured guest, just as Alec waited for me now. 'Lunch will be ready in an hour,' Alice told us. 'You've plenty of time to talk.'

We made small talk, Alec and I, but he soon sensed that something was wrong. 'You want to tell me about it?' he said, and to my surprise I nodded, uncertain where to begin. I'd the awful need to unburden myself. I took a moment to find my voice before I began hesitantly with the events of the previous night, from there going back to that other night and then all the way back to that time when I'd known Callen. I told him what McQuillan wanted from me and then grew silent while he sat quietly gazing into the fire, judging me. Despite the fact that I saw myself being judged, I still felt a weight lift from my shoulders, but when I looked at Alec, the weight returned a hundredfold. He owed me nothing. It was I who owed the debts, and had incurred another. I was frightened that he'd turn me away, but I knew that one thing I had in my favour was his love for Alice. If it hurt her to send me away, then he wouldn't do so.

Alec sat looking at the fire, and I could only guess at what it was he saw there. 'So that's why you ran?' he said. 'Ah, Willie, if only you'd come to me.' He sighed as if at the wasted years and raised his head. 'You know,' he added, 'I've always had a feeling there was something suspicious about that fire. There were so many unanswered questions. Why was there no lid on the paraffin tin? How had she sustained her burns when the door of the room had been closed? The experts could tell, you see, but she had suffered so much and none of us had done anything ... '

'You'd suspected that something was wrong before the fire?' I said.

'Not in the way you mean. Just that it wasn't right to leave a child with an old man. People saw it as another Heidi, but she was such an unhappy creature. Your father mentioned it once. "What can we do?" he asked me, and I told him there was nothing we could do. Months later he was dead and there was no one left to care.'

'I'm sorry,' I said. 'I didn't know that this would be so painful.'

'No.' He waved my words away. 'The past always returns to confront us. We bury our pasts like we bury our waste, but the stink seeps back up.'

'You can't blame yourself,' I said. 'What could you have done?'

'I wasn't thinking of that,' he said. 'It's what we do to our own that haunts us – what we do to those we profess to love. Forty years ago Alice and I were married. We wanted a family, a house full of children. I'd a dream, too, of being a writer; it was in my blood like a virus. But it withered away, or I became immune to it, or maybe I just didn't want it badly enough. I think now that was the problem. But the other dream died, too. We'd no children. For me it was just a minor blow, but for Alice ... She wanted to adopt a child – even one would have pleased her – but I refused. I told her it was fate. We'd see the world instead. I was so blind. What does it matter now that we've seen it? What will we leave behind – a house, a newspaper? Money? Is that it? Even my grandfather left the woods. Is that my legacy, the fact that I didn't cut down the trees?'

I'd no answer for him. I'd looked at his life and seen only

perfection, yet it was like any other life. Raise a stone and there beneath were the same hopes and betrayals, the dreams turned to dust, and death to make a mockery of it all. I thought of the giant who went about lifting the roofs off houses to peer in, of the priest in the confessional... To even learn the sad details of a single life was surely horror enough?

'You mustn't mind me,' Alec said. 'I've too much time to brood. When I brood I see the wrongs I've done. And what of you, Willie? I wanted you to fulfil my own ambitions. I nurtured you and pretended that it was for you. Offering you the job here now wasn't for you. It wasn't even for Alice. It was for myself. Everything we do is for ourselves. You ask me what should you do? What can you do except follow your own needs. It's what we all do, what we have to pay for. We're taught about heaven and hell, reward and punishment, but there's no such thing. Life punishes and rewards. Nature's a cycle. Birth and death, and life in between.'

I turned and looked out of the window. The rear lawns stretched away to the shelter belt of cypress trees and above them I saw the tops of the broadleafed trees in the wood. In the right-hand corner was the orchard – apple and plum and pear trees. I'd played there as a child, had picked the fruit when I could reach it. One day I'd found an apple on the ground and brought it to where my father and Alec sat on the patio. It was a windfall apple, Alec explained. It couldn't be eaten because there was a maggot in it. He lead me down to the orchard and picked another apple for me. It was a time when I thought the world would never change, that my father would never die and I'd never grow old. But already the world was changing and the malignant growth that would kill my father was even then beginning to eat his stomach.

'I shouldn't have come,' I said. 'I'll go and leave you in peace.' I made to rise but he stayed me with his hand.

'This is a small place,' he said. 'We know everyone's business. I've been told already about you and Elizabeth O'Malley. Only you don't know what to do any more. You ask my advice but I want you to know what sort of man advises you – one who'd use another for his own selfish needs. Never mind that we use each other all the time. So why would you want advice from someone like me?'

'Nothing's changed,' I said. 'Do you think I've told you everything about my own life?'

'None of us ever do,' he said. 'But if you want my advice, don't ever let another person hold power over you.'

'She's spoken to Lizzie already,' I said. 'She's threatened to tell her everything if I don't go along with her.'

'Let her tell away,' he said. 'If Elizabeth loves you she'll accept you for what you are, not for what you once were or what happened twenty years ago. And there's another thing you obviously don't know: there's no Sissy Bradley any more. They took her body from the river nine months ago. She'd get drunk and go down by the river... The coroner recorded a verdict of misadventure, though no one really believes she just fell in.'

'I didn't know,' I said, hardly able to believe it.

'Keep clear of McQuillan,' he said. 'She's been seeing other men about the town. I don't know what Callen thinks of it. He must know. There was one man who beat his wife. She was hanging about with him. Maybe he batters her, too. Who can tell?' He stopped to look at me. 'Keep away from her,' he warned again. 'She won't talk to anyone or go to the Gardaí. She's got to live here, too. Life has wronged her, but wronging someone else isn't going to make it right.'

'You're right,' I said. 'She's just seen a chance for some easy money.' I wanted to believe it, willing myself to forget the intensity of the emotions she'd shown and the instability I'd sensed in her.

'Don't think like that,' Alec said, as if he could read my thoughts. 'People can hate a long time.' He stared at me and then looked into the fire and silence grew around us.

'Does your offer still stand?' I asked. 'I wouldn't blame you if you changed your mind. I'd understand.' I watched him, waiting for an answer, thinking of how he had said that everything one did was for oneself.

He turned to look at me. 'The offer still stands,' he said. 'If you'll accept.'

'It's what I want,' I said.

He nodded and smiled and nodded again. 'Come on, then,' he said, 'and I'll show you the garden.'

We went out into the thin November sunshine and walked the gravel paths which criss-crossed the lawn. On the rose-bushes an occasional flower still bloomed. We walked down to the orchard where the fruit trees seemed to me as they'd always been. We were the ones who'd changed. I chanced to look back at the house and caught a glimpse of Alice inside the patio doors, watching us, and I had the feeling that I was looking at a ghost. I must have shivered because Alec asked me if I was cold. 'No,' I said, 'I'm not.'

Alec examined the trees, testing the suppleness of the branches. There was something on his mind; I could sense it. I didn't want to press him – we'd touched enough darkness for today – but he brought it up after lunch, when I was leaving. 'I hope you know what you're doing, Willie,' he said as we stopped by the gate.

'Doing?' I echoed the word as a question, but I knew what he meant and I resented his intrusion. I didn't want another giving voice to the doubts that assailed me.

'With Elizabeth. She's hardly more than a child.'

'She's nearly eighteen,' I said, an edge to my voice.

'Maybe I'm too old,' he said. 'It's just that I don't want to see you hurt. Either one of you. And she has her whole life before her...'

I didn't speak. In the woods some rooks screamed. Perhaps they'd been screaming all along. Their screams might have taken me back to that night again, but instead I felt myself propelled into a future where I found myself alone. I stared about in panic, seeking some anchor for that future day, but there were only the lawns and the trees and the house and the man beside me, staring in puzzlement. 'I'll go,' I said, wanting to get away. I'd told them I was going away for the weekend to visit a friend in Galway. It had been easy to lie to them.

'Take care, then,' Alec said, 'and we'll talk next week.'

I thought of what he'd said to me as I made my way back to the hotel. I thought of McQuillan, too, and his advice on what I should do. I imagined her coming to the hotel this evening and finding me gone. What then? That was something I'd no control over. But I did have control over what Lizzie might learn. This weekend I'd tell her whatever she needed to know.

18

I picked up Lizzie on the outskirts of Castleford as arranged. She was shy with me, and when I leant across to kiss her she offered me her cheek. I was aware of how young she was and Alec's warning echoed in my mind. Yet I was like a man who'd just awoken with amnesia to find that the only memories he possesses are those from his youth.

I drove in silence, filled with wonder at her presence. When we spoke it was of trivialities. Bridie had gone to her friend's house and they were going shopping tomorrow. The Keoghs had found a babysitter for the night. She'd prepared two shepherd's pies for her father and he only had to warm them up. It was all so banal, yet I clung to every word.

'He didn't mind you going away?' I asked. I was thinking of what Alec Whitley had said about this being a small community and people knowing about us. Surely her father knew about us too?

'No,' she said. 'If he's got money for drink that's all that matters.'

'Does he know about us?'

She nodded. 'But let's forget about him. This is our weekend.' I was happy with that. Sometime over the next two days I'd find a way to tell her about McQuillan, but until then the time was ours.

We came into Galway as darkness gathered and the water

in the fountain in Eyre Square looked like an oil gusher in the gloom; Padraic O'Conaire sat silently on his plinth, staring out with stone eyes from under the brim of his broken hat. I found a parking place and we crossed to the hotel. I took Lizzie downstairs to the bar where, to my surprise, she ordered a Coke. 'I want to enjoy this weekend,' she said, 'and alcohol makes me feel funny. Anyway, I don't need it.'

'We'll stay here tonight if you like,' I said.

'It must be expensive,' she said, looking about her. She reminded me of a child in an exclusive toy shop looking at all the things she cannot have. For a moment reality intruded. This was the girl I wanted to marry but in my position a wife would have to be much more than a lover. Lizzie was but a child. She knew so little of my world, where predators circled like sharks, seeking prey just like her. She should marry a man from her own community, someone who, if he didn't love her as much as I might profess to love her, would at least not leave her open to that.

Alec Whitley's words re-echoed yet again, but I turned a deaf ear. This was our weekend. We had two nights to spend together and, as Lizzie had said, we'd best make the most of them. For all I knew they might be all we'd ever have. Before we returned to Castleford I'd have to tell Lizzie about the past, and I didn't know how she would react. Alec was right when he said that McQuillan would go to Lizzie for revenge, not to the Gardaí, but she wouldn't tell Lizzie about the night she burned her grandfather. She'd tell her about Callen and Sissy Bradley and Judith Kelly. McQuillan would know that it was the sexual revelations that might destroy our relationship.

After the drink I booked a room and brought up our bags from the car. Lizzie was impressed by it all and walked about the room touching things. I lay on the bed and beckoned her, but she shook her head. 'You're a terrible man,' she said.

'Come on,' I said. 'Make a terrible man happy.'

She laughed and looked about the room again and then turned back to me. Her face was framed by the dark hair and I saw it tense up as she tried to come to terms with whatever part she saw herself playing. Did she see herself as the loose woman away for the dirty weekend, alone in a hotel room with someone who was old enough to be her father? Or did she see this as an interlude she might later recall – something she could cling to when the monotony of everyday life ground her down? In that future time when she might remember this moment with fondness, would I have a place in her life?

This was the moment when my amnesia was cured and the whole of life came rushing in to overwhelm me. I found myself back in the real world, confronting the reality I'd pushed away, coming to realise that love wasn't just a game. With it came fear of the future; how could one ever know what lay ahead? One moment could change everything. A speeding car, illness, a dropped cigarette – love could die as simply as that. I knew that the memories would live on, but you can't love a memory. And love could die in other ways, those ways and means we use so carelessly every day of our lives to kill affection – indifference, habit, pride, selfishness...

I climbed off the bed and crossed the room and took her in my arms. She didn't resist and I wondered if she thought that this was expected of her, that this was how a women paid for the weekend away, for the expensive gift – with a shudder I realised that a bottle of perfume would suffice – for the protestation that they were loved.

I kissed her and she responded. Only our passion and need of each other existed, and it was this we fulfilled, the sheets cold against our skin when we climbed between them. Warmth quickly enfolded us as the room filled with our moans and whispered entreaties and endearments. She said: 'I love you,' and I spoke the word love in return and then there were no more words. In the moment of release I imagined that I heard her say 'no' again and again. But maybe the word came from my own lips, uttered among the cries, beating against them to echo and re-echo about the room. Afterwards we lay spent, cocooned in that moment of human communion that's eternally renewed in the coming together of flesh.

We slept, and I dreamed I was entwined in someone's arms, and when I woke I found the dream was true. Lizzie was still sleeping and, careful not to disturb her, I raised myself up so that I could gaze on her face and see her in repose. She was more childlike than ever, and I wanted to protect her from the world. She must have sensed my gaze because she woke and blinked. She smiled and I bent to kiss her, no trace of passion remaining.

'You are a terrible man,' she said. 'But I think I might love you.'

'I know I love you,' I said. 'In fact so much that I told Alec Whitley I'd accept his offer.'

'You're going to come back?' She hadn't really believed me before, but I couldn't blame her. Men always practised deceit to get what they wanted, and how could I know what promises might have been made her before? And McQuillan must have sown doubts; she was here now, like a presence between us.

'It doesn't matter about her,' Lizzie said as if reading my thoughts.

'It doesn't?'

'No,' she said. 'Not anymore.'

'Come on then,' I said, her assurances dispelling my worry at what I'd still to tell her. 'I'm taking you out on the town.' I was boisterous and cheerful and filled with enthusiasm for this new life, the words of the love songs coming true, my feet itching to dance as we all itch to dance when the music plays.

'I smell like a brothel,' she said. 'You do as well.'

'Ah ha. So you've had experience of these things?'

'Not as much as you've had, I bet.' She punched my chest and then bent to kiss the spot. Her hair brushed my skin and I closed my eyes and tried to banish all the things that were between us – age, experience, the past – but they clung to me like barnacles.

'Come on,' I said again, 'while the night is young.'

'You get out first,' she said.

'You're not telling me you're shy?' I imagined her as she'd been that first day at the old house, and couldn't equate her with the person before me now, her crossed arms hiding her breasts. 'I'll run a bath,' I said and slipped out from between the sheets and pulled on my underpants. I ran the bath and came back with a towel which I draped about her shoulders. I kissed her and she slipped out of the bed and stood watching me, the towel clutched tight at the front. 'Go on,' I said. 'The night's out there waiting.'

'Thanks,' she said. She smiled and went into the bathroom and I lay on the bed until she came back out. I took a bath myself, and when I emerged, she was dressed in a simple, beige woollen dress that moulded itself to her body. 'I borrowed the dress,' she said. 'I wanted to look my best for you.'

'You always look your best,' I said.

'Go on,' she said. 'You're pulling my leg.'

'I mean it,' I said. 'And I'll buy you dresses, as many as you want.'

'I bet you make that promise to all the girls.'

'No,' I said, putting my arms about her. 'I never made that promise before.' I could feel her breasts against my naked chest, the touch of the wool not downy, as I might have imagined it to be, but rough against my skin. She smelled of soap and water and youth and health, and I felt that in her company I'd live forever.

Reluctantly I let her go and she sat at the dressing table to put the finishing touches to her make-up. When I was dressed, I stood behind her to watch. She brushed her hair, the colour changing in the light, and on impulse I took the brush from her and brushed her hair until I felt the static would discharge in a bolt of electricity.

She rang before we left to see if Bridie was all right, and it seemed everything was quiet in Castleford. Downstairs the receptionist recommended a restaurant and a young man who was booking in couldn't take his eyes from Lizzie. As I turned from the desk she possessively took my arm and I was overwhelmed with love for her.

The doorman summoned a taxi, secure in his coat and gloves against the cold, his eyes filled with admiration. And in that very moment I felt that everything would be OK. Lizzie would dazzle everyone she came into contact with. She was more than just a body. She was a person now and I was seeing her with love.

It was warm in the taxi and we held hands like teenagers. We drove through the narrow back streets of the city where the buildings seemed to tower up like skyscrapers. The driver knew the restaurant. 'You have to try the Chicken Kiev,' he said, and we did, laughing with the waiter and telling him that it came highly recommended. The place was busy but we were lost in our own world where nothing intruded.

We talked about our lives. I told her of my father and she reached across the table to hold my hand. I told her how my parents had met on a Brooklyn Street, how the Jewish family my mother had worked for there had always written to her and had been grief-stricken to learn of her death.

She told me in turn of her mother and how her own world had disintegrated when she died. It was a strange topic of conversation, yet it never became morbid; rather, it drew us closer together. We were sharing with each other the things that mattered, things we'd never shared before with anyone else. We were both reluctant to leave and didn't go until the dregs of the coffee went cold in the cups.

We called a taxi and, in one of those odd coincidences life throws up, it was our former driver who came. We were like old friends, and in the few minutes it took us to reach a pub he recommended, he told us of his family. His daughter was at university, 'your age,' he said, swinging round to look at Lizzie; his son was an engineer in Germany. It was a glimpse of a life, more than we might ever hope to know about the majority of the people around us. 'What time do you want to be collected?' he asked, 'and I'll come back for you. A special service for the young lady who reminds me of Katie.' He laughed and I knew that he didn't question the disparity in our ages. Maybe he saw that we were in love. Maybe he was aware that his own daughter might never find such happiness.

We told him to collect us at eleven and then we entered a world I'd never experienced before. I was no lover of tradi-tional music nor of the Irish language, but it was in a small oasis where such things are still nurtured that we found ourselves. Around us – some people made a few feet of space available for us on the end of a wooden bench – we heard the language alive and vibrant, not dead and sterile as I remem-bered it from my schooldays. The musicians were in another corner of the bar and the music issued from there with hardly a pause. A woman sang, a haunting song, and though I didn't understand the words, I could tell from the emotions in her voice that she sang about unrequited love. I took Lizzie's hand in mind and held it, no fear in me then that I'd ever lose her.

I don't think we spoke a hundred words between us while we were there, and yet I was never so close before to another human being, with the possible exception of my father. The music whirled about us, seeming wild and abandoned one moment, the next sad and haunting and beautiful. We were reluctant to leave but we'd promised the taxi driver we'd meet him at eleven, and he was waiting outside for us when we emerged. He wouldn't take a tip. 'It's been a pleasure,' he said, and his eyes confirmed that he spoke the truth.

The evening had drawn Lizzie and me even closer and there was no embarrassment as we undressed and climbed into bed. We didn't make love immediately; we lay in each others arms, talking quietly. After we made love we slept, entwined together until the maid knocked in the morning with our breakfast. There is something extraordinarily intimate in sharing a meal with another person, but to share it in the warmth of a bed with the one you love is the ultimate experience. I discovered that Lizzie didn't like eggs and I ate her egg and stole from her plate, while she in turn stole from mine, and we laughed like the children we'd become in the innocence new love bestows.

After we'd eaten we put the tray aside and curled up again, no desire for her within me now. It was enough to lie beside her in wonder at her presence. I pushed the future away – even the day that lay ahead of us – but the outside world beckoned. 'I want to buy you a present,' I told her and I took her out into the city and we wandered arm in arm from shop to shop and I bought her a dress and perfume and a chain and locket in which she said she would keep my picture.

We had lunch and returned to the car to find a parking ticket tucked under the windscreen wiper. I ceremoniously dropped it in a litter bin while she pleaded with me not to do so. 'You'll be fined twice as much,' she said.

'Never,' I said. 'I'll go to prison first.' There was a Garda standing across the street and I pointed towards him. 'I'm going to give myself up,' I said, and she grabbed my arm and, hysterical with laughter, dragged me back to the car. 'Where to now?' I asked and she suggested that we go for a drive. 'OK,' I said. 'A drive it is. We'll let the horse show us the way.'

I took the Limerick Road, pointing out Merlin Park Hospital where I'd spent two weeks as a child. We drove through Clarinbridge. At Kilcolgan I showed her the metal man on his bicycle and for a moment she believed he was real. I turned right on the edge of the town and took the road for Kinvarra, and on through the Burren to Ballyvaughan, the grey expanse of limestone seeming to go on forever.

At Fanore I braked suddenly and pointed out the pair of wellington boots sticking out of the barrel by the pub. 'Someone's fallen in,' I cried, and again for a moment she believed me. Then as I began to laugh she punched me and we grabbed each other and kissed and clung together oblivious of where we were until a horn tooted behind us. We broke apart and I pulled onto the side of the road to let the vehicle pass. As it did so the horn blew stridently and a grinning male face stared at us from the passenger's window. I could have sworn that I saw envy in his eyes in that moment of contact between us. 'You must have been here before,' she said now, 'to know about that.'

'Years ago,' I said. 'A friend had a cottage here and he let me have it. I used to fish off the rocks for mackerel and every day I'd tramp the Burren, covering anything up to twenty miles. It was May and the flowers were everywhere...'

She didn't speak, as if she sensed that these memories were important to me. But she could never have guessed at what they really held – how my stay here had been a last chance to hold onto my sanity in a world that was spinning out of control; a world I'd tried to slow down in a thousand bars and with a million bottles of whiskey. Or so it seemed then. I'd been trying to blank out the memories that had followed me from Castleford, end the nightmares they'd given birth to, slay the beast that was crouching in its lair, waiting to devour me. But in the daytime when I awoke there was another one waiting, and it was to escape from it that I came to Clare and tramped the acres and acres of limestone, certain that if I didn't slay it now the men in white coats would take me away and lock me up forever. It was here that I'd discovered that we can never slay the beast, only learn to live with it. Either that or succumb to madness. I knew it was still out there waiting for me. It was patient and merciless and would wait forever.

I drove on, taking the coast road for Ennistymon. At the Cliffs of Moher I turned off and parked in the deserted car park. 'Come on,' I said. 'We've got it all to ourselves.'

It was dark now and O'Brien's viewing tower was like a flaw against the sky. We walked to the bottom of the steps leading up to the tower, cuddled tight together against the biting wind sweeping across from the Aran Islands. On our left the face of the cliffs dropped sheer into the darkness and we held each other, awed by the sight.

The cold drove us back to the car, the lights of Ennistymon glowing in the distance. We were both hungry and I decided to turn back and head for Lisdoonvarna. We had dinner in the Hydro Hotel and over coffee we talked again about our pasts. We were reluctant to leave, but there was nothing for it except to drive off into the night and retrace our route.

Back in Galway I parked again in Eyre Square, and up in our room we undressed with urgent haste, eager to lie together, to love each other and forget the waiting shadow of old father time who comes even for kings.

In the morning we had breakfast and we might have been

an old married couple, secure in the love that has lasted a lifetime and will last for what time remains. We lay for a while afterwards listening to the city come alive below us, calling us to come and be a part of it. We took a bath and after I'd paid the bill we joined it.

I drove out to Salthill, ignoring the newsagents we passed. The story that had meant so much to me now seemed of little significance. Tomorrow those pages would be used to light the fire, as Doyle had already pointed out to me.

At Salthill I parked on the front. The strand was almost deserted, just a few strollers braving the cold. The sea was grey and wind-tossed and the noise of the moving water ebbed and flowed with the breaking waves along the shore. It seemed an appropriate place to tell Lizzie what she had to be told, for it was by the sea that McQuillan had faced me with her demands.

I held Lizzie for a few minutes, her closeness making it all the more difficult for me to begin. But she must have been attuned to my mood for she pulled away and looked at me, her eyes betraying uncertainty. I smiled but she saw through me. 'What's wrong, Willie?' she asked. 'Is it me? Amn't I what you expected?'

'It's not you,' I said. 'You're everything I've ever dreamed of. I... I still can't believe what's happening to me.'

'So what is it? There's something the matter, isn't there?'

'Yes,' I said, 'but it's nothing to do with you. It's about the past, about things that happened long before you were even born.'

'You can tell me,' she said. 'I won't mind.' She stared at me and must have seen something on my face that warned her. 'Is it McQuillan?' she asked, and when I nodded I saw the pain on her own face. 'You can still tell me,' she added. 'I'll try to understand. I promise.'

But despite that the telling came awkwardly to my lips. In the grey light of the late morning, the words seemed to take on the stink of corruption which lay behind those things I'd seen Callen do long years before. I'd not been a willing partner – in fact had never succumbed to his taunts and offers – but that was no consolation now. In the awkward phrases of confession – for what else was I doing? – those deeds seemed stark and brutal and ugly, and surely damned me as much as they damned him.

Lizzie tensed up with each word and began to withdraw from me so that by the time I'd confessed to her we seemed beyond reconciliation. 'I had to tell you,' I said. 'I can't have secrets from you.' I took her hand in mine and it was small and cold and vulnerable. Her face was pinched, as if with cold, and set against my excuses. 'Don't you think it's best to hear the truth from me than from her?' I asked.

'Why would she do it?' she asked. 'If there's nothing between you now, why would she do it?'

'I don't know,' I lied. 'Maybe she sees me as her last hope. She feels I owe her something.'

'For what she gave you in the past?'

'I suppose so. But you must understand that I'm not a teenager. I've... There have been others, but I didn't love them. I didn't love McQuillan. I love you and no one else. I told Alec I'd take the job, but only for you – to be near you. I never wanted it to be like this. I wanted time to show you that I love you. I wanted you to get to know me. But you have to know the real me. I'm not a saint – just a man in love and trying desperately not to kill that love. Now it's in your hands. You can kill it or let it live. If you kill it, you'll kill the only good thing I've ever had. That's what I'm giving you, Lizzie. I'm giving you everything I possess. Don't throw it away because of something that happened a lifetime ago.'

'But Callen and her,' she said. 'How could you?'

'I don't know,' I said.

'Maybe it's him,' she said. 'Did you think of that?'

'It's not him,' I said. 'He was with McQuillan on both occasions when the girls went missing. Look, the past has nothing to do with what's happening now. Callen was only a boy then, like me. We were almost as young as Bridie is now. Would you condemn Bridie for making a mistake?'

'No,' she said. 'I wouldn't.' She didn't look at me and I eased my grip of her hand. But she didn't pull away and I could hope again. 'We'll go,' I said. 'I'll buy you lunch and show you Connemara.'

We stopped at a roadside café for lunch – roast beef which was adequate and apple pie and cream, and coffee which tasted bitter. Connemara was bleak, and silent, and as we passed through Leenane with cloud clinging to the mountain tops and the inner reaches of Killary harbour reflecting the sky, an unexpected shaft of sunshine picked out the rocks and paths on the Devil's Mother, the fissures like living veins of rock.

We saw Croagh Patrick like a broken arrowhead stuck in the ground and less than an hour later we drove into Castleford. I didn't care now who saw us. The town seemed as it had always been, but I had changed. I'd found what it was I'd been seeking, and now that I'd found it I was in danger of losing it. When Callen lured me under the bridge, how could I have known then that I was blighting the love I might possess one day in the future?

We collected Bridie and she told us of the stir my article had caused. Councillor Moran had denounced the Gardaí for suppressing the information and at the same time managed to denounce me for making it known. It had made the national news and I'd got what I'd wanted, but now I'd swap it all for a kind word or a loving gesture. At the house I left the engine running.

'I won't ask you in,' Lizzie said. 'I have a lot to do on a Sunday evening.'

'Can I call tomorrow evening?'

'If you like'

'Would you like?'

'Yes.' She nodded.

'I don't want to press you,' I said, 'but don't let what happened in the past come between us. We didn't know each other then. If we did I'd have behaved differently. Give me a chance. That's all I ask. Will you do that?' She nodded again and then leaned across to kiss me on the cheek. 'I'll call tomorrow evening,' I said. 'If I'm not lynched by then.'

'Be careful,' she said, and it was as good as a declaration of love.

'I will,' I said. 'And thanks for the weekend. I'll never forget it.'

'I won't either,' she said, getting out, taking her bag and the things I'd bought her. 'Goodnight,' she said, 'and thanks for everything.'

'A smile,' I said, 'before I go.' She smiled and it was a precious gift to take with me, to cling to later in the big bed that was empty and lonely and cold.

19

The next morning I found that a message had been left for me at reception asking that I call to the Garda station, and I went there after breakfast. A Detective Inspector questioned me, and though outwardly he appeared calm, I suspected that he was angry. 'Have you seen yesterday's *Sunday Chronicle*?' he asked.

'No,' I said. 'I never read the papers.'

He let it go. 'You wrote an article,' he continued, 'containing confidential information. We'd like to know where you got that information.'

'Confidential information?' I said, puzzled. 'Perhaps if you told me exactly what was confidential, I could answer your question.' I'd a part to play – the journalist reluctant to divulge his sources – and I'd play it to the best of my ability.

The detective didn't see it quite that way. 'Please don't play games, Mr Leitch,' he said. 'This is a very serious matter. We need all the help we can get. There may be other lives at stake. Aren't you aware of that?'

'It's because I was very much aware of that fact that I wrote what I did,' I said. 'I felt people were entitled to know the full extent of the danger facing their children. Or don't you think they were entitled to know?'

'We have to consider many things,' he said. 'We made a decision which we still happen to think was the correct one.

Obviously you don't agree. But you must agree that we should have access to any information that may help us catch the killer. We've a very good idea where you got your information from. All we need from you is confirmation of the source.'

'Haven't you ever heard of a journalist's privilege?

'This is a murder investigation, Mr Leitch.'

'I didn't get it from the killer, if that's what you mean,' I said.

'We have to be certain of that.'

'I got it from Joe Hawley,' I said, 'purely by chance. But of course you know that already. He'd be the first person you spoke to. Now I've got a question. Can you tell me the nature of the assault on Majella Hawley?'

He stared at me as if amazed at my nerve, but he stayed a professional to the end. 'I can't tell you that,' he said.

'I've been thinking,' I said. 'If the girl was kept alive for days, then this wasn't an opportunistic crime. It had been planned. He didn't just happen to bump into her accidently and kill her in a panic.'

'Not necessarily,' he said. 'His meeting her was probably accidental. He just took the opportunity presented. He did what he did to satisfy his perverted sexual needs. That's what the shrinks say. They use a lot of mumbo jumbo to explain it, but you don't need any mumbo jumbo to describe an evil monster. I prefer to think of him as such.'

'But why did he keep her alive? Had it anything to do with the type of assault he carried out?

'No comment.'

'It must have been so that he could further indulge his perversions,' I persisted. 'Isn't it obvious? And you think that if he takes another victim, he'll keep her alive for some time and you'll have an opportunity of rescuing her? Is that why my article's upset you?'

'I can't comment,' he said firmly. 'Now if you'll excuse me, I have work to do.'

'Have you heard anything new since the article?' I asked.

'I'm going,' he said, looking at me as if unable to understand what breed of person I was, and left me. But he should not have blamed himself for that. I didn't even understand myself.

Once outside I drove back to the hotel and rang Jones. From the tone of his greeting I could tell he was pleased, but he wasn't a man to dwell on success. 'Got anything else for me?' he asked, his mind already on the next issue, and I told him I hadn't. 'You coming back here then,' he asked.

'In a few days,' I said.

'Fallen in love with the place? Or is there some other reason?'

'A rich widow,' I said.

'Well, don't forget the news,' he said. 'That's what I pay you for.'

'There won't be any news,' I said. 'Not unless he's caught or strikes again. According to your expert, that's not due for weeks yet.'

'Experts can be wrong,' Jones said, and rang off.

I'd hardly hung up when the phone buzzed. It was Alec Whitley. 'When are you going back to Dublin, Willie?' he asked.

'Probably on Wednesday,' I told him.

'Maybe you could spare a few hours,' he said. 'There's one or two people I'd like you to meet. Unless you're tied up, of course. If you are we'll make it tomorrow.'

'I can make it now,' I said, glad of the chance of having something to occupy my mind until tonight. 'I'll see you in fifteen minutes.'

When I met Alec in his office, he didn't mention the

article and I was grateful for that. He introduced me to the editor and then we went to lunch, where I met a local businessman who was a shareholder in the paper. We discussed my proposed employment briefly and then the conversation flitted from subject to subject. I realised that I was being sounded out, but this was to be expected in the circumstances. The shareholder might trust Alec's judgement but he wanted to see for himself what he was getting for his money. Perhaps what I'd written had been drawn into question, but if it had been there was no hint of it.

After lunch, Alec, the editor and I went back to the office and chatted for a while. Only when the editor left did I become aware that Alec had something on his mind, and I asked him what was troubling him.

'I was wondering if you'd seen McQuillan?' he said.

'No,' I said. 'And I don't want to see her.'

'I just wonder,' he said. 'I know I told you to keep clear of her, but maybe you should see her and clear up matters. Don't leave them hanging...' He hesitated. 'I think it might be best. Get it over and done with. So we all know where we stand.'

'You think she's going to be a problem?'

'I wouldn't think so. It's just loose ends...'

'I've spoken with Lizzie,' I said. 'McQuillan's not going to get any joy there. Though if you think it might be best to see her ... '

'It might,' he said.

'I'll see her then,' I said, suddenly feeling apprehensive. There was no reason for it. There was nothing McQuillan could do. But the apprehension wouldn't leave me be.

'Right then,' Alec said brusquely. 'We'll not discuss that again. Now, what about dinner tomorrow evening? Can make it?'

'I'll let you know in the morning,' I said, unwilling to

commit myself now. If I returned to Dublin on Wednesday, then tomorrow evening would be my last one with Lizzie until I returned.

He nodded and then the telephone rang. 'I'll go,' I said. 'I'll ring tomorrow morning.' I left him then, and as I drove back to the hotel, Alec's advice was on my mind. McQuillan had to be faced sometime. Maybe it would be best to get it over and done with.

When I drove into the car-park she was waiting for me, huddled up in the recess of a boarded up doorway. As I parked the car she came hurrying towards me. I wound down the window, and as she leant down to look at me, I saw she was shivering and her hands were blue with the cold.

'I thought you'd gone away,' she said. 'They wouldn't tell me anything at the hotel. Did you tell them not to tell me?'

'No,' I said. 'I didn't tell them anything.'

'I waited Friday night,' she said, 'like we'd arranged, but you never came.'

'We'd arranged nothing,' I said. 'Can't you understand that?'

'We had,' she said. 'You... you promised.' There was something in her voice that might have been despair, and I turned away, seeing her as I had on that night she'd beaten her grandfather with her fists and had held the door shut against his last desperate efforts to escape. I thought of all she'd endured, but I could find no pity for her. I remembered the weekend with Lizzie, sleeping with her in my arms and waking to see her soul bared to my gaze. I wanted that forever.

I couldn't now imagine a life without Lizzie, couldn't imagine drifting back to the life I'd known before I met her, the evenings spent alone in my flat with the whole world seemingly outside the window, beyond reach. That life of one night stands, of furtive encounters, of condoms donned and surreptitiously disposed of, disease waiting at every turn for the unwary or the careless. I wanted stability and permanence – what my father had found when he met my mother. I'd years to face yet before I reached the moment he'd reached, and I didn't want to face those years alone.

'I made no promise,' I said. 'I'd no reason to. Can't you understand? I want nothing to do with you or your demands.'

I might have struck her. She flinched, and her face darkened as if a shadow passed over it. I felt uncertain and the thought came that maybe I was making a terrible mistake. Her features seemed to be pulled out of proportion, twisted into a grotesque mask. 'You promised,' she said. 'Why did you lie to me?'

'I didn't promise,' I said. 'Or lie.'

'You... you're going to write the book without me?'

'No,' I said. 'There isn't going to be a book. And before you start making threats again you should know that I've told Lizzie everything. Now, you can go to the Gardaí if you want, but nothing will come of that. You're the one who'll suffer – who'll have to go on living here. And Sissy Bradley won't be able to help you, will she?'

'You fucker,' she said. 'You used the information I gave you and now you're going to... With her...' She stood up and I thought she would beat on the car with her fists.

I got out and she stepped back. I expected anger, even hatred, but it was with satisfaction she watched me. It was as if I'd done what she'd been expecting all along. 'See the Gardaí if you want,' I said again. 'I don't care.'

'I won't,' she said. 'Not now.' Her voice was quiet and resigned. I'd been wrong all along. She'd only seemed invincible.

'Fine,' I said. 'I'm glad you're seeing sense. And I hope you get what you want. If you want to get away badly enough, then you will.'

'Oh, I'll get away,' she said. 'You don't have to worry about that.' I'd the feeling that she wanted me to go and I didn't need bidding. I walked away from her across the car-park and not once did I look back.

20

That evening, fog drifted in off the sea, shrouding the town in silence. Over the hours since my meeting with McQuillan, my apprehension had increased and was my sole companion as I drove out to Lizzie's. Twenty-four hours is a long time when the world might change in a moment.

When I reached the house the lights were welcoming beacons looming out of the darkness. As I parked, Lizzie came out to meet me and I took her in my arms, and as I held her I was reassured that everything would be all right. 'I missed you,' I said, holding her as if she were fragile.

'I missed you, too,' she said. 'I'd hoped you'd come today. When you didn't I thought you were angry with me. You're not angry, are you?'

'No,' I said. 'I'd never be angry with you.'

We kissed, not the kiss of lovers but of those who know how close they have come to losing all. She clung to me and I recaptured something of what I'd had over the weekend. She held my arm until we reached the door of the cottage. Inside we found Bridie curled up on the armchair engrossed in her favourite soap opera. 'Hello,' she said, not taking her eyes from the screen. 'It's really cool tonight.' Excitement bubbled in her voice as she anticipated the drama ahead. 'I can't bear waiting to see what's going to happen? Can you?'

'No,' I said. 'I only wish I knew a little bit more of...'

'Ssshh,' she said. 'Here they come.'

On the screen a young couple met under some trees. They argued and the man took the woman in his arms and kissed her. She resisted a moment before succumbing. Slowly the camera pulled back until we saw another girl on the edge of the screen, watching with wide-eyed astonishment, a mirror image of the face of the child across from me. Just then the credits began to roll and Bridie grimaced. 'Oh, we have to wait again,' she complained, but she was unable to conceal her thrill of anticipation as she rose. 'I have to go,' she said, 'so you two can be alone. You wouldn't go off with another girl, would you?'

'Bridie!' Lizzie admonished.

'I only asked,' the child said.

'Well, don't.'

'I know where you were at the weekend,' she said. 'So there.' She looked at me conspiratorially, curiosity and pleasure touching her face. 'I won't say anything though. I know how to keep a secret.'

'You'd best get your coat,' Lizzie said. 'It's seven.'

'I'll see you,' I said.

She stopped at the door to look back. 'Don't forget to watch it,' she said. 'It's going to be really mega tomorrow evening.'

'I won't forget,' I promised.

The ritual that ensured Bridie reached the house was enacted and then Lizzie came to me. 'I thought you wouldn't call,' she said. 'If you hadn't I don't know what I'd do. What you wrote frightened me. It was on television last night and everyone seemed so angry. I thought you'd get in trouble and have to go away.'

'I'm here now,' I said. 'I'll always be here if you want me.'

'Promise,' she said, all of her insecurity in that one word.

'I promise,' I said. 'But I've got to return to Dublin on Wednesday. I've lots to sort out before I can come here to work. It could take weeks – maybe longer.'

'But won't you be coming back before that?'

'Of course. I couldn't keep away.' She smiled but it couldn't hide her uncertainty. 'McQuillan's still bothering you?' I asked.

'No.' She spoke too quickly, not having yet mastered the means we use to make the normal intercourse of life possible.

'I saw her today,' I said, and she stiffened. 'I told her that I'd told you everything, so I don't think she'll bother you again. But if she does, remember I've told you the truth. That's all there is to it. Now we won't speak of her again.'

I could claim that we'd banished McQuillan and for Lizzie it might have been so, but for me she was still there at my elbow as Lizzie and I made love. Afterwards we dressed and sat by the fire with tea and cakes. I tried to slow time down but too soon we had to go out into the night, where fog hung about the outbuildings and dampened the sound of our footsteps. Somewhere a dog barked, an eerie disembodied sound. The headlamps turned the fog milky white and the hedgerows into great heaps of darkness. At the bungalow we kissed before Lizzie got out. 'I'll see you tomorrow,' I said, and she nodded and raised her hand in goodbye.

On the bypass the fog seemed less dense and I made good time back to Castleford. At the hotel I decided to have a Guinness, but as I hesitated at the entrance to the bar, I saw Callen there with another man. I assumed that he was here to see me and I stepped back. I was trying to decide what to do next when the receptionist emerged from her office. 'Mr Leitch,' she said, 'Elizabeth O'Malley just phoned for you. She asked you to call her back urgently. I have the number here.'

'Did she say why?'

'No, Mr Leitch. She didn't.'

'Would you call her for me,' I asked, trying to figure out what she might want, my mind filled with forboding.

I watched the receptionist dial and then she handed me the receiver.

'Willie,' Lizzie said in my ear, and somehow I knew the worst even before she told me that Bridie was missing.

'You're mistaken,' I said. 'She can't be missing.' I was aware of nothing but an awful feeling of emptiness. Fear hadn't touched me yet. 'I'll come out,' I said. 'Everything'll be all right. You just wait there.'

'I have to,' she said. 'I can't leave the children.'

'I'll be there in a few minutes,' I said, and cut the connection with my finger. 'What's the number of the Garda station?' I asked the receptionist and she told me.

I dialled and a Garda answered and I told him what had happened. 'Can I have your name, please?' he said, his voice calm and unhurried.

'To hell with my name,' I said. 'Just get your fucking arse off the chair.' I slammed down the receiver and stood for a moment trying to regain a hold on reality.

'Can I help?' the receptionist asked.

'Pray,' I said. 'You can pray.' I turned and ran, shutting my mind to everything but the objective of reaching Lizzie as quickly as possible. The fog was lifting as I drove out on the bypass. It lay in pockets, and as I encountered each one, it seemed as if I were going through a series of doors. One by one I was entering new countries to which I'd neither map nor guide, and from which I might never return. There was little traffic and the whole countryside seemed hushed. As I drove, a whole series of images passed before my eyes like poor quality snapshots: Bridie as she turned at the door to look at me;

the evening I first saw her curled up on the armchair; the evening I stopped to talk to her. And I knew with certainty that if anything had happened to her, I'd never be able to forgive myself, that my damnation would not be to suffer the torments of hell but to be damned for eternity with the memories.

But it made no sense. She'd got to the house and wasn't it unlikely that she'd have gone out again? Surely she would never leave the children. But could I be absolutely certain she'd got there? Could Lizzie have been mistaken because of the fog? Suppose Bridie had been taken on that short journey. The trees sheltering the bungalow loomed ahead in a swirl of fog and I swung in through the gateway. As I did so, the front door opened and Lizzie was silhouetted in the doorway. Seeing her, I knew Bridie had not been found. Lizzie came running towards me and was a rag doll in my arms. If I released her she'd crumple up at my feet. But I didn't want to let her go. While I held her I could imagine life. Once I let go, the horror, which so far I'd managed to keep at bay, might come breaking in upon me. She spoke but there was no hysteria. Shock at the moment protected her. 'Why?' she said. 'Why Bridie?'

'There's a simple explanation,' I said. 'Are you sure she got here?'

'She was here,' she said. 'She always made tea at nine. Her cup's there, half empty.'

'Maybe she's got a boyfriend,' I said, 'and she's out with him.'

'She's only twelve,' she said. 'And she'd never leave the children.'

'Have you looked everywhere?' I pushed her to arms length, willing her to admit that she hadn't done so.

'She's not here,' she said. 'She's been taken.'

I was about to speak when a vehicle approached at speed. It pulled in before us and its lights lit up Lizzie's face, frightening me with the change which had come over her in half an hour. Mercifully the lights were switched off. Only the blue revolving light on the roof remained illuminated and it turned her face into a poorly painted image of a plaster madonna.

There were four Gardaí, two in plain clothes. They were competent – not once did they betray the anxiety they must surely have been suffering. Quickly they ascertained the bare details. There was so little to tell, it took but a minute. They were gentle and understanding, aware that this was what they had dreaded since the body of Majella Hawley had been found.

The uniformed Gardaí were detailed to check the garden and, despite Lizzie's protest that she had searched the house, we searched it again. We searched every room, aware that it was pointless. We took care not to disturb the sleeping children.

We found nothing, and the two uniformed Gardaí were sent to search the nearby fields. Beyond the garden the whole world seemed to be spread out, enormous and without boundary. Even if Bridie were out there, it would be impossible to find her. The other two Gardaí conferred together while Lizzie and I watched. An hour before, we'd been locked in an embrace. Now we stood apart. Only the other day I'd imagined that I'd regained my innocence. But after this I'd never imagine such a thing again.

The Gardaí finished conferring and approached us. 'Could she have gone home?' one of them asked. 'Maybe she was taken ill.'

'I'd have seen her,' Lizzie said. 'We came from the house and we met no one.'

'We'll check anyway,' the Garda said.

'My father will have to be told,' Lizzie said.

'Where can we find him?' the Garda asked.

'In Burke's,' she said. 'And the Keoghs will have to be told. I can't leave the children alone. You can contact them at the factory.'

'I'll see to it,' the Garda said. He and his colleague returned to the car where a voice crackled on the radio.

'I'm frightened,' Lizzie said. 'I can't stop imagining...' But she hadn't really begun to imagine yet.

'She'll be OK,' I said, putting my arms about her.

'Who?' she said. 'Who could do such a thing?' I had no answer for her. 'She wouldn't have gone with a stranger,' she added. 'I'd warned her. So why did she leave the house? She must have been forced to go.'

Again I didn't speak, didn't bother pointing out that she was almost certainly mistaken. There was no sign of force having been used. The indications were that if Bridie'd gone with someone, she'd gone willingly. It made me think again that she had a boyfriend. Any moment now she'd return and make us look like fools.

The Gardaí returned and told us that reinforcements were on the way. 'It's him, isn't it?' Lizzie said. 'He's got her. You won't find her alive. Isn't that right?'

She turned and fled into the house. I was tempted to follow her but didn't. Instead I remained with the Gardaí in the darkness.

The uniformed Gardaí returned with nothing to report. They were sent to the O'Malley house to search there, and I went with them. As we stopped by the gate the normality was frightening. For a moment I could believe that we'd go into the house and find Bridie curled up on the armchair. But she wasn't there. The living-room was empty, the fire burned out. On the rug I saw a spot of dampness from our love-making.

We searched the house, aware that we'd find nothing. In Lizzie's and Bridie's room I felt like an intruder, even more of an intruder on their privacy that my intimacy with Lizzie had been. I checked the wardrobe and as my hands touched the clothes hanging lifeless on the hangers, rage surged through me. I slammed the door closed and stood for a moment to compose myself before I looked under the beds. I knew I'd find nothing and I felt a fool, imagining the killer laughing at me.

We found nothing in the house. As we searched the outhouses, the reinforcements arrived. I felt a surge of hope at seeing them, but it was short-lived. We gathered in the yard beneath the glare of the light, while beyond its range the darkness lay thick, compounded by the fog which again was closing in about us. It seemed to mock us and the orders of a detective that we were to search the surrounding area. It was a gesture on his part – nothing more. In the darkness one could walk within yards of a body and not see it.

But we searched. We went in twos, myself and the Gardaí and O'Malley who had returned from the pub, and men from the neighbouring houses. Word seemed to have travelled quickly. We stumbled over the rough ground, the damp grass soaking our shoes and socks and the ends of our trousers. We called her name again and again, but no answer came. We clambered over fences and our clothing snagged on barbed wire and sometimes we tripped and fell, but we went on, human fireflies calling out into the night, searching and hoping.

'This is crazy,' I said to the Garda who was with me, impotence making me angry. 'I'm going back.' I turned and blundered off into the darkness. Visibility was hardly the width of a field. I saw a hedgerow at the extreme edge of my vision and stumbled towards it, but in the fog I lost my bearings and I wandered in the fields, the voices of the Gardaí all about me.

I found the house by accident, and as I approached it, the first man I saw was Halligan. He was deep in conversation with a detective I'd seen at one of the press conferences. Some journalists milled about, watched over by a Garda. I went on into the house and found Lizzie there with a neighbour woman.

'You... you haven't?' Lizzie said and I shook my head. She turned away and stared at the heap of ashes. 'It's my fault,' she added. 'I should never have sent her there.'

'Are you certain she hasn't a boyfriend?' I asked, wanting any sort of hope to cling to.

'She was only a child.' Lizzie swung towards me. 'You saw her. She was only interested in television.' She stared at me, a vulnerable schoolgirl. Because she hadn't been a virgin I'd taken her to be a woman. But that girlish look I'd glimpsed from time to time was the real person. Like all youth she'd just wanted to grow up too soon.

I turned away. In my mind I saw Sissy Bradley and Judith Kelly. They had been but children.

'Are they still searching?' Lizzie asked.

'They are,' I nodded.

'Why aren't you searching?' she said. 'Didn't she mean anything to you at all?'

'They won't find her tonight,' I said. 'The best chance of finding her will be tomorrow after first light.'

'If she's still alive.'

'We have to pray that she is.' The other woman arranged her face in a look she assumed was proper for the occasion.

There were footsteps outside and Halligan entered, followed by his colleague. 'Would you mind leaving us,' he said to me. Stubble darkened his face and gave it a hard edge.

'I'll be outside,' I said to Lizzie, but she didn't acknowledge me. I nodded to Halligan and walked out.

They had called off the search. The Gardaí were returning, grouping in the yard, talking among themselves. A cigarette glowed in the darkness and somewhere in the fog a radio crackled. I stood watching until Halligan's colleague came for me. I followed him into the house despite a desperate urge to flee. But convention stayed me. I was as much a child of Pavlov as any other. Only the killer, out there now with his ugly needs and urges, had thrown off the shackles.

Halligan was alone in the living-room and showing signs of stress. Perhaps he'd hoped that Lizzie would have had a lead for him and that hope had come to nothing. With me, too, he would find only disappointment. 'Who knew of your liaison with Miss O'Malley?' he asked me. 'Who knew that her sister Bridie would be alone at Keogh's tonight?'

'You think she was taken by someone who knew?'

'If she was taken,' Halligan said, 'it was certainly by some-one who knew that very fact. It was no opportunist who took her. This was planned. Whoever planned it knew you'd be with Miss O'Malley and that the child would be alone at Keogh's.'

I nodded. McQuillan and Callen sprang to mind immedi-ately. They'd known. Callen had been at the hotel, but I didn't know how long he'd been there. According to Lizzie, Bridie made her tea around nine. I'd seen Callen at about ten-thirty; that barely left him much more than an hour. And if he were responsible, was it likely that he would have casually gone for a drink afterwards? He had an alibi for the other occasions as well.

Halligan was waiting for my answer. 'Look,' I said, 'it was common gossip about the town that I was seeing Liz... Miss O'Malley. And it must have been well known that she and Bridie looked after the Keogh children. I think you should be looking at this from another angle. Why did Bridie leave the house? Everything points to her having gone willingly, so she must have gone with someone she knew. The father or brother of a schoolfriend perhaps. I... I don't know. Lizzie or her father would know. Interview her friends, her teachers...'

'We're following all lines of inquiry,' Halligan said. 'At first light we'll organise a search. In the meantime, if you think of anything that might help us, let us know immediately.'

I was dismissed and I went back outside. The Gardaí were leaving and the neighbouring men hung together in a group in the yard. I saw Doyle a little distance away and I went over to talk to him. 'You think it's him?' I asked. There was a shadow of beard on his jaw and his eyes betrayed fatigue.

'It's him all right,' he said. 'He's out there now laughing at us. But we'll get him.' There was a finality to his words that boded no doubt. They would find him all right. But would they find him in time?

I saw Halligan and the other detective emerge and I excused myself and went back into the house. Lizzie was in the living-room staring out the window. I crossed the floor and put my hands on her shoulders, but she swung about as if stung and drew away. Her features seemed cut from granite, some hidden reserve of strength holding her together for now, but she might crumble like sandstone at the next blow. 'They're going to search in the morning,' I said. 'They'll soon find her.'

'They'll find her all right,' she said, 'but what good will she be to me dead?'

'She won't...' I tried. 'She'll be all right.'

'I'm so frightened,' she said.

I held out my hands and now she came to me and I embraced her. There was nothing in the past to compare with this. I'd never loved so much nor felt so helpless before. 'We'll find her,' I said. 'You'll see.'

'I couldn't live without her,' she said. 'I'd never forget...' But she would forget. It was part of our survival mechanism. There would be reminders, of course. That was part of life, part of the price of being human. But they would never be as bad as the actual reality.

'I was going to go back to town,' I said to Lizzie, 'but I'll wait if you want.'

'No,' she said. 'You go. My father is here. And Mrs Moran.'

'I'll see you tomorrow, then,' I said, and I left her.

When I got back to the hotel, there were many people milling about. A couple of journalists I knew fired questions at me, which I answered as best I could as I edged my way through reception to the stairs. In the sanctuary of my room, with the tumult from below muted, I paced up and down and stared out of the window. The monument and river both were reminders of death and I avoided them. The fog which formed halos around the streetlights now seemed less dense. Above the rooftops across the river the sky was clear and the moon had its own halo.

I tried not to think of Bridie, of where she might be and what might be happening to her, but my mind wouldn't let me be at peace. It tortured me with visions of my own desires and fantasies, held in check by convention. But the killer was subject to no such constraints.

I would have considered myself a practical man and I tried to channel my thoughts in a constructive way. Tomorrow would be a busy day and how could I know what I might have to face? What I needed now was sleep and rest. I undressed and climbed into bed. The streetlights created shadows and all about me there seemed to be shapes and movement. I shut my eyes but my mind took the darkness and illuminated it with terrible images once again, and it seemed as if I would never have peace.

I slept eventually and in my dreams I was pursued, by whom or what I did not know. I tried to outrun it, but always it was there like my shadow. When I awoke the shadow was still there. I knew that only if Bridie were found alive would I ever shake it off.

21

We assembled in the morning at the Town Hall, and there was no mistaking the sense of excitement and unease that permeated the atmosphere. You couldn't help but look at your neighbour and wonder if he was the one.

Halligan spoke to us briefly and quietly. Then we were divided into small groups with two Gardaí in charge of each, and using Ordnance Survey maps we plotted out the areas we'd search. I saw O'Malley in the crowd. He was broken, like Hawley, and I wondered why I'd ever hated or feared him. I saw Hawley, too, and Devlin and Callen, but kept well away from them.

A local company provided buses, one of which took a group of us out to the bypass, near Keogh's. As we drove there I was acutely aware that my future might depend on what we'd find. The group I was with were assigned to search along the bypass – rough grazing land where weeds grew black and shrivelled. Spreading out in a line, we searched the fields but found nothing. Beyond that was cutaway bog and here the size of the task facing us dampened our spirits. The area was honey-combed with bog-holes filled with black stagnant water and drains overgrown with heather, and it would take an army to search it thoroughly.

We trudged on with a terrible sense of hopelessness. We knew we were wasting our time but no one had the heart to admit to it. At lunchtime we returned to Castleford where the hotel provided soup and sandwiches and tea. I took a moment to go up to my room and phone Jones, taking care not to give any hint of how closely I was caught up in the present events. 'We've sprung him,' Jones said. 'Now it's up to the hounds.'

I just hung up and went back downstairs. Here I learned that Garda inquiries had thrown up a lead. A car had been seen behaving suspiciously out on the Duagh Road. We were taken there and began to search, and they might have been the selfsame fields we'd wandered over that morning: we found nothing. Gradually our searching became more haphazard, but we persevered until darkness thickened about us and the Gardaí called it off. We were cold and dispirited and wet from the drizzle which was beginning to fall.

Back at the Town Hall, Halligan thanked us for our co-operation. 'We hope to organise further searches tommor-row,' he said, 'on the basis of the information pouring into the incident room. I hope that we can rely on you men to come out with us again.'

I retreated to my room in the hotel and took a bath. I rang room service and ordered an omelette and forced myself to eat a little. I knew I had to go to see Lizzie, but I was dreading having to face her. I lay down on the bed and closed my eyes. I must have nodded off because the next thing I was aware of was the telephone buzzing. I picked up the receiver and the receptionist informed me there was a woman on the line.

I thought it was Lizzie and so wasn't prepared for McQuillan's voice. 'Willie?' she said.

'Yes.' I was abrupt. My mind was still muddled from sleep.

'I need to talk to you,' she said, despair in her voice.

'I'm tired,' I said, irritated by the call, by my lack of sleep and the long fruitless day.

'I have to see you,' she said. 'I want you to come and meet me.'

'I've nothing to say to you,' I said, trying to remain calm. Nothing would be gained by anger. 'Don't call me again.'

'I've got some information,' she said.

'About Bridie? Do you know if she's...?' But I couldn't put my fears into words. To speak the words might give them reality. 'Is it Callen?'

'I can't talk on the phone,' she said, and now there was a myriad of different emotions in her voice. 'Can't you just fucking well come?'

'OK, OK,' I said. 'I'll come. Where are you?'

'I'm in the phone box outside the post office on the Duagh Road.'

She was waiting when I got there, her arms clutched tightly across her chest. Seeing her I felt overwhelmed by fatigue, by fear, by the unknown. She sat into the car and I was frightened to look at her in case I'd see the truth on her face. I asked her instead what she had to tell me, aware of the tension that hung like a physical aura about her. 'Come to the house,' she said. 'Then I'll tell you everything.'

'But where's Callen? Is he there? Is it him?'

'He's safe,' she said. 'He won't harm anyone again.'

'Do you know where Bridie is? If she's still alive?' Hope caught in my throat like phlegm.

'I know where he took her,' she said. 'He told me he'd killed her, but I don't know. He hated you, you see. He knew everything was closing in about him, but he wanted revenge before...' her voice trailed off and she sat beside me, staring out at the drizzle.

'Where is she?' I demanded, gripping her arm.

'Take your fucking hand off me,' she said, breaking my grip. 'Come to the house and I'll tell you. You wanted a story. Well, this is the best story you'll ever get. I'll even keep you out of it if you do what I want. Your secret will be safe with me. I don't want revenge. I only want to get away.'

I felt numbed. There were other implications in her words I didn't want to face. 'We'll go to the Gardaí,' I said, fighting my emotions. 'They're the ones to deal with this.'

'No,' she said. 'We have to talk first. We have to decide what I'm to tell them. They'll want to know about Callen. Why he did this. What I know about him – about the past and everything...' Fear touched me again, but now it was for myself. 'I want to get away,' she added. 'You want to stay here. I want to sell what I know for money to escape. We can still help each other and get what we want. What does it matter what you and Callen did thirty years ago? If it hadn't been you he took under the bridge, then it would have been someone else. Even if you tell them about the past, it won't bring her back, will it? So why can't you just fucking well come with me. Maybe he lied about killing her. How do I know. Just come and then you'll see.'

I did as she asked, fear and self-preservation and hope governing my motives. I knew I was giving myself up to her, but I'd no other choice. 'Tell me what happened,' I said, desperate to know.

'You'll see for yourself,' she said. 'Soon enough.'

'But when did you find out? About Callen...?'

'This evening. But I should have suspected all along. As you should have suspected. You knew what he liked, what he wanted. When I was a child and used to babysit for a neighbour, he'd come to the house. I used to let him... You know... You were under the bridge with Sissy and Judith... You knew he liked them young... bare... If the Guards ever found out that you used to be with him, that you didn't tell them...'

She lapsed into silence, giving the threat time to sink in. Now there was only the noise of the tyres on the road, the swish of the wipers and the sound of my breathing.

'It didn't stop in England,' she went on, finding her voice again. 'It got worse. He became involved with some group. Most of them were interested in boys but Callen claimed he wasn't a pervert. He was normal. He only liked girls.' She laughed, a hint of hysteria in the sound.

'We were always on the move. I wanted to get away from him, but I was trapped. He knew too much about me. He was clever. He always took care to trap anyone who might be useful to him. That's why he hated you. Then some years ago he got caught and was sentenced to six years in prison. There was a riot there and three sex offenders were taken hostage. He was one of them. The rioters tried to use them in bargaining with the authorities, but they wouldn't budge.'

'The rioters castrated one of the hostages with a razor blade while the other two had to watch. They told Callen he was next, but a few minutes before the deadline, the authorities gave in. He never recovered though, and when he was released he decided to come back here. He promised to give it all up – he didn't want to go back inside again. I thought he'd given it up, but he hadn't. He wasn't home the evening Jacinta Devlin disappeared. He told me he was with someone planning a burglary. Obviously he couldn't tell that to the Gardaí when they questioned him, so I had to back up his story that he was with me. I believed him; it suited me. I was with someone myself that night. He's an important man in the town and he told me that his wife would say he was with her. They didn't want any scandal. So I told the Gardaí that Callen was with me and that seemed to satisfy them.'

'You gave him an alibi?' I took my eyes from the road to stare at her.

'I didn't think he could kill anyone,' she said. 'He didn't even want proper sex. Just a look and a feel and... You know that.'

'But how do you know all this now?' I asked.

'He told me. I confronted him this evening and he admitted everything. He wanted an end to it all.'

'But what about Majella Hawley. And Bridie...?'

'He wasn't with me the night Majella disappeared. But I'd already lied once to the Gardaí. It was easier the second time. But with Bridie... He was out last night. He knew she babysat for the Keogh's. I'd told him. I'd told him about you and Lizzie – your arrangements. He thought you were trying to get him. When he saw your article he went fucking crazy. He thought the Gardaí had leaked the information in return for what you knew.' She hesitated – seemed to be trying to figure it all out herself. 'When Bridie went missing I knew it was him. This evening I confronted him and he told me everything.

'He picked up Jacinta one night and she didn't seem to mind. He gave her money and told her it was their secret. But she was clever. Or stupid. She saw her chance for more money. Maybe she approached him. I... I don't know. But he picked her up again one night and took her out to Duagh. His uncle left him the cottage there when he died three years ago. Anyway he'd some crazy idea that he could keep her there for good. He'd have her there and she wouldn't be able to tell either. But she was sick and got pneumonia or something. Then he picked up Majella that Monday night and kept her at the cottage for two days before he got scared and killed her. I think he took Bridie there, too, but I don't know. He wouldn't tell me anything about her.'

I opened my mouth to speak but clamped down on the words. There was nothing to be gained by words. Bridie was dead. By coming here I'd killed her as surely as if I'd strangled her myself. I didn't know what to do.

As if fate didn't want me to have to make a decision just

then, I came to the turn off for Callen's place. I stopped the car and we got out and she caught my arm as I moved to open the gate, her mouth a dark cavity when she spoke. 'He's in the shed,' she said. 'Over there.' I followed her pointing finger, taking in the old stone building, a dark mass against the lighter sky. I walked towards it and she followed me. 'There's a light switch inside the door,' she said, and my fumbling fingers found it.

Callen hung from a rafter, a grotesque effigy of the man I'd known. The knot on the rope was beneath his left ear and his head lolled away from it. His eyes had rolled upwards and his tongue protruded between his lips. His scuffed shoes were barely inches from the floor and he could have easily reached the concrete blocks on which he'd stood to place his head in the noose. 'We'll have to cut him down,' I said to McQuillan.

'Leave him,' she said, the two words laced with hatred and bitterness and contempt.

'I can't,' I said. 'He might still be alive.'

'He's dead,' she said vehemently. 'Let him stay dead.' Her words forced their way through to my muddled brain, but there was no real reaction yet. This was part of some nightmare from which I'd soon awake.

'We have to call the Gardaí,' I said. 'They have to be told. Jesus, don't you realise you're in serious trouble?'

'I'm in trouble,' she said. 'That's some joke. You're the fucking one in trouble. He tried to kill me this evening when I told him I was going to turn him in. Do you know that? I got away and hid in a neighbour's shed. After about an hour I came back here and found him ...' Colour tinted her pale cheeks and she began to pull frantically at the buttons on her jacket, opening them. Beneath she wore a yellow blouse and now she fumbled at the buttons at the neck and opened three of them. She caught the edges of the blouse and pulled them apart, showing me her cleavage and the frilled edge of a bra. 'See,' she said, and I couldn't avert my eyes from the white flesh which wasn't white at all but a dirty bluish purple. 'It was him or me,' she said. 'He's killed four children already. He did this too, and you say I'm in trouble?'

'Four?' I could only cope with the one word.

'The other was a long time ago,' she said. 'And don't tell me that you never suspected.'

'Judith Kelly? You're lying. Jesus, you're lying.' I felt afraid.

'He told me everything,' she said. 'He wanted me to know it all before he killed me. Judith was going to tell on him. You had told her to. So he arranged to meet her down by the river pool. He said it took only a minute, that she hardly struggled. When she was dead he threw her body in the river. Then he broke the plank on the bridge and made it look like an accident.'

I closed my eyes, my mind filled with images: a child in blue knickers scrambling up the bank by the bridge, running at my urging; Callen cursing and calling to her to come back. I was saving her, I thought, from what Sissy Bradley had endured, yet was only sentencing her to die. I saw the pool of water that collected down by the bridge on the Duagh Road when there was heavy rain. I saw Judith Kelly's head plunged beneath the surface, the air bubbles rising. She was a slight child – couldn't have weighed more than six or seven stone. What could she have done when he grabbed her and pushed her head under the cold dark water and held it there, her body exploding with its need for air, water filling her lungs? It wouldn't have taken long, but she'd have had sufficient time to know she was going to die.

I clenched my eyes tighter, but the images persisted. I saw Callen's face from that time twisted with something I was too young and inexperienced to understand. I was back under the bridge that first evening Sissy Bradley joined us. Without even being asked, she'd reached beneath her school skirt and pulled down her knickers and squatted before us. The knickers fettered her ankles as she exposed the secret of her child's body to us. Callen reached out to touch her, his eyes never leaving my face all the time he stroked her. 'You can touch her if you want,' he'd said. 'She doesn't mind.'

I wanted to touch her, wanted to place my hand on that bare mound of flesh which in the magazine had been hidden from my gaze, but I didn't do so. 'Touch her,' he'd said, tempting and defying me. 'You won't touch anything better. The hair's so light you can't even see it. She's just the right age. Any older and it starts to become coarse. But the light downy stuff...' I saw him fumble with his zipper and the child move towards him, her hands reaching out...

Now I had learned that he had never grown out of that need or desire or habit, had never matured to the point where a woman would have sufficed. I knew now what the detective had meant yesterday when he spoke of the killer's perverted sexual needs. I couldn't bear to think of it – to think of her naked and Callen with a razor or whatever it was he used to shave his victims.

'Oh, God.' I swung about to face McQuillan.

'No one knows,' she said. 'No one but you and me. All those who knew are dead. It's our secret now.'

'Secret?'

'About Sissy and Judith. I won't tell the Gardaí. No one has to ever know. That's why I wanted to talk to you first.' She watched me, the power now in her hands. 'You can still have what you want,' she added. 'Lizzie, the job on the paper, the story. I'll tell you everything. I have to get away. I can't go on living here. Not now. I'd wanted to get away for so long but I didn't know how. Then you came and I saw my chance. I knew it was only a matter of time before Callen... before he started again and we'd have to run. I didn't want to have to go without anything. Once, in England, I got a job in a laundry. They had a contract for a chain of nursing homes. Many of the patients were incontinent. You... you can't imagine it.' She stopped but I couldn't speak. 'Do you agree?' she said.

'I don't know,' I said, shaking my head like a dumb animal.

'You can't bring them back,' she said. 'Even if you tell the Gardaí about the past, the dead still stay dead.'

I still didn't speak. I turned back to look at the creature that once had been a human being like me. No power on earth could bring him back or undo what he'd done. McQuillan was right. Only the living mattered.

'Well?' she said, her voice betraying her desperation. All her life she'd paid for what she wanted. Now she couldn't be certain if she'd enough to give. Would her silence about my past buy her freedom? Was I willing to pay? Could she know that I had as much to lose as she did?

'I won't say anything,' I said. 'And now I'd best inform the Gardaí. I'll call them from the post office.'

'Take me with you,' she said. 'I... I don't want to wait here.'

'Go in the house,' I said. 'I won't be long. He can't harm you now.'

I drove to the post office, called the Garda station and asked for Doyle. The door of the box didn't close properly and a cold draught blew about me. While I waited for Doyle, questions whirled about in my mind. There would be time enough for both questions and recriminations later. 'Just listen,' I said when Doyle came on the line and he listened, not interrupting once.

'I'd be prepared for the worst, Willie,' he said when I finished.

'But Majella Hawley, he kept her alive...'

'It's different now,' he said. 'But let's hope you're right.' His words transported me back to that afternoon I'd met him at the hotel. He'd spoken about responsibility, but then it had only been a word. 'I'll get things moving,' he said. 'Go back to the house and wait.'

'No,' I said, suddenly coming to a decision. 'I'm going on to Duagh. I have a good idea where the cottage is.'

'I'd advise you not to,' Doyle said. 'This is a Garda matter now.'

'Did you know her?' I asked. 'Did you?

I hung up and walked back to the car.

22

I drove on into the darkness. The hedgerows loomed large in the light of the headlamps; beyond them, the dark fields seemed empty and lifeless. I passed some roadside dwellings and in the distance the lights of scattered farmhouses winked. It was difficult to accept that normality, whatever I might now imagine it to be, still existed.

The road was narrow and twisting, and as I climbed higher the black formless fields gave way to heather and gorse and withered bracken. This in turn gave way to forestry plantations which seemed to cling precariously to the hillside, and when I reached them the trees shut me in, towering high into the sky on either side. The rain was easing and the sky seemed to be clearing. I glimpsed it above the tree tops, a lighter shade, as if there were another world up there beyond reach. I'd covered fifteen miles, the road deteriorating the higher up I went. I knew I had to cross the bridge over the Duagh river but after that my memory was hazy as to the exact location of the cottage. I'd been there half a dozen times with Callen, but that was many years ago. After another mile I crossed the bridge, but my memory failed me and I had to stop at a farmhouse to ask directions. An old man pointed out the route and told me that no one lived there now.

As I drew near I began to be taken over by thoughts of what I'd find. I had hope – it was all I had – but it was festering with fear and doubt. Would Callen have dared to leave Bridie alive? Would he have felt that she was safe at the cottage – would never be found? Might he have left her alive, certain that he could return again and again? To think of it made my skin crawl, yet I clung to the hope.

According to McQuillan, he'd taken Bridie to punish me. He'd warned me away from McQuillan that first night and must have assumed that I'd not heeded the warning. At the time I'd found it laughable, but now I saw a reason for it. He'd been frightened that McQuillan would tell me what she knew and that she'd provided him with an alibi. When she'd confronted him this evening and told him she was going to the Gardaí and probably boasted that she would sell her story, he must have realised that it was finished. Was it only then he'd decided that death was his sole option? But if he'd only decided this evening, wasn't there a chance, however slim, that Bridie was still alive?

Yet McQuillan only confronted him this evening. Bridie went missing last night. So his decision to pick on Bridie had nothing to do with what happened this evening. He must have known for some time that it was all but over. He'd picked on Bridie as his final act of vengeance against me and the world. I realised why he'd been in the hotel last night: he'd been there to taunt me. While we'd searched the countryside, Bridie had been in the van, probably in the hotel car-park, and only by killing her would his revenge be perfectly sweet. But why did she go with him? He may have tried to lure her with some excuse, but why did she go?

I was so caught up with my thoughts that I almost missed the turn-off. I braked sharply and swung off the road onto a narrow track. Here the trees grew right up to the edges and seemed to engulf me. The headlamps picked out a rusted gate and I stopped and got out, shivering in the thin cold air. As my vision adjusted to the darkness, I realised that the night was no longer soot black. Only deep beneath the trees was there impenetrable darkness, and I imagined nocturnal creatures staring at me from the murk.

I took my torch from the boot, opened the gate and moved forward. The track was rutted and overgrown and it made walking difficult. As I stumbled on, the ground opened up to a clearing of maybe an acre. The cottage stood at the farthest corner, crouched beneath the trees, hardly more substantial than a shadow. I made out the shape of a chimney against the backdrop of sky and trees, and what I took to be the sheen of windows. I hesitated, not wanting to go on, regretting that I'd not waited for the Gardaí.

Bridie must have come here last night, I thought, must have seen what I now saw, must have walked or been dragged along this very same track. What thoughts ran through her mind then? What thoughts when she'd found herself alone in the dark with Callen, for surely she must have known by then what he was?

I went forward again towards the cottage which became more substantial with each step. As I drew near I heard a sound behind me – what might have been the cry of an animal – and I swung about in a panic, switching on the torch, flashing the beam all about. But there was nothing there and I went on, the cottage clearer now, a squat building with two windows to one side of the door.

It was here Bridie had been brought, and how many others? Perhaps there were others he'd let go – those who hadn't threatened him. Or was it only when he'd killed Jacinta Devlin that his blood lust had been roused? After that did he have to kill, just as he had to do that other...? My mind baulked at that thought. Even killing seemed more acceptable.

215

The track narrowed to a footpath, and now the trees seemed to loom above me although they were still some distance away. They seemed to want to lure me from the open space into the shadows and I felt afraid. Afraid of the open space itself; of the shadows beneath the trees; of the cottage which stood dark and silent and forbidding. I wanted to turn back, to run to the car and wait, but how could I fail Bridie?

I reached the cottage but couldn't gain entry. I shone the torch and noticed that the door was rotten. I stood back and kicked it but it held firm. Frustrated, I put my shoulder to it and after three heaves it gave way, and I found myself staring into what I felt was a dark cavern. My torch picked out a stone fireplace, a couple of armchairs, a pine table and chairs, white roughly plastered walls. Permeating it all were smells of damp and must and disuse. I was aware of this as I stepped inside, listening. But there was only the sound of my breathing and the moaning of the wind in the chimney. 'Bridie,' I called. 'Bridie.' But there was no answer. I shone my torch about and saw a light switch by the door. I pressed it and a bare bulb hanging from the ceiling lit up the room.

There was a door opposite me which I knew led to the kitchen and the bathroom, one on my right at the side of the chimney breast which led to the only bedroom. I hesitated, needing time to gather myself. I had to force myself to walk across the worn vinyl to the bedroom door, terrified that it would burst open and that some thing would leap out at me. Not a ghost – I held no fear of ghosts. It was a human form that held terror for me.

Somewhere the house creaked as I hesitantly reached out to grasp the doorknob. It felt heavy and cold as I turned it and pushed the door open. In the light from the living-room my ghostly reflection stared at me from the mirror of a wardrobe which stood against the bedroom wall.

I turned on the light and saw an iron bed and a wardrobe, a dressing table and a ragged cane chair. And on the far side of the bed a photographer's white umbrella and light. I shrunk from it as my mind registered its significance.

I stepped into the room and moved to the foot of the bed. It was then I saw the bundle of clothing in the corner. I didn't need to be told that they belonged to a child and that the child was Bridie. I felt my stomach contract. I edged round the bed to examine my find – a pair of blue jeans, a red and black striped sweater, a child's underclothes, a white sock with a band of red stitching, a pair of white sneakers with pink trim.

I swung about and stared at the photographic equipment. To even think of Callen with that... I came back round the bed and saw my face in the wardrobe mirror, drawn, haggard and damned. I wanted to smash my fist into the image, but instead I opened the wardrobe door and looked inside. It was empty. I closed the door and stood for a moment trying to imagine what had taken place here: Callen with a camera, with his face bloated and stomach protruding, his short fat fingers. The image was all but unbearable.

I had to force myself to return to the living-room. I searched the kitchen and bathroom, but found nothing. I went outside, intending to search further, but the night seemed to have become darker and there was little hope of finding anything with just a torch.

At the rear of the cottage there were some outbuildings. One of them, a stone-built shed with an iron roof, was the only one possessing a door. It had a heavy bolt, a new padlock securing it. I banged on the door and called Bridie's name, but no answer came. I put my shoulder to the door, but realised almost immediately that I couldn't break it down on my own. I circled the shed, but there was no window through which I might gain entry.

I searched the other outhouses, one of which was partly filled with haybales, but found nothing. I returned to the cottage, a drowning man now with his whole life flashing before his eyes. Only there was no sense of progression. My life was jumbled up in a thousand different images, images from childhood mixed with images from yesterday and today. Had I taken an hallucinogenic drug I couldn't have been more muddled or confused.

I wasn't aware of time, didn't become aware of it until I heard car engines and went to the door to see their headlights sweep the sky and then hear the Gardaí as they came up to the cottage. I thought of what McQuillan had said to me. 'If you don't say anything about the past, I won't either.' But if I spoke or not it wouldn't bring back any of the children. My head told me that Bridie was dead, only my heart still hoped. But if she were dead, what was to be gained by talking? Callen was dead. He couldn't be touched any more. Only the living would suffer.

I might want McQuillan punished – she'd given Callen his alibi, had given him the opportunity to kill again – but she'd suffered enough already. Or so I told myself, thinking that Lizzie and I could still have a future. While the past remained a secret, I could still hope.

Halligan led the way, accompanied by a Detective Inspector, Doyle and others I didn't know. It only took a moment to fill them in and Halligan organised an immediate search of the surrounding area, leaving the questions and recriminations which must have been nagging him for the moment. He then went into the bedroom and examined the bundle of clothing. 'Are they hers?' he asked me. 'Would you know?'

'Who else could they belong to?' I said. 'They're... The fucker must have taken photographs.' I walked out to the living-room as Doyle came in to inform Halligan about the locked shed.

I went out to the shed with them – Halligan, Doyle and the Inspector and another Garda. In the tension of the moment they seemed unaware of my presence. 'Break it down,' Halligan ordered. A half-dozen shoulder charges were needed before the door flew open and we saw the interior, piled to the rafters with bales of hay. 'Take them out,' Halligan ordered, and we began to remove them, Doyle and myself and the Garda, while the Inspector held a torch. There were two layers of bales, built interlocking like a brick wall. Behind them we found a cavity.

No one spoke but we began to work more quickly. I could hear our breathing in the small confined space and sensed the hope that gripped us. I tried to remain calm but my whole body was trembling. We'd removed almost half the bales when the Inspector leaned over and shone the torch into the cavity. It was just wide enough to contain what I saw in the light – a human shape beneath a dirty quilt. 'Jesus,' I said. 'She's there.'

Doyle and the Garda renewed their efforts. I, too, attacked the bales with a frenzy. 'Bring the doctor here immediately,' Halligan said to the Inspector, and as he slipped out, we pulled the last few bales aside, giving access to the cavity.

Halligan stepped forward with his torch and gently pulled down the quilt. Mercifully she was faced away from us so that I didn't have to see her face. She was naked, her body starkly white in the light, her hair about her shoulders as if it had been arranged thus to cover her nakedness.

I didn't doubt that I was looking on someone who was dead. She was just a shell. Sick with anger and sadness, I thought of the fear she must have endured, of the thoughts that must have overwhelmed her, and I had an awful need for vengeance. I wished that Callen wasn't dead, so that I could have killed him myself. But he was safe. No one could touch him anymore. The dead were the lucky ones. It was the living who were cursed.

'Come on,' Doyle said, grabbing my shoulder, his anger and frustration palpable.

I didn't want to go. It was only a body, I told myself, but I didn't want to leave her. But as I did turn to go, Halligan spoke, his voice calm. How he remained calm in the circumstances, I do not know. 'She's still alive,' I heard him say. 'Hurry up with the doctor.'

I remember that I cried out – disbelief, hope, joy, anger, all jumbled together. I made to move forward, but Doyle held me. Then there was a flurry of activity and a man carrying a black case entered the shed. 'Come on,' Doyle said, 'you're only in the way here.'

He lead me outside while Halligan issued orders. I couldn't come to terms with what was happening. I was vaguely aware of Gardaí gathering around – of their sense of relief at finding the child alive. A car was brought to the end of the track and I watched Doyle carry Bridie down to it, wrapped in the quilt, the doctor following him.

I thought of Lizzie. She had to be told. I hurried away, unnoticed. Half-way across the clearing I turned to look back. The lights lit up the front of the cottage, backdrop of trees and sky dark in contrast, but I no longer felt afraid.

23

Lizzie must have been watching out because as I swung into the yard I saw her in the headlights, her face as blank as that of a doll whose features haven't yet been painted on. A slash of colour could create sadness or mad hilarity – and I realised what the future would have held for me if we'd found Bridie dead.

I got out of the car and I knew from her face that she thought I'd no news or bad news. So I had twice the pleasure when I took her in my arms and told her we'd found Bridie alive, and that she'd been taken to the hospital.

'I was certain she was dead,' she said. 'I'd been praying and praying... Only I didn't think God would answer my prayers. Not after what we'd done.' She pulled away and I saw her eyes were bleary from crying and lack of sleep.

'Your prayers have been answered,' I said, 'so be thankful. Come on, and I'll take you to the hospital.'

'I...' she said, shaking her head in bewilderment. She'd been prepared for the worst, and needed time to reconcile herself to the positive outcome.

'Come on,' I said again, taking her arm. 'Let's get your coat and we'll go,' and this time she came with me.

The neighbour, Mrs Moran, was in the living-room, anticipation and excitement in her eyes. The two women embraced and then Lizzie told her that Bridie had been taken to the hospital.

'I must go to her,' she said, walking robot-like to the bedroom.

'Bridie'll be needing a few things,' Mrs Moran said to me. 'I'll get them.' She fussed around importantly, assuring Lizzie that she'd tend to the fire and lock up and leave the key under the stone by the gate.

Once we were in the car, Lizzie asked me what had happened. I told her we'd found Bridie at a cottage in Duagh, omitting any mention of Callen or McQuillan or how exactly we'd found her. I reached out and squeezed her shoulder, feeling life beneath my fingers like a promise. 'Who?' she asked quietly. 'Do you know who did it?'

'It was Callen,' I said. 'He's dead: he won't hurt anyone anymore.'

'He was your friend,' she said. 'She was, too.'

I thought she meant Bridie and was about to agree, but then I realised that she spoke of McQuillan. 'They were never my friends,' I said. 'I knew them once, that's all.'

'Bridie liked you,' she said. 'She wanted to babysit for us. It gave her pleasure. She thought life was like what she saw on TV. She'd a child's idea of love. She wanted us to be in love. To think she almost died for the pleasure we've had... It's what I have to live with from now on.'

'You'll get over it,' I said, and we were silent for a while.

'Has my father been told?' she asked eventually. 'Do you know?'

'No,' I said. 'I don't. Do you know where he is?'

'He's probably gone back to Burke's,' she said.

'I'll see that he's told,' I said as we drew into the hospital. We found Doyle waiting for us. While a doctor took Lizzie away I asked Doyle if her father had been told. 'Superintendent Halligan will be dealing with that,' he told me. 'I'll check up on it when I get back to the station. I'm waiting for someone to take over from me here.'

'Thanks,' I said. 'I appreciate it.'

'It's OK,' he said, shrugging his shoulders, calmer now. There were flecks of grey in his hair and scurf on his collar. We sat in grey plastic chairs in the corridor while people hurried by. Telephones rang and outside an ambulance's siren wailed. I couldn't bear the inactivity and I got up and wandered down to the end of the corridor and stared out of the window to where the lights of the town promised life.

Doyle came to join me. 'I still can't believe it was Callen,' he said. 'But then, it had to be someone.'

'What happens now?' I asked.

'We search at the cottage in the morning for Jacinta Devlin's body. The Super thinks she's been buried in the woods there.'

'I don't think...' I began, but stopped. I'd been about to tell him that McQuillan had told me that Callen had kept Majella Hawley alive at the cottage before he'd brought her body back to be buried in Castlewood. If he'd risked bringing Majella's body back when there was a search on for her, why would he have buried Jacinta there? It was so easy to let something slip; I'd have to be careful. 'About Bridie?' I said. 'Was she assaulted?'

'No.' He shook his head. 'I don't think he touched her. God knows why. Maybe he hoped to come back again. We don't know.'

'No,' I said. 'Anyway thanks for telling me. I appreciate it.' I stared at his reflection in the glass, a ghostly image superimposed on the orange lozenge of a streetlight. 'Have you spoken to McQuillan yet?' I asked, anxious to know what she might have told them.

'Not yet,' Doyle said. 'The Super will interview her tomorrow. We're holding her overnight. We'd have to anyway, for her own safety. Feelings will be running high.'

I nodded. 'I don't think I'll take Lizzie home,' I said. 'She'll only be bothered by the press there. I think I'll take her to stay with Alec and Alice Whitley. You might let Halligan know. I'm sure he'll want to see her. I'll go and phone them now.'

Alec answered and was relieved to learn that Bridie was fine. He knew she'd been found but had no other information. He was only too glad to be of help and told me to bring Lizzie around whenever I wanted. 'Alice will have everything ready for her,' he said.

When I went back Doyle was leaving and I sat with the uniformed Garda who'd taken over from him until Lizzie came to join me. I held her while she cried, my hands measuring the tremor of her body. It was like touching the trunk of a tree and feeling the movement of the branches in the wind and being utterly powerless to stop it. 'Don't,' I said. 'It'll be all right. You'll see. Now I'm taking you to Alec Whitley's for the night. They'll take care of you.'

I thought she might protest, but she offered no objection and I led her out to the car. As we drove off she told me Bridie was still muggy – that Callen had drugged her with some sleeping pills – and probably wouldn't be fully awake or aware until the next day. But the doctor had told her that she'd be fine once she got over the trauma. 'She's young,' Lizzie said, 'and he said that, with help, she'll make a complete recovery.'

'That's great,' I said. 'You see. Everything's going to be fine. Isn't it?' She nodded and I wondered if she really believed that Bridie would ever fully recover. 'I spoke with Sergeant Doyle about your father,' I told her now. 'He'll make sure that he's told the good news.'

When we reached Whitley's, Alec answered the door. He called Alice and I was never more glad to see her. She didn't ask any questions, just took charge immediately, ushering Lizzie down the hallway, staying us with a gesture.

'I didn't know where else to take her,' I said to Alec.

'She'll be fine here,' he said. 'Alice will look after her. We'll wait in the study.' No fire burned in the grate and the room no longer possessed the warmth I remembered from my earlier visit, but I was glad of its sanctuary. I couldn't remain silent and I recounted for Alec the events of the evening. As with Lizzie and with the Gardaí, I was aware of the omissions in my story. Even with Alec I was trying to pretend that there had been no past. Maybe if I told the story often enough I'd come to believe my version.

I waited for Alec to speak, to touch on the past, but he didn't have the opportunity to do so. At that moment Alice called him and he came back within a minute. 'Alice thinks that Elizabeth should see a doctor,' he told me. 'Just to get her something to help her sleep. I'm going to phone our own GP and ask him to call.'

Elizabeth. It was as if he spoke of someone I didn't know. I watched while he made the call and when he hung up he told me that the doctor would come round immediately. 'He's a good man,' he said. 'He'll take care of her. Now I'd best tell Alice.'

He left me alone again and I'd a few minutes to gather my thoughts, but they were too chaotic to rein in before Alec came back. He walked to the fireplace and stared at the empty grate. 'This business,' he said, not turning to face me. 'What happens now?'

'I don't know,' I said.

'They'll be interviewing McQuillan,' he said. 'You realise that?'

'She won't speak of the past,' I said. 'She's in enough trouble from providing Callen with alibis as it is. It'd only make it worse for her. Anyway it was all a long time ago. It has nothing to do with now.' I spoke as if to convince myself that it was so.

'Ah,' Alec said. 'It's just that if she did speak...' He let the implication hang in the air. He'd promised to stand by me, but perhaps there was a limit to his promise.

We were interrupted by the arrival of the doctor, a small man with a mop of grey curly hair. Alec took him upstairs while I waited in the hallway. Alec came back down, followed shortly by Alice. 'Willie,' she said, holding out her hands to me. As she held me I was aware of how thin she was, how brittle her bones seemed beneath her clothes. The future was like that, brittle as old bones.

We waited in the hall until the doctor came back down and told us he'd given Lizzie something to help her sleep. 'She'll feel much better in the morning,' he said.

As Alec saw him out, Alice asked me if I'd like to see Lizzie. 'She's in the back room,' she said. 'She's probably feeling drowsy already, so don't delay too long. What she needs now is sleep.'

But she wasn't drowsy and the hand she reached out to me from beneath the bedclothes was vibrant with life. 'Willie,' she said, and I wondered how a single word could convey so much love. I took her hand and she pulled me to her and reached up with her other hand to encircle my neck. 'Willie,' she repeated, 'don't ever leave me. Promise me that.'

'I promise,' I said, certain that it was forever despite the lies and the deceit and the continuing need for them. I held Lizzie until Alice came up and told me that I should leave. I didn't want to go but I kissed Lizzie and promised I'd call to see her the next day. 'You stay as long as you wish,' Alice told her. 'And Willie will be here all the time. He won't go away now. Isn't that right, Willie?'

'That's right,' I said. 'I won't ever go away again.'

Lizzie smiled at us, her face as white as the pillow she lay on, the dark hair more like oil than it had ever been before. I smiled at her and looked about the room before I went out, noting as if it were important to do so the pastel walls, the curtains and matching quilt cover, the white built-in furniture, the pictures of Victorian scenes.

Alice followed me downstairs where Alec waited for us by the door of the study. 'Coffee?' Alice asked. 'Or something stronger?'

'No, thanks,' I said, torn between wanting to stay and wanting to go. 'I'm tired. I need a good night's sleep myself.'

'Goodnight then, Willie,' she said, putting her arms about me, kissing me on the cheek.

Alec came out to the car with me and we stood in the darkness. 'I'll go,' I said. 'We'll talk when this is all over.'

'There'll be plenty of time for that,' he said.

I left him there in the driveway, a ghostly figure seen in my rear-view mirror as I drove away.

In the town I saw groups of people scattered here and there, shock and excitement clinging to them like ectoplasm. The posters with Jacinta Devlin's image hung faded on the poles, no need for them now. I drove down by the Garda station where a crowd had gathered, and I thought of McQuillan having to run that gauntlet. But her ordeal here was almost over. This place could harm her no more. Despite what she'd told me, I knew that she must have suspected for some time that Callen might be the killer. It was why she'd approached me in the beginning. She'd seen me as her only means of escape. Had I agreed to help her, I thought she'd have told me of her suspicions then and Bridie would never have been taken. But then, if I had not returned; if I'd never got to know Callen or McQuillan... I could go on forever with that but it would gain me nothing. I had to turn from the past and look to the future, give thanks each day that we had found Bridie alive.

I'd no logical explanation as to why Callen hadn't killed her. Maybe there never would be a satisfactory one. Maybe the words of that song my father once sang was the only explanation: there but for fortune... As a child I hadn't understood what the writer had meant. I did now. There but for fortune... That's what we all were, hostages to fortune. Maybe I should just accept that, and live with it as best I could.

24

The night was one of fitful sleep and snatches of dreams. In one of them I was back in my old room with the oilcloth-covered table and the tree outside my window. There was someone hanging on the tree and I saw it was my father. Only he had Callen's face. I shrank from him, but he put his hand through the glass and reached for me. His swollen tongue filled his mouth, forcing itself between his clenched teeth. The hand drew closer, cut and bloodied, and I screamed. I don't know if I screamed aloud, but when I woke I imagined I heard the echo of the scream in the dark room.

Blind terror took me over and I had to have light. It took me a couple of attempts before I could fumble on the bedside lamp and banish the images my mind superimposed on the dark corners. I clambered from the bed and crossed to the window and pulled the curtains aside. The town was sleeping. I pressed my forehead to the cold glass, closing my eyes and breathing deeply to quell my agitation, and slowly the terror diminished.

The cold drove me back to bed but I didn't switch off the light. After some time I slept and no dreams troubled me.

After a quick wash and shave I had coffee and toast in the dining-room, and as I finished eating, the receptionist paged me. There was a phone call for me and a letter which had just been delivered. It bore a Castleford postmark, and the writing on the address was laboured. I thought it was a poison-pen letter and that it hadn't taken whoever had sent it too long to get their vituperation onto paper. I went back up to my room, throwing the letter on the dressing table while I took the call, which was from Jones, excited with new developments. 'It's going to be some story,' he said.

'I suppose,' I said, 'but you'll have to get someone else to cover it. I'll deal with it only for today.'

He was surprised and pressed me for my reasons. 'I'll tell you everything later,' I said. I'd expected him to be angry, but he must have detected something in my voice, for he let me be.

I called the Whitleys and spoke with Alice. She told me Lizzie was still sleeping and had had a peaceful night. She herself had just been in touch with the hospital and Bridie was comfortable, the word hiding the awful reality of what she'd endured. I asked Alice to give Lizzie my regards and to tell her that I'd call later. For the moment I was Jones's man.

I made my way downstairs again and out to my car, and headed for the Duagh hills. There were cars parked along the roadside for a hundred yards as I approached the turn-off for the cottage. I left my own car at the end of the line and walked from there. Parked in the track were marked and unmarked Garda cars and two Garda vans which had brought the searchers. This was to be a Garda-only operation.

Two uniformed Gardaí were on duty at the cottage and shed. Halligan must have known that the area was too large to police and that he couldn't hope to keep the press or onlookers out, so he'd protected vital evidence and had his men concentrate on the search, leaving the press and onlookers to fend for themselves. I heard voices among the trees as I climbed over the barbed-wire fence separating the cottage grounds from the woods. It was starting to rain and the trees only offered partial shelter.

Halligan was concentrating the search on an area to the rear of the cottage. Later I learned that all he had to go on for his suspicions that the body was buried there – if anywhere – was that the wire there was slack due to a broken stake and afforded the best place of entry to the woods. An area had been cordoned off with yellow tape stretched from tree to tree, and here the Gardaí searched for a spot that had been disturbed. I walked along the boundary of yellow tape, watching the Gardaí as they searched the soggy ground. The rain was falling heavily now, but despite this there was a sense of expectation in the air. This was the final act in the drama.

Several questions still nagged me. Why had Bridie gone with Callen that night? Why hadn't he killed her? Why had he gone to the hotel and left her in the van? He must have known that her disappearance would be quickly noted and that there was a possibility that the Gardaí would set up roadblocks and search every vehicle entering or leaving the town. I'd thought initially he'd done it to taunt me, but surely he hadn't been that much of a fool? McQuillan had said that he'd been terrified of going back to prison. So why then had he taken such stupid risks? But who could ever know what drove him or motivated him?

A sudden shout alerted me to the fact that something was happening, and I ran back to the taped-off area to see the Gardaí on their knees gently and carefully clearing away the top layer of rotting vegetation. I watched as with feverish fingers the men unearthed the body of Jacinta Devlin. The photographers' flash bulbs threw a surreal light over the scene. I thought of the Devlins and the hope I'd given them. Maybe they could mourn now.

I'd seen enough to enable me write something for Jones tomorrow and there seemed little point in catching pneumonia; I decided to return to Castleford, change into some dry clothing, and go to Lizzie. I needed her presence to quell my fears of what could have been and banish the sickly smell of corruption which seemed to emanate from me.

I walked back to the car, wet and cold. The heater caused my damp clothing to steam and I opened the window. Away from the immediate area the air seemed clean and fresh and I drew it down into my lungs. The worst was behind me. It was all over now.

Back at the hotel there was a message to say that the Whitleys had taken Lizzie to the hospital and she would meet me there. If I hadn't been wet and cold I might have set off just then, but I needed a shower and a change of clothing. Up in my room I showered, letting the water run hot until my body tingled. I came back out, towelling myself vigorously. Then I noticed the letter on the dressing table.

I was so certain that it was a poison-pen letter that I almost threw it unopened into the bin, but curiosity made me pick up the envelope and tear it open and extract the two sheets of blue, lined paper. I had never seen his writing before, but as I glanced at the laboured script, I knew it was Callen's even before I saw his name at the bottom of the second sheet.

'I know it's over,' he wrote. 'I know that you and McQuillan are against me and you're going to inform on me to the Guards. But I don't want to end up in prison again. So there is only one way to end it. I was going to kill McQuillan first but this way is better. I know she told you everything and that you're thinking that you will be writing her story in your book. But you should be only writing the truth. If you want to know the truth I have hidden what you'll be needing under the bridge. You know where to be looking for it. I know that you might not want to be writing the truth. But you'll have to. McQuillan might not have told you where Bridy is. She's in a shed at that cottage at Duagh that we used to be going to years ago. She thinks I killed her. If you want to know why I didn't kill her you'll have to be asking Bridy that.'

I wanted to believe that it was a hoax, but I knew it wasn't. I held the paper between my fingers, trying to pretend I'd never seen it. But I knew that I couldn't do so. Just as I knew that I couldn't ignore what was hidden beneath the bridge, my imagination giving it a thousand different possibilities.

Just minutes before I'd been looking forward to seeing Lizzie, but how could I face her until I knew what was beneath the bridge? Maybe there was nothing there. Maybe Callen had been deranged when he wrote the letter. In it he'd spoken of wanting to kill McQuillan, but hadn't he tried and failed? And how could Bridie know why he'd left her alive? Had he actually told her so? It made no sense. It was a mark of the state I was in that I hadn't realised that the letter must have been posted before McQuillan said she had faced him with her suspicions and threats and he'd tried to kill her. So prior to that he must have known that there was no escape except the rope.

I got dressed, took the letter with me and headed out on the road for home. I thought of my father as I passed the turn-off – of the decency Alec Whitley had spoken of and that he had thought I might have possessed too. I was my father's son, but now he'd be ashamed of me.

The light was growing dim as I reached the bridge and parked. It was still only early afternoon but black storm clouds had rolled in off the ocean, darkening the world. In the distance the Duagh hills were shrouded in mist. Reluctantly I got out of the car and went down under the bridge.

It was gloomy beneath the arch and the wet stone glistened even in the dim light. I stood for a moment at the entrance, aware of a forbidding and oppressive atmosphere, and I had to force myself to move forward. The loose stone was about half-way along on the right-hand side, and I removed it, aware that it had been disturbed recently.

I knew I shouldn't touch what was there – that it was evidence – but I had to know. I took out the camera first – an old Polaroid model with one flash cube still attached, the plastic twisted by the heat. Behind it there was a large brown envelope, folded in two, along with a man's shaving kit in a leather case. I didn't open it to examine the contents. It was later I learned that it contained soap and a shaving brush and a razor and pubic hair, kept like the first white men in the Old West kept the scalps of their Indian victims.

I instinctively knew what the envelope contained, but I didn't want to look at them here, so I climbed back up to the car, taking my find with me. I turned the car about and headed back to Castleford: past the turn-off for my old house; past the entrance to the woods; past the school; past Dempsey's bar where in another lifetime I'd met McQuillan and Callen and the madness now taking me over had been set in motion. At the square I swung left into Bridge Street intending to return to the hotel, but instead I drove straight on, out past the castle to the Point. I parked where I'd parked the night I'd come here with McQuillan. For some moments I just sat and stared out at the turbulent sea.

I picked up the brown envelope and held it in my hands. I hesitated before eventually opening it and removing the Polaroid pictures it contained. When I stared at the first one there was no mistaking the face of Jacinta Devlin or the fear that showed in her eyes. I recognised the bedroom at the cottage and the threadbare bedspread she lay on.

Callen appeared in the second picture, and I knew as I looked at him with his drooping belly, matted with black hair, and his short erection sticking out below it, that the image would never leave me. And surely then it was the sickness I felt at seeing him that prevented my mind from grasping the evidence the photograph provided. Someone other than Callen had taken the picture. But I wasn't prepared to accept that. He could have used a time delay mechanism, I reasoned. There hadn't been one in our hidy hole beneath the bridge, but he could have got rid of it. But if he hadn't, then who had taken the picture? Who had been his accomplice?

I picked out the third photograph and was transported back to the very first time I'd gone under the bridge with Callen. The picture was of poor quality – it hadn't developed properly. McQuillan posed on all fours, her heavy breasts hanging down like udders, not quite concealing the fleshy roll of her stomach. Her mouth was clenched shut and her eyes were blank lenses staring into darkness.

The picture meant nothing by itself. If Callen wanted to take photographs of McQuillan that was their business. The picture could have been taken at any time and inserted here to implicate her. Wasn't that what he'd implied in the note, that she was equally guilty?

I held the pictures in my hand, frightened to look at the remaining ones. It was as if I'd a premonition – actually knew what the pictures would contain. Yet despite that I hoped. I think that I might have even prayed that the pictures would be other than what I was coming to believe they would be. But in the next one McQuillan stood by the bed on which Jacinta Devlin lay. Whose face showed the most fear, I couldn't say.

I think I whimpered. I threw the pictures from me onto the passenger's seat, as desperate to get out of the car as I'd been those few nights ago. The ozone was bracing, but it only made me feel more nauseous, my stomach churning like the sea. I stumbled away from the car and retched emptily, hearing the sea crashing against the rocks again and again. Darkness was gathering, a bright line at the horizon dividing the land from the sea, the two great areas of darkness kept apart by the light. When the light vanished and the darkness merged, it would surely engulf me.

My mind was numbed, unable to come to terms with what I'd seen and by its implications. I knew where duty lay – I who'd placed so much emphasis on duty – but in duty lay an end of everything. If I took what I now possessed to the Gardaí, McQuillan would tell them everything and I'd never again be able to stand upright in the winds that would blow. Yet I could not face Halligan and pretend that none of it existed. And to run again was unthinkable.

I thought of Lizzie waiting for me at the hospital. 'She needs you,' Alice had said, but how could I offer myself to her, contaminated as I was by so much knowledge and involvement? I could have seen the truth a long time ago, if I'd had the nerve to confront it, but I had not wanted to see it because I had been a part of it: I was there at the beginning, and would be there at the end now.

I had the answers to the questions that had nagged me. Why Majella Hawley had been kept alive for days and why she was buried in Castlewood. I remembered McQuillan telling me that first night she came to the hotel that Callen was in a foul mood because his van had broken down the night Majella disappeared. They must have picked her up that night as she walked from the town and before the van broke down. They hadn't been able to take her out to the cottage, so they must have hidden her at their house and waited for the van to be repaired. But they'd panicked and killed her. McQuillan had then driven the van and dropped off Callen with his bundle at the entrance to the woods, returning later to pick him up. That was why no one had seen a vehicle parked there. I'd also wondered why Callen should have brought Majella's body back from Duagh to bury it in the woods as McQuillan had implied he'd done. But he hadn't done so. Majella had never been to Duagh.

I knew, too, why Callen was at the hotel last Monday night. Not to taunt me as I'd thought. He'd been looking for me and McQuillan, certain that she was with me. Maybe he'd thought he could blackmail me into not writing anything more. He'd been convinced that McQuillan had given me the information that Majella Hawley had been kept alive for two days and was going to let me have the rest.

But McQuillan hadn't been with me. She'd been out driving the van. It hadn't been in the car-park at all. She'd been on her way to Duagh with her terrible load. I knew now why Bridie had left the Keogh's house without a sign of a struggle. She hadn't gone with a man but with a woman. She'd no reason to fear McQuillan. Why should Jacinta Devlin or Majella Hawley have had a reason either? I was certain now that she had been with Callen when he picked them up. What had she said to me? 'I didn't care what he did as long as he left me alone.'

But she hadn't taken Bridie for Callen, though she would have told him that she had, that it was her way of showing him faith. She'd taken Bridie to have revenge on me, and to create more sensation. I'd said to her myself that if another child went missing then there might be sufficient interest in a book about it all. She'd planned it, sucking me into her web, driven by whatever had twisted her mind – those long years of childhood in which she'd endured the demands of her grandfather, the long years of Callen's demands, my own demands, which, though of short duration, might have been the worst of all to accept because they'd been answered with love. She'd been a hostage all her life to the black desires and needs of men, desires and needs born in darkness.

It was all over. There could be no going back. It was fitting, if anything in all of this could be so thought of, that it should end here at the Point. I knew now why Callen had left Bridie alive, and what it was she could tell me. He'd told McQuillan he'd killed her so that she'd feel confident of getting what it was she'd wanted. She would believe that, and at the end see everything destroyed when Bridie spoke.

Or had he wanted to give us a choice? How could I know that he didn't think that I'd consider killing Bridie to get what I wanted? If she were dead and I destroyed this evidence, then McQuillan would be free and so would I. Maybe he thought we were two of a kind.

I stood for a while looking out towards the sea, watching the darkness merge at the horizon. When the bright line disappeared and the darkness was a shadow over the sea, I went back to the car. I sat there with the pictures and the camera on the seat beside me while fog rolled in off the sea like a grey tide and flowed over me. I started the engine and drove off.

There was a small crowd gathered outside the Garda station, but they paid me little heed as I entered, the horror I carried contained in a battered holdall I kept in the boot of my car. In the reception area I saw Doyle and beckoned him over. 'I've something here you should see,' I said. 'Is there somewhere private we could go?'

He took me to a stark functional interview room containing a table and two chairs. I handed him the note and he read it and then looked at me. I knew it was the last normal human look I'd receive for a long time and I held onto it before handing him the holdall. He took it and I pulled out a chair and sat down. I knew it was going to be a long day and night and that when it was over all I'd possess was the life I once saw myself cursed with.

25

I returned again to Castleford when bluebells patterned my garden and the wind-battered daffodils lay broken and dying in the borders. I couldn't say what was drawing me back. Maybe I wanted to see the place again, to visit my parents' grave, a duty I'd failed to fulfil on my first visit. Maybe I'd wanted to see Alec Whitley and Lizzie, maybe Bridie too. Maybe I'd found a shred of hope.

I'd been on the dry a week, the first time I'd been fully sober since November. The time in between was like a blurred film when I tried to recall it. My first real memory is of a day before Christmas when D'Arcy called, a gesture that ultimately helped restore some of my faith in humanity. He brought food – God only knows who'd told him of my plight – and invited me for Christmas. I didn't accept and now I can recall neither Christmas nor New Year.

D'Arcy, like Gatsby, turned out all right in the end. He called again and begged me to leave the drink be. When I didn't respond he let me alone for a while. He called again two weeks ago and had the decency to go into my filthy stinking kitchen and make us both a coffee. I'd been in the sitting-room, recovering from a particularly bad binge, and the coffee made me sick. I'd retreated to the bathroom, and when I returned D'Arcy had gone. I sat on the couch while waves of self-pity washed over me.

But he reappeared, from where I didn't know then, and sat down to talk to me. There was no coaxing now. The gist of his talk was that if I wanted to fuck up my life, that was my business. But if I didn't wish to do that, if I wanted to drag myself out of the mire, then he'd help me.

'I'm leaving the *Chronicle*,' he told me. 'I've had an interest for a few years in a free paper that's distributed in Limerick. A friend set it up and I helped finance him. Now he's decided to sell out because of ill-health and I've bought his share. I want to do my own thing for once. Isn't that what you younger people call it? Doing your own thing?'

'Fuck off,' I said.

'Well, whatever you call it, William, that's what I want to do. I'm going to run it, edit it and, if necessary, deliver it door to door. Only I need someone to help me, someone like your good self with some experience of the business. This friend had a wife but I'm not so blessed.'

'And you want me? You must be mad.'

'Very likely,' he said. 'But you're the ideal candidate. Where else would I get someone with your capabilities at the salary I'm offering? I'll give you a week to think about it. Give me your decision then. But be sober when you tell me.'

'Go fuck yourself,' I said, too ill when he left even to go out and drink myself to oblivion. Instead I dragged myself to a bed which stank even worse than the kitchen, and there with the help of a bottle I kept on the bedside table, I bought myself a few hours oblivion and peace. It was the following day before I had an explanation for where D'Arcy had been the previous evening. I'd got up late and had gone into the kitchen to make a coffee. At first I thought I'd gone insane when I saw the kitchen had been tidied, the ware washed, the leftovers of a dozen takeaway meals cleared away, the filthy floor swept.

I went into the sitting-room then and sat on the couch and cried like a child. I cried for Bridie and Lizzie, for Alec whose beloved Alice, D'Arcy had told me on one of his visits, had had a stroke on the last day of the old year and had died as the bells were ringing in the new. Most of all I cried for myself, for what I'd had and for what I'd lost. I cried until there was no emotion left and there was room for new emotions and for hope.

I gave D'Arcy his answer within a week, going to his house bathed and shaved and sober, wearing shirt and tie and an old suit that had hung in the wardrobe for years. 'I'll accept your offer,' I said, 'providing the terms are satisfactory. And that you tell me why you want to help me.'

'I was in love once myself,' he said. 'A long time ago. Now to the terms.'

We argued them out, more for the sake of it than for any other reason, and then had coffee together before I left. A few days later I put my flat on the market. When it was sold my ties with Dublin would be broken, and maybe that's why I returned to Castleford – I wanted to break the ties still lingering there.

Following my find under the bridge I hadn't seen Lizzie or Bridie or the Whitleys again. I'd spent most of the night in the Garda station and had come out in the early hours of the morning to a crowd of onlookers and television and newspaper men. All sorts of rumours were circulating, and I was relieved to gain the sanctuary of my room at the hotel. After paying my bill, I left via the fire escape, with the porter's connivance, and headed for Dublin. I hadn't been back since.

At the time there had been a slight chance of charges being brought against me. But nothing came of it. McQuillan had been interviewed before I produced my find and had told her story. Afterwards she'd tried to implicate me by claiming that she'd told me of Majella Hawley having been held alive for two days; in fact that she'd told me everything then. But I stood by my story that I got the information from Joe Hawley. Halligan knew that if I had known I wouldn't have stayed silent when Bridie had been abducted. He also sensed that there was some truth in what McQuillan had said, but he had no hard evidence against me.

Now as I crested the rise and saw the sprawl of the town, I stopped the car as I'd done that November evening I'd last come here. I didn't know what I wanted or what I hoped to achieve by returning. I think I'd a foolish hope that I'd meet Lizzie and begin where we'd left off.

I waited a few minutes, then drove into the town, past the church and on down Main Street to the cross, turning left into Barrack Street, going down by the Garda station which seemed horribly ordinary now. I drove on until I came to the graveyard and parked outside the gates.

I found my parents' grave on the hillside with its marble tombstone. I didn't kneel nor pray, but just stood bowed in the cold for a few moments and remembered. I was taught that it was God who created us, who gave us souls, who knew everything about us even before He breathed life into our bodies. If that were so, why then had He allowed my parents to meet? Why had He breathed life into me? I stood and wondered, and thought yet again of the strands that had drawn us all together in this place. I thought of my father who'd fled to America, seeking what he was only to find and hold for such a short time. He'd come here hoping to fulfil a dream, but dreams were the domain of the young. In school I'd been taught that the dead, like God, watch over us. If that was what heaven held for me – to look down eternally on this speck we call earth, to see it spinning in the vastness of space, to see us crawling over it like maggots – then I'd settle for oblivion.

It was cold with a sharp wind blowing off the sea, and I didn't stand about too long. I searched for the other graves, but only located Judith Kelly's. I didn't pray here either for she had no need of prayer. I only hoped that there was a grain of truth to something else I'd once been taught about the dead, that they were in some heaven somewhere, praying for us who were in need of redemption. Let them be there and praying for us but not able to see. Let them have that small mercy.

I wouldn't find Alice Whitley's grave here – she'd have been buried in the old Church of Ireland cemetery with her ancestors. Callen hadn't been buried here either – how could he have been put here with his victims? He'd been buried with his uncle out at Duagh with but a few protesting voices raised against it. In the end, what he'd done had been overshadowed by the fact that McQuillan had been his accomplice.

What most people seemed to forget though was that they had both been innocent once, just as I had been. We were all born innocent, and life or circumstances or fortune made us what we had become. The newspapers had spoken of the victims – of Judith Kelly, Jacinta Devlin and Majella Hawley – and of their families. But Deborah McQuillan had been a victim too – still was and always would be. Indeed without doubt she was the saddest victim of all. I assumed that at her forthcoming trial she'd be found to be insane, a verdict that would appear to apply some sort of logic to what she'd done and help quell the fears that possessed the so-called decent people among us.

I left the graveyard and returned to my car and drove to the offices of *The Mayoman*. Alec rose to greet me, and though his grip was firm I knew he was uneasy. I sympathised with him about Alice's death. In a sense his loss mirrored my own, though he'd had Alice for a whole lifetime.

He thanked me for my sympathy, and as we chatted about

trivialities, I realised that he was embarrassed by my presence, that he had nothing to say to me anymore. I wanted to go, cursing myself for having come, and I rose to my feet. He didn't try to detain me. It was only as I reached the door that he really spoke for the first time.

'Elizabeth works in Burke's now,' he said. 'She's getting over what happened. You should leave her be. After all, you've done enough harm here.'

His words angered me. I'd thought of him as my friend, and I shook my head, seeking words to damn him. 'You blame me?' I said. 'I didn't kill them. I didn't ever kill anyone.'

'There are people,' he said, 'whom evil pursues. They may not be the cause of it themselves, but it follows in their wake. Alice died of a massive stroke, yet she had never been ill a day in her life. It was what happened... Look, Willie, just leave Elizabeth be. And maybe God will forgive you.'

'God?' I said. 'You talk about God and forgiveness.'

'Everyone needs forgiveness,' he said. 'Someone has to forgive. If the dead can't forgive us and the living won't, then that leaves God. Whatever you may think Him to be.'

I nodded. 'Goodbye, Alec,' I said. 'I'm sorry, more sorry than you'll ever know.' I walked out, shutting the door behind me, leaving him with his memories. Back in the car I drove on to Main Street and parked across from Burke's. I no longer knew what I should do. Not that I'd really had any idea from the first. I wanted to see Lizzie, to talk to her. Maybe I wanted the forgiveness of which Alec had spoken.

I felt exposed, was certain that people would recognise me, and how could I know what their reaction might be? I sat for half an hour, hoping I'd even get a glimpse of her, but she never appeared. I was on the point of driving away when suddenly children appeared on the street. I watched them as they made their way home, without shepherds now. It was amazing really how quickly people forgot. I thought that maybe they'd forgotten me and was again thinking of crossing to the shop when I saw Bridie.

Seeing her was a shock. When I'd left Dublin, I'd thought of meeting her, too, but now I knew I couldn't face her. I watched her coming down the street with a friend, both of them stopping by the entrance to Burke's, chatting together.

I watched them, aware that this was the only life I'd ever have. 'Leave Elizabeth be,' Alec Whitley had warned, and God might forgive me. I didn't need God's forgiveness. I needed to forgive myself. But I wasn't ready yet. I needed time. It was strange that. Months ago I'd thought myself cursed with time.

The two children parted and Bridie turned to look across the street, seemingly straight at me. But even if she saw me, I was but a face glimpsed through a car window. She called something to her friend – something about tomorrow – and then went into the store.

I started the engine and drove off. Maybe when I'd forgiven myself, I could begin to hope. Perhaps that was the most important thing we possessed. Not dreams or ambition or desire. Maybe not even love. But hope and time. As I crested the rise in the road and the town disappeared from my rear-view mirror, the two words echoed in my head like a promise.